MW00638286

I WILL CLOSE MY EYES

A NOVEL

AMY FILLION

Copyright © 2023 by Amy Fillion

All rights reserved.

No part of this book may be reproduced in any form or by any electronic or mechanical means, including information storage and retrieval systems, without written permission from the author, except for the use of brief quotations in a book review.

Amy Fillion asserts the moral right to be identified as the author of this work.

For Jason and our boys
May we embrace the time given to us

ALSO BY AMY FILLION

Adult Novels

The Marks You Made

Grace and Ally

Surprise Me (Grace and Ally Book 2)

One Day (Grace and Ally Book 3)

Secrets of Spaulding Lane: Nancy

Secrets of Spaulding Lane: Marni

Secrets of Spaulding Lane: Rose

Little Things

Broken and Breaking Free

Children's Books

Fairville (Room of Reveries Book 1)

FenneGig (Room of Reveries Book 2)

Esmerelda and the Courageous Knight (Room of Reveries Book 3)

Wonderwell (Room of Reveries Book 4)

SkyTopia (Room of Reveries Book 5)

The Ancient Curse (Room of Reveries Book 6)

A Magical Farewell (Ro0m of Reveries Book 7)

PROLOGUE

I woke up this morning, the day of Barbara's funeral, and I fell out of bed.

It wasn't the first time. Oh, no.

But it felt like it.

It always does when I fall.

Luckily, this time I didn't break anything, just bruised myself up right and good. I know that Deidre will be here soon. She works at this facility, drives that new car of hers to get here. That thing—what's it called? A hybrid, that's it. All these new inventions, the new technology, all the newness. I can't keep up. Things move too fast for me these days.

I stopped driving many years ago now. It's the eyes, you know. They're milky with cataracts that conceal the vivid blue that once glimmered, and I even scare myself sometimes when I glance in the mirror. I look like a creature in one of those scary movies I once liked to watch. When I was young and carefree. When I'd clutch onto Merle for comfort, not even knowing I was doing it, until my knuckles shone white.

Merle…

I can't clutch onto much of anything now, can I? These arthritic fingers won't let me, twisted as they are like gnarled tree roots or dead branches reaching out, reaching up, taunting. My knuckles are bulbous and elevated, and the tips of my fingers face the floor like an old crone about to cast a spell on a pesky stray cat rubbing against her leg. A leg, perhaps, that feels like mine: achy and sore. I seem to channel that crone now. Don't touch my delicate skin or I'll wince in discomfort and wish for nothing more than the ability to cast that spell.

I'm not nasty. Oh no. Just tired. Achy. Old.

And with a nostalgia that won't dissipate. At times it haunts me, now that so many loved ones from my formative years are gone, relegated to mere memories that creep into my dreams when I gently close these paper-thin lids of mine and drift away…

I'm one hundred and one years old. Shut your eyes now. Go on, do it.

Can you see me? Can you imagine? What image do you have in mind?

I attempt to extricate myself from the carpet of my residence, a small one-bedroom apartment in a facility that boasts of independence. If this old body of mine needs help, it's just a button away. Deidre is my girl. She's this young thing, no older than I was when—no, no, not today. I can't go there. Where it used to bring me pleasure, Memory Lane has taunted me of late. So I'll let that thought go. For now. Until I'm back in this room, staring through the small window next to my bed at the mass of stars in the night sky, naming the constellations, and remembering those days, yearning for those days. And I know that then, a smile will play on my lips. They'll be here. *He'll* be here.

Deidre is in her early twenties. She told me her exact age once. This I know. But I forgot. That happens sometimes, you know. She reminds me of Barbara, my old friend. My best friend. In stature, Deidre's the opposite of me. She's tall. Golly, is she tall. I have to look up to see those beautiful chocolate brown eyes of hers. She wears her thick brown hair, which reminds me of my younger days, in a braid. Always. Sometimes two braids plopped against her chest. And that smile. Sometimes it's that smile that motivates me to begin my day.

I'm feeling weak, so I remain on the floor, and Deidre finds me there mere moments later. Just a button away. It's helpful sometimes, the resourcefulness of this residence of mine. "Martha, girl, how'd you end up on the floor again?"

Girl. When I first met this sprightly young woman, the word confused me. Girl. I was no girl and hadn't been for years upon years upon years. Girl. But then, I learned that this was a term of endearment, and that, paired with that smile of hers—well, it always sends my heart into little flutters of pleasure. I suppose that's one good thing at my age, yes? That my heart still knows how to react, that pleasure can be found in the simplest of gestures. I lost that once. More than once, if I'm telling the truth. But it always found its way back to me.

One of life's many miraculous mysteries, that is.

Deidre puts her palms under my arms and gently helps me to stand. I try to grasp onto her shirt for balance, but these darn gnarled fingers of mine hinder my completion. I have to press down with my palms instead. But that's okay. Deidre has me. She always does. She's become a true friend to me, this young, spirited woman. I've learned in all these

3

many years of living that sometimes age is just a number. I acquired the ability to stare into someone's soul from a young age. Right into the depths. And, with Deidre, what I intuited the day we met was all I needed to open up. I let her in right away. She makes my heart smile.

Once she has me upright, I lift my head and look into those beautiful eyes of hers. They're eyes I've gotten to know well, right down to the one yellow dot that looks as if, one day, it manifested from goodness knew where and nested itself right into the mocha warmth of the iris, grasped on comfortably, and sighed.

Sometimes I wonder why people don't make eye contact more often. These days, it's all heads down, looking at screens, talking to folks behind computers. I used to own a cell phone, if you can believe that. But not anymore. If someone wants to call me, they can connect to the phone here in my apartment. But I do have a computer. I even have the same email account I created when the internet was a new wonder, when we had to dial up in order to connect, when that crackly tone indicated that the synapses were firing and we'd be on the World Wide Web shortly. Hold tight. The same email address after all these years—a marvel, really. I don't check my inbox often. It's mostly spam, anyway, and by golly, I don't need a computer virus or—and I still blush to think—for these blurred eyes to behold pornographic images.

I stand here now and press down on Deidre's arms, my thigh throbbing.

"You okay there, Martha?"

Deidre had called me Mrs. Mayhew when we first met, and I was glad. None of this calling-your-elders-by-their-first-names-upon-introduction nonsense. Wait, instead, until they permit you to use the less formal title. Perhaps it's a generational mindset that has never dissipated. Back in my day, my father would have…

Dad.

Let me pause and close my eyes. Let me conjure a vision, see his face. I didn't think I could go there today, but perhaps it's just what I need. My father. At times, I catch myself calling him Daddy as if I were six years old again, a little girl running into her father's arms. I see his features, his smile. I hear his voice, even now.

Anyway, I digress. I do that a lot these days.

Deidre called me Mrs. Mayhew for about a week, and then I just stood there and shook my head. "Call me Martha," I told her. Even after a week, I could tell she'd be a good friend. The goodness of her soul shone through. And my friends call me by my first name.

"Good as I'll ever be," I say now. I drop my hand and rub at my thigh with a wince. She looks down at me, her hands still tucked lovingly under my arms, though their pressure has lessened. I'm standing on my own now. I often wonder what she sees when she looks at me. Does she see what I see when I stare into the mirror in my compact bathroom? Old, tired eyes, hair that has gone white as snow.

My hair is still rather thick. I pride myself on my hair, though Daddy always told me that pride came before the fall. It's just hair. But I've learned that there's a difference between pride and conceit, and conceited I am not. My white hair is worn short now in my old age. It's easier to care for this way.

I often wonder if Deidre scrutinizes every wrinkle on my face. The lines are so prolific, it's a marvel that I have any smooth skin left to detect. Does she see the age spots that mottle my skin? I used to know their number, but now they're so many that I lost count years ago. Does she feel

5

the veins protruding from my hands when she holds them? Does she make a conscious effort not to grasp on too tight for fear she'll break the brittle bones of my twisted fingers?

Deidre. My, do I love her. I will miss her when I'm gone, when I leave her behind to join those that have departed before me.

But not yet. No, not yet. Today I have a funeral to go to. This slight, fragile body of mine and this still acute mind are going to say goodbye to Barbara. I've lost a lot of people in my long life, especially in the past few decades, but this one hurts something good. I'll need Deidre by my side. I'll need her presence, her love, to counteract the sorrow seeping down to the very marrow of my bones.

Barbara, the best girlfriend I ever had. God has been good to us, hasn't He? While I've lost so many people, either because of death or a mere happenstance of life and the paths we chose to take, and I've attended entirely too many funerals—so many that I've lost count now—He blessed me with a best friend that lived almost as long as I have.

Deidre drops her hands to her side, smiles down at me. "Want help getting ready for the day?" she asks.

I shake my head, close my eyes, and think of Barbara. "No, dear." I pat Deidre's arm. "I'm okay now, thank you. You've done good. I can get ready. I'll see you at ten o'clock."

"I'll be here," Deidre promises. And I know she will be.

She leaves my apartment and closes the door softly behind her. I slowly make my way to my bathroom. I feel the chilly air seep under my nightdress. I shiver. I've always had the tendency to feel cold. For as long as I can remember, really. I was a petite girl and then a petite woman. Perhaps that was why I was always cold then and why I'm cold now, though I don't know. Is that really the way that works, anyhow? Now I am not only petite but fragile. If I place my palm on my hip, I can feel the bone jutting out, sharply pronounced. I'm a waif of a woman, I know. But it can't be helped. And it's not for lack of eating, for I do love to eat. I always have. Good food fills the soul. It began with my mother, this love for food.

It takes me a while to lift the nightdress off my body, and I'm careful to deposit it onto the counter instead of letting it slip to the floor. It's too hard for me to bend over and pick things up now. The distance always feels miles away, and my ancient body protests those movements.

I turn the faucet on in the shower. Hot, please. I hold onto the railing and ease my way in. My legs need to navigate only the most minor hurdle; they've thought of everything in this facility for old people. And that's another thing, if I'm allowed to digress once again. Elderly is a kind term, it's true. It makes the bearer of the word feel like they're offering a bit of respect when they use it to describe another. And yet, call me old, for that's what I am. I am old. I am not offended by the word; in fact, I wear it like a badge of honor. I might have a difficult time with this body of mine. My eyes might not see as well as they once did. I might not be able to dance, to spin, to take pleasure in so many of the things I once could. But I've lived now for over one hundred and one years. How many people can say that? And I have all my faculties about me, don't I? My memories might hurt sometimes, and they might not always be entirely reliable, but they are mine to keep, to harbor, to retrieve. And more often than not, the hurt dissipates, and I'm left with a wistful, appreciative smile. So call me old. I will look at you and grin, and my heart will tingle, for I have been blessed in life—

this long, sometimes arduous life. I am grateful to be an old woman.

It takes me a long time to finish my shower, not only because my movements are slow but because I relish the feel of the hot water on my delicate, paper-thin skin. But I am showered and dressed and have a light breakfast settling in my stomach by the time Deidre knocks on my door. I call to her to come in.

"Hey, girl," she says. "You ready to go?"

I look down at my loose black dress and my practical slip-on shoes that are a bit too tight around my swollen ankles. I am sitting in my favorite rocking chair in the corner of my small living area, which I have positioned to look out and into the courtyard of this facility where I will spend some of my last days, perhaps all of them. Who's to say? An old couple—though not as old as me, I'm sure—walks amongst the small flower garden. They sit on a bench. He leans into her, and even from this distance, I can see her smile.

An image of a man I loved dearly enters my mind, but I push it aside. For now. He will return.

I turn my head to Deidre. "I am ready." I smooth my palms over my dress and slowly stand.

I am going to say goodbye to my best friend. My Barbara.

BARBARA

They say your earliest memories can start at the tender age of two, and I believe it because I remember the very day I met Barbara. It was 1925, and Barbara and her family—her father, mother, and two older brothers—moved next door. My childhood home was a small double-story brown-shingled Cape Cod nestled comfortably on half an acre of land in a small cul-de-sac in southern New Hampshire. I will never forget that home, for a couple of reasons. One is because I grew up in it, and it would remain in my life for years to come. Another is because of the godawful bright red panels on either side of the four small first-floor windows on the front of the house. And when I tell you they were bright red, I make no exaggeration. I can still see them in my mind's eye, and even in the black-and-white photos I have, the boldness seems to pop out at you, screaming, shouting, "Here I am!"

My mother, even then, was unconventional. Nobody was going to tell Ruth Laplant what to do. And that included my father. Thank the Lord he wasn't a controlling man. It wasn't in his nature. And this, I believe, was why they complemented each other so well: he, demure, easygoing, and she—my beautiful mother—exuberantly exerting her strength to all those that were fortunate enough to cross her path. She loved life, my mother. She lost her own mother in childbirth, and the baby, my mother's younger brother, died on that abhorrent day as well. My mother was old enough at nine years to remember that and remember it well. Although I wasn't there myself, of course, she described the scene in so much detail that it feels as if the images in my mind are my own: the screaming, the moaning, the eyes rolling in the back of her mother's head. The blood. A body going limp, then another, much smaller body, entering the world blue and still, never taking a breath to sustain his life. While such a circumstance, such a sight, might have affected others negatively, it had the opposite effect on my mother. Oh, she mourned, I assure you, but she determined that very day, knowing then how precious life was, how it could be stripped from you in an instant, to live hers fully. She didn't know what was in store for her, but she knew there was beauty to be found, even if you had to weed through the thick, encumbering grief to find it. Her mother had taught her that. And it was that belief she held strongly to, even until her dying day.

My mother.

Those red panels were one of the many ways she spoke to the world in a time in which women were relegated to a lower status than men—even if I didn't understand that when I was growing up and those panels were one of the many causes of embarrassment for me in my formative years.

At first, I saw Barbara from a distance. She was in the short, narrow driveway of the house just to the left of mine, a home that mirrored my own, though the shingles on her Cape Cod were a dark gray. The panels were also gray, though muted, far from the shocking conspicuousness of my own.

I was three and a half years old that summer of 1925, and yet, I remember the day like it was yesterday. There she was, this little girl that looked to be about my own age, standing in her new driveway, her feet firmly planted on the concrete in a pair of well-used Mary Janes set over gently stained white stockings that climbed up her shins and rested just below the knee. Her dress was a loose, floral, short-sleeved beauty, also well worn—my, but did I love dresses in those days—with a high neckline that rested against her delicate collarbone. I wanted to run over to her, touch her dress, look into her eyes, for even then I could read someone's soul. My heart smiles at the thought of that day when I first spotted the young girl that would become my best friend throughout this long, eventful life of mine.

Who was she?

And then I saw them: her brothers, or so I assumed; two beefy boys older than she was. They intimidated me, even from the distance at which I was watching them. They sped out of the dilapidated family vehicle, the elder chasing his younger brother with a determination even I could detect, his lips pressed into a line and the devil shooting darts from his eyes. He caught up to his little brother, and when he did, I watched Barbara step back. In her arms, she clutched a doll that had been hidden until that very moment. She took another step back and then another until she hit the side of the car and could go no farther.

I watched in shocked silence as the eldest boy grabbed his younger brother by a suspender and yanked him back. The suspender snapped out of place, and the younger boy lost his balance and fell with a thump I imagined I could hear against the grass of the modest front yard.

The boy who had fallen released a high-pitched, pleading scream. The older brother grasped the younger's shirt sleeve and yanked. The shirt ripped from beneath the fallen boy's trousers as one of his palms planted on the ground, and the other lifted in a sign of surrender.

And then the father—or the man who, I assumed at the time, was the father—rushed toward the boys. He disentangled one from the other. Words were spoken at such a low register that I couldn't decipher them. The elder boy looked up and into his father's face, his expression still set with maddening determination. The younger brother lifted himself from the ground with resignation but also apparent relief. He swiped the dirt from his bottom and hung his head.

And the little girl—my Barbara—clutched her doll to her chest, taking everything in.

A tall woman exited the house and slowly made her way over to the commotion. She ran her palm over the top of the younger boy's hair. She glared at her eldest. And then the four of them—the two boys, the mother, and the father —retreated into their new home, leaving a petrified, wide-eyed Barbara in the driveway.

I couldn't wait any longer. I was compelled forward, so my feet obeyed. I walked to meet her in a driveway I had never set foot on before, even though this home was nestled directly beside my own. An older couple had owned the house before Barbara and her family, and they kept to themselves, so I had never been invited over, and I didn't dare encroach on their privacy, even in a time when privacy was less desired than it is today.

"Hi," I said, my voice low but certain. Curious.

I must have startled the girl because she nearly jumped out of her Mary Janes at the sound of my voice beside her.

"Who are you?" she asked me, wide-eyed, still clutching her doll.

"I'm Martha," I said. "Who are you?" No use for preamble. I adore the blunt nature of the very young. They don't beat around the bush, as you say. They get right to it. At times, I wish adults would do such a thing. It would certainly make matters a whole lot easier.

"Barbara." She brought the doll even closer to her chest.

"What's her name?" I motioned to the doll with my chin and then dared reach out my hand and stroke her golden hair, much like Barbara's own, though this girl before me had hair that was stringier and more unkempt than her doll's. Barbara let me do so without even the slightest movement to retract her beloved doll farther from my touch. I loved the girl immediately.

And then I gazed into her eyes, light brown with a splattering of green. And they spoke to me, right then and there. And I knew. I knew we were destined for each other, Barbara and I. Right then, every ounce of my three-and-a-half-year-old self burst forth. I lunged. I flung my still-chubby little-girl arms around Barbara's neck and tugged her to me with a yearning even I didn't know I possessed at the time. She stiffened within my grasp but only for a moment. I felt her melt into me. And when I let her go, my cheeks already aching from the force of my smile, my soon-to-be best friend looked into my eyes—blue, unlike her delicious light brown—and offered me a smile in return. I would grow to love those smiles, each and every one. Her cheeks dimpled when her smiles were wide and genuine, and I never once, in all these years, questioned the authenticity of a single one when given to me. I relished them, was humbled by them. Because Barbara Brown didn't offer them to just anybody, and even when she did, I knew. I knew when they were genuine or when they were forced.

"I live over there," I said, pointing at my house. Barbara followed my finger with her gaze and then looked back at me. She didn't verbally reply, but she shrugged, and her lips pressed into a slight smile that seemed to say *okay*.

"We're neighbors," I tried again.

And her smile widened.

"Were those your brothers?" I asked. My eyes wandered to the front of her new home, its door left wide open.

Barbara nodded, though her smile had disappeared just as suddenly as a baseball hit by a bat, and I swear I could even hear the loud *crack* of her deflation. I knew then to tread carefully when it came to her brothers.

I grasped her hand. "Want to come over?"

She looked at my house then at her own. "I have to ask Mommy."

"Okay," I said. And I waited for her to move. I sensed her hesitation, but then she slowly made for her front door, with me at her side, our hands still entwined. She paused at the threshold and peeked her head inside. I followed her gaze, curious.

And then her eldest brother, in a flurry of movement, entered the living area from the kitchen at the back of the house. "What do you want?" he asked his sister with a sneer. "And who the hell are you?"

My eyes went wide. I had never heard such language, especially from one so seemingly young. I felt Barbara's hand tremble in my own. I wasn't scared, though, not then.

In my naïveté, I didn't know that I should have been.

"Oh, Barbara." My new friend's mother had entered

14

the room and looked at her daughter first, hovering within the threshold of her new home, then at her eldest son, whose countenance was still set in a sneer. My, but I didn't like him. "Who is your new friend?" Her voice was so soft, I had to strain to hear her.

"Martha," Barbara whispered.

"Hello, Martha," Barbara's mother said to me. "I am Mrs. Brown. And where did you come from?"

"Next door," I said, the inflection of my voice rising animatedly on the last word, despite the lack of enthusiasm surrounding me. I was three and a half, after all, and though my intuition had emerged, I still lacked the ability to read a room well at times, especially since my own familial circumstances were highly positive.

"How very nice," Mrs. Brown replied. "I am glad our Barbara has made a new friend already."

I nudged Barbara with my elbow, coaxing her to ask her mother if she could come over to my house, but Barbara didn't make a sound. She stood there staring at her older brother instead. I supposed it was up to me to make the move.

"Can Barbara come over?"

"Go to your house?" Mrs. Brown asked.

"Yes."

She looked from me to her daughter. "You want to go to Martha's house?"

Barbara nodded, the movement slight but discernible.

"Okay, then," Mrs. Brown said. "You may go." And then to me, "I will have to meet your mother soon, Martha. Especially if you and Barbara are to be friends. And now that we are neighbors."

"Okay," I said. All I felt was indifference to Mrs. Brown's statement. I just wanted to pull Barbara back outside, run over to my house, show her my room, and let her play with my toys. No other little girls lived on our small cul-de-sac. I was beyond thrilled!

"And which house do you live in?" Mrs. Brown asked.

"Red windows," I stated.

Mrs. Brown's eyes widened ever so slightly, but I noticed the gesture. "Okay, then," she said. "Barbara, you may go."

And then Barbara smiled. Needing no further motivation, she stepped backward, and then she and I turned, hands still entwined, and set off as fast as our little legs would carry us, across her driveway, into my front yard, and through my front door.

The aroma of a summer stew wafted to my nostrils—oh, how my father loved his stew, even in the summer months—and I knew that I'd partake of a delicious lunch shortly. I pulled Barbara forward into my living room, but before I took more than a few steps, someone suddenly whisked me from the floor. I lost my hold on Barbara's hand, and my stomach flopped with the fast speed of the movement. I felt my father's strong hands under my arms. He planted me back on the floor and I couldn't help but giggle. My father always had the ability to elicit that response from me. It was one of the things I loved best about him then.

"Look who it is," he said. "Martha Moo."

I giggled again. I wasn't yet old enough to find embarrassment with my father's term of endearment.

"Daddy!" I said, the word coming out in a burst through my lips, my smile wide.

My mother appeared, her sunflower-splattered apron snug around her thin waist. Genetically, I had always taken after my mother. Even then, she was thin and even frail-looking despite her adamantly strong personality. My father, on the other hand, was tall and broad, and I felt dwarfed within his arms, a feeling I loved even into adulthood: safe and secure. His hands were unusually large, even for his stature. As a little girl, I believed those hands could do anything. They were undoubtedly able to crush, to smother. But they also had the ability to cuddle, to hold, to caress. He held my world, my very existence in those hands, and I idolized him.

My mother lifted me gently. I wrapped my legs around her waist and my arms around her neck. "Oof," she complained with mock exaggeration. "Martha, you are just getting too big for me to hold, aren't you? Pretty soon, I won't be able to pick you up at all! You're nearly a full-grown lady!"

I smiled with adoration into my mother's blue-gray eyes. "I'm not a lady," I said.

"Oh," my mother countered. "But you nearly are." She plonked me back on the floor and then stooped in front of a timid Barbara. Her bottom nearly touched the back of her high-heeled shoes. My mother loved heels and wore them even when in the house. She claimed they made her appear taller and accented her ebullient personality. I had to agree, and at the age of three and a half, I would often steal into my parent's room, rummage through their closet, and borrow a pair of my mother's heels. I would place them on my little feet and attempt, with much difficulty, to traipse around the house in them. I often stumbled and fell but righted myself immediately, pretending that nothing was amiss, and got right back to it. In my latter years, I learned the delicate nature of walking in heels, but unlike my mother, I found I did not care for them.

"And who have we here?" my mother asked, addressing Barbara with a soft smile.

"Barbara," I said exuberantly.

"Hello, Barbara," my mother said. "I'm Martha's mom. You are welcome here in our home. And where do you live?"

"Next door," I offered.

"Thank you, Martha," my mother said, still stooping so she was eye-to-eye with my new friend. "But I would love to hear Barbara speak for herself."

I frowned but closed my mouth, pressing my lips together tightly.

"You have moved next door?" my mother asked. I watched Barbara clutch her doll tightly to her chest and shuffle her shoe back and forth against our carpet. She gazed at the floor.

My mother, unfazed, continued to speak. "I'm so glad that you have moved next door," she said. "Martha has no friends on our street, and I have so hoped for another little girl that she can play with. I imagine you and she will become the best of friends." She attempted to catch Barbara's gaze with her own. Barbara lifted her head only slightly, but I could see that my mother had gained her attention. "I hope you come over often, Barbara. I'm so very glad you're here."

Maybe it was Mother's soft voice. Maybe it was her words. Maybe it was the addition of my father, arms crossed over his massive chest, leaning back inconspicuously, a smile playing on his lips that bespoke his warmth despite his physical appearance. Whatever it was, Barbara relaxed, and I watched as her lips curved upward, the movement slight but perceptible.

My mother slowly reached her hands out toward Barbara and placed her palms on Barbara's forearms. "That is a beautiful doll you have there," she said, and

Barbara's smile widened a bit farther. "What is her name?"

After a moment of silence, Barbara uttered, "Edith."

"That is a wonderful name," my mother replied. "May I hold her?"

Barbara looked down at Edith then back up at my mother. She hesitantly offered my mother her precious doll. My mother brought Edith to her chest and rocked her from side to side, humming a tune I knew well. She hummed that very tune to me when I was hurt or emotionally disturbed and needed coddling. Mother kissed Edith's forehead, smiled, and handed the doll back to Barbara. "Martha has a doll in her room. Would you like to go see her?"

Barbara nodded, blinking once.

"Martha," my mother said, turning to me, "would you like to take Barbara to your room? Then I will call you girls down when the stew is ready, and we can have a nice lunch. How does that sound?"

"Good," I said.

"Then it is settled," my mother announced. She stood, smiled, and gently ran her palm from the top of Barbara's head and down the back of her hair. "Go on, now. You girls have fun."

I needed no further urging. I grabbed Barbara's hand and tugged her toward me. In my peripheral vision, as I hastened out of the room with my new friend, I saw my mother snuggle against my father's chest and my father wrap his arms around her shoulders. The sight was common enough, so I thought nothing of it. I just wanted to show Barbara the many wondrous toys in my room!

...

19

That day marked the beginning of my lifelong friendship with Barbara Brown. Days turned into weeks, weeks into years. We started school together, both at the age of six. Barbara met me in my driveway every morning so we could walk together. Unfortunately, upon their mother's insistence, so did her two brothers.

By then, the chubby limbs of my toddler days had elongated into those of the girl I would remain for the next several years. Petite in stature, yes, but thin, too, almost waifish, despite the urgings of various aunts to "fatten up." My physicality was inherently genetic. I ate. By golly, did I eat. My mother found pleasure in the kitchen, and my father and I were her culinary muses. My father especially. "Ruth, you've outdone yourself with this one," and "Ruthie, we having that casserole you made last week? You know the one, chunks of meat and all that good stuff. This body of mine could use some of that wholesome cooking right about now", were sentences I knew well and at an early age. Cooking and then taking pleasure in dining together marked my childhood. My father would eat his fill at the compact kitchen table—typically two or three helpings of whatever my mother had prepared—then sit back in his chair, throw his hands with exaggeration over his stomach, and grin contentedly. "Another good one, Ruth." And this would always please my mother—not just that he had enjoyed her cooking, oh no—though she did appreciate that. It was the way he always thanked her, paid mind to her, that my mother loved. It didn't matter what it was that my mother had done, big or small. My father noticed it and remarked upon her efforts. He did so until the very day he left this earth.

So, no, it was not because of lack of sustenance that I grew to be a thin girl and then a thin woman, but my physical appearance did tend to have an effect on my girlfriends, especially in high school and even into my adult years. The girls around me would bemoan that I ate anything and everything my heart desired, and my body didn't retaliate. I always brushed away their remarks; my parents had never placed emphasis on anyone's body weight, so I hadn't grown up believing one type of woman was more attractive than another. Fortunately, this mindset remained with me.

I stood at the edge of my driveway on the very first day of school with Barbara, the two of us with our arms inter-linked, our opposite hands occupied with carrying our metal lunchboxes. Mother had packed my lunch that day, and even after all these years, I remember what it was: little tea sandwiches and cream-cheese-stuffed celery sticks. And she treated me to a piece of pineapple upside-down cake that she had made the previous weekend. My, but my mother made the most delicious pineapple upside-down cake.

Barbara was nervous that morning, I could tell. She held her body rigidly, with Edith clutched tightly to her chest, while her arm was linked with mine. My parents had come out to bid us a wonderful first day of school prior to Barbara's brothers joining us, and my mother, bless her soul, got Barbara to smile. My mother then had us pose for a photo with the Vest Pocket Kodak camera that my parents had purchased when they married, a slightly odd-looking miniature contraption, especially by today's stan-dards, though we are speaking about a piece of technology that was produced over a hundred years ago, are we not? Goodness, just to think about it, just to remember it…

My parents said goodbye and headed back indoors just before Barbara's brothers, unfortunately, joined us in my driveway.

"Why you got that stupid doll?" her eldest brother spat. "Let me have it." He reached his beefy arm toward his younger sister, making to grab the doll from her arms. Barbara gasped and spun so her back blocked her brother's attempt.

"You leave her alone, Robert Brown, you big ol' meanie!" I yelled. By that time, I had known Barbara's oldest brother for just over three years. I was six and a half now and starting school. He might have been ten, but I didn't care. Not at all. I had learned, even on that first day when I had met my best friend, that her brother wasn't someone I wanted to associate with if I didn't have to, but I held firm when required to be in his presence. And, unlike Barbara, I didn't live with him and therefore, didn't have to put up with his antics on a consistent basis, so I could exert myself more readily. I didn't enjoy my excursions to the Browns' home, and Barbara never seemed to want to be home herself, so my parents adopted my best friend as a kind of surrogate sister for me. She was at my house all the time in those early years, both day and night. From time to time, her mother would insist that Barbara stay home with her family, but more often than not, Barbara even shared our meals, which was all for the better, for it gave my mother an extra mouth to feed and offered an excuse to experiment in the kitchen. Barbara, like my father, was always complimentary, no matter what my mother served. I, on the other hand, had a propensity for bluntness even then. Perhaps that was another trait I inherited from my mother, for she didn't seem to mind and was often direct herself. In fact, if she spooned something into her mouth and didn't like it, she'd grimace and immediately tell whoever was at the table that by no means would we be forced to eat what she had prepared. Some days, this pleased me greatly. Most days, though, my mother's meals were delicacies to me.

"I ain't no meanie," Robert said. His hand darted to Barbara's side as he attempted to claim Edith once again.

"Robbie, stop!" Barbara cried. "Stop!"

Barbara's youngest brother, the middle child, was named Eugene, and I had grown to like him well enough. He was a quiet boy, so quiet, in fact, that I often marveled when I heard his voice. He would often go about his days unobtrusively. If that boy could have been a fly on the wall instead of a solid human being and a part of the Brown family, he would have been. Eugene, his eyes trained on the concrete of my driveway, stood several feet away from Barbara, Robert, and me. Sometimes I wished he'd stick up for his sister. Wasn't that what brothers were supposed to do? Well, I didn't know. I was only six, after all, and had no siblings of my own. But that was what I had heard, and Eugene did quite the opposite. More often than not, he fled when his brother was near.

"You sure *are* a big ol' meanie, Robert Brown!" I shouted. "Leave her alone! That's *her* Edith!"

"Stupid," Robert grunted as he lunged forward. "Doll."

"Robbie!" Barbara was shedding tears now, fat droplets that stained her cheeks and plonked upon the lace of her dress at her collarbone. Oh, her poor dress. She didn't own many nice clothes, and she had been looking forward to wearing this new dress on her very first day of school. Now her brother was ruining it, not only because of Barbara's elicited tears but because he was now—

"Robert Brown!" I shouted and smacked his arm away from his sister as hard as I could, which was apparently pretty hard for a six-year-old because he halted and turned his head to look at me, his eyes wide but his nose all

23

scrunched up and his jaw clenched. Barbara cowered, but I didn't back down. "You leave her alone. We're just trying to get to school, you know."

"I know," Robert said. "But nows I gotta deal with a sister at school. And she ain't bringin' that stupid doll."

"What's it to you?" I asked, hands on hips. "Why do you care?"

The corner of Robert's lip turned up in a sneer. "I just do," he said.

"Why?" I demanded again. I needed an explanation.

"No business of yours, Martha Laplant."

"It is when you're being a big ol' meanie to my best friend," I replied and stomped my shoe on the ground in a juvenile huff.

"He…" I turned at the sound of Eugene's voice. Had he really just spoken?

"What?" I asked. Robert and Barbara had turned at the utterance too.

Eugene looked back at the ground and shook his head.

"That's what I thought," Robert retorted.

And then, quick as lightning, Robert lunged back into action, snagging Edith from Barbara's arms and holding her up in the air so she had no chance of regaining her prized possession. "Robbie!" she cried. Her face was red and tear streaked. "Robbie, no!" She jumped in her Mary Janes, arms outstretched, but to no avail.

"Robbie!" Barbara cried again as I shouted, "Robert Brown, give that back!"

"No!" Robert said. His face was expressionless now, not set in a sneer, not malicious. It was hard for me to read.

And then my father ran out the front door of our house. He was wearing his work suit; I knew he'd climb behind the wheel of my family's Ford shortly. He caught up to us rather quickly with those large strides of his. "What's the meaning of this?" he demanded.

"Robert's being a meanie," I said. "He took Edith from Barbara."

My father glared down at Robert, who had the sense to look abashed. "And why'd you take the doll away from your sister?" my father asked.

Robert's gaze fell to the ground, and he lowered his arms to his sides, though Edith was still clutched tightly within his grasp. "No reason," he said.

"No reason…"

"Sir," Robert added.

My father narrowed his eyes. No further words were necessary. Robert slowly handed Edith back to his sister.

"Barbara, you tell me if Robert takes your doll away from you again," my father instructed.

"Okay," Barbara said, her voice meek. I knew she didn't dare look at her brother. And I knew, too, that there was no way on God's green Earth that my best friend would ever tell on her brother. That was when Robert would retaliate, one way or another. Oh, but I would. I would tell. He could do nothing to me.

Or so I believed at the time.

"And you, young man," my father said to Robert. "That's no way to treat your little sister."

"Yes, sir," Robert said, his voice low. Although he acknowledged my father's words, I knew he didn't take them to heart. He was only saying what he thought my father wanted to hear.

"Now, off you go," my father said. "All of you. Don't want to be late on your first day of school."

"Bye, Daddy," I said. Although I had already said goodbye to my parents, I took advantage of the moment to stand on tiptoe and wrap my arms around my father's broad lower back. It was as high as my slight stature would allow. My father removed my arms to allow himself the mobility to stoop forward. Then he gave me a tight squeeze. "Love you, Martha Moo," he said. I closed my eyes and drank it all in: his voice, his smell, his very essence.

"Love you too, Daddy," I whispered. And then I let go, grabbed Barbara's free hand—Edith was back safely in the crook of the arm carrying her lunch pail—and set off down the street toward the one-room school building where I would spend my weekdays.

...

In October of 1929, the stock market crashed. I didn't know this then. Not really. I overheard my parents talking to each other about it when they did not know I was listening, but as a girl of just seven and a half, I let it pass me by. It was a whisper spoken between adults and not something a child of my age should have to worry about. I know now that it was something of great importance, that crash of the late twenties that led to the Great Depression, but my parents, thoughtful souls that they were, never let it slip to me then, in those early days, that something was greatly amiss. Oh, I'm sure they talked plenty amongst themselves when I wasn't aware, when they were in a room that I did not share, or when I was off walking the streets and the woods with Barbara. It wasn't until the early thirties, really, that I became abreast of the distress our nation was suffering.

"Where's Robert?" I asked. "Is he sick?" Barbara and I were both ten years old and walking to school. Eugene had stepped ahead of us when he spotted a friend on the narrow dirt road. A leather strap was wrapped around my books and slung over my right shoulder, and I held my metal pail in my left hand, the food my mother had prepared for me nestled inside. I had noticed our household meals had changed in the past couple of years: less meat, more broth. And my mother didn't bake nearly as often as she once had. But I had the mind of a sheltered young girl, so I didn't think much of it. Mother had begun volunteering with the Volunteers of America, so I assumed her work had been taking up more of her time, and so she spent less of it in the kitchen. I didn't know much about volunteering at the tender age of ten and less about the Volunteers of America. But, although we lived in a small town ourselves, there was a larger city not too far from us, and my mother traveled there quite frequently throughout those dreaded days that would become known as the Great Depression. My parents were determined to do their utmost to ensure my childhood wasn't turned upside down, and I know now, as a woman who has seen a myriad of years, that they must have sacrificed a great deal then for my childhood to appear as normal as possible.

Oh, my parents... Even now I close my eyes and see their faces form lovingly in the darkness behind my lids: my mother's smile as she greeted me with painted lips, always with a pair of her beloved heels on her feet; my father's grin as he'd lift me from the floor, often speaking words of endearment, something I would learn pretty early on wasn't typical for a man of those times to do.

So no, it wasn't my parents or anything colossal that occurred within my immediate family of three that apprised me of the changes in our country.

It was the Browns.

"Robbie can't go to school anymore," Barbara said.

I frowned. "Why not?"

"Papa says he needs to work, so Robbie went with him today."

"Work? I don't understand."

"We don't have money anymore, Papa says. He lost his job last year, you remember?" I nodded, so Barbara continued. "He says we were lucky that he found another one, but it doesn't pay good. Mother is afraid we're going to lose the house. Lots of people have, you know."

I shook my head slowly. No, I did not know.

Barbara looked at me with raised brows. "How can you not know? It's happening everywhere, or at least Mother and Papa say. It happened to Papa's brother. He lost his house, and his family had to move in with Papa's other brother."

"Oh, that's terrible," I said then wrinkled my nose. "But lots of people live together. I have an aunt, and she has lots of family living in her house." I truly didn't understand. My family was a sort of anomaly in small-town southern New Hampshire back then. Unlike today, it was quite common for extended relatives to live together under one roof.

"Yeah," Barbara said, "but Papa's brother, he didn't want to move. So it's different."

"I guess," I said, as I shuffled my Mary Janes—shoes that, until that very moment, I didn't realize were too small for my growing feet—against the packed dirt of the road.

"So," Barbara continued, "Robbie has to work. To make money to give to the family, Papa says. Papa says it's his duty as the oldest boy."

"But Eugene doesn't have to work?"

"No," Barbara said. "Not yet. But we don't know what

will happen. Mother is scared. I can tell. And she even told me so."

"What…" I looked at my best friend walking beside me, looked down at her dress, too small for her tall frame, and at her golden hair, which looked rather disheveled that day. I was afraid to ask the question that had formed in my mind, but I simply had to know the answer. "What will happen to you, Barbara?" I felt my lower lip quiver with emotion. "Will you have to leave school too?"

"No," Barbara said, allaying my worst fear with that single word. But I still felt my heart constrict and my stomach ache. "Not yet. Mother doesn't know what will happen. She said only time will tell, but that Robbie should be able to help. At least a little bit, for now."

I pondered for a moment and then asked, "Will he ever come back to school?" I didn't know why I cared so much. Robert was someone that I kept as far away from as possible. I didn't care for him. At all. I should have been pleased to hear that he wouldn't bother me or Barbara on our way to school any longer. Or at school, for that matter. He'd be gone, working. And I believed in any other circumstance, this would have filled me with a carefree pleasure. But that day, walking with my best friend at my side, I knew that things would never be the same. What had been held from me for so long had come to light, even if I didn't yet fully comprehend its ramifications.

"I don't know," Barbara said. "He's fourteen now, old enough to work, Papa says."

"Do you think he'll work for always now? Never go back to school?" I couldn't envisage it. School, for me, was miraculous. Starved for knowledge, I learned new words and how to read and write in school. I even discovered a love for history within the walls of our schoolhouse. And books. Oh, those blessed books. Our teacher, Mrs. Maccomb, a young, fresh-faced woman, who had been my teacher since my initiation into school, had a large bookcase gloriously filled with books of all kinds: textbooks, fiction, nonfiction. And she allowed us to take those books home with us to read at our pleasure. I devoured books at my leisure, sometimes propped up in bed at home, other times sitting against the trunk of a tree in the woods that lined my small backyard. I am convinced to this day that it was young, sprightly Mrs. Maccomb that instilled a love of the written word within me, which would only proliferate as the days progressed. My eyes aren't what they once were, but I still read. Oh, you can bet your buttons I still read. Books make my heart smile.

Barbara shrugged. I watched her schoolbooks bounce against her bottom as she walked. "I don't know," she said. "Probably he'll never come back."

"Oh," I replied. I suddenly felt forlorn. Not because Robert would never grace our presence at school again—ha!—but, putting myself in his place, I feared suddenly that I could be next.

My mother saw my expression later that day when I arrived home from school. She looked a bit disheveled, too, and I wondered if she had been volunteering while I was gone. "What is it, my darling girl?" she asked. She removed the strap holding my books from my shoulder and gently brought them to rest on the hard, narrow steps that ascended to the second floor of our small home. She led me to the couch, a rather uncomfortable piece made from a dark wooden base with upholstery of a bold design that I remember well, since it would sit in our living room for years to come. "Out it comes," my mother said, as she smoothed a tendril of hair off my forehead.

"Are you taking me out of school?" I asked. The entire day had progressed in a panic. At first, the thought was a mere seed, and then it grew and grew until I found myself struggling to concentrate on my studies, my mind otherwise occupied with this fearful possibility.

"Whatever do you mean?" my mother asked me. "Where is this coming from?"

"Robbie Brown has to work," I said. "He wasn't at school. He won't be. Maybe never ever again."

"Ah," my mother said, offering me a wan smile. "Now I see." She pressed her lips together, apparently thinking for a moment, and then she said, "I will not be taking you out of school, Martha. Not ever. Not until you have finished all your schooling days and are ready to enter the world as an educated young woman."

"But Barbara says that lots of people have to work now, that even lots of people are losing their houses, and—" I looked up at my mother, tears prickling my eyes. "Will we have to sell our house? Will we have to move in with someone else? I don't want to be with aunts or uncles or cousins or grandparents. I want to be with you. Alone. Here."

My mother smiled softly. "We will not be leaving this house," she said. "Not if your father and I can help it."

I looked at her, my confusion evidently plain to see, since my mother smiled again and reassured me. "We are okay, Martha. Yes, it is true. There are others that have not done so well these past years. Our country is… in trouble. But it will not last forever. I promise. And your father and I… Please don't worry. Leave the worrying to the adults, won't you?"

Tears dripped from my eyes, but I bit my lip and

nodded. I trusted my mother explicitly. I didn't believe she would fabricate anything.

"Now," she said, as she lovingly touched my arm and offered a bright smile that seemed to transform her features, "tell me all about school."

...

Months passed, and the new year of 1933 rang in. And then, days later, my eleventh birthday. My mother and father allowed me to invite my friends over for a celebration, and though I know now how modest that celebration was, it made no difference to me at the time. I didn't need gifts or a large fanfare. All I truly needed at eleven years of age was the company of those I loved most in the world—especially my parents and Barbara—as well as our imaginations, which proved an asset in those days.

We spent our time in the house until we girls began a game of tag and knocked one of my mother's figurines off a table in the living room. "Out you go," she instructed us. Bundled up in our winter gear, we children headed outdoors to resume our game. When we were through, our bursts of joyful breaths lingering in the cold air, climbing higher and higher until the mist dissipated, I suggested we make snowmen, and my friends all merrily agreed. We formed three teams of two to construct our snowmen and then asked my parents to join us outside to choose a winner. My mother, being the woman she was, said we all won. But my father, God bless him and his ways, looked directly at me, my face framed beneath my thick, woolen hat, and declared, "It's Martha Moo's birthday, so naturally, she's the winner." The girls weren't upset; rather, they cheered, and then my mother suggested we all head inside for hot chocolate and some birthday cake.

Hot chocolate! I hadn't tasted hot chocolate in—goodness, it must have been a couple of years!

My eyes widened, as did my friends', and we all rushed into the warmth of my home, stripped out of our winter gear, and hastened to the kitchen and to the mugs that already waited for us on the counter. Steam billowed from the tops of the mugs, the aroma tantalizing. A very welcome birthday surprise, indeed!

We crowded along the counter and each grabbed a mug, enjoying our first sips immediately. I laughed at Barbara as she lowered her mug from her mouth, and I saw some chocolate adhered to her upper lip. She licked it off with the tip of her tongue and a hearty giggle.

And then music began to play. I turned my head at the familiar tune, "Some of These Days" sung by Bing Crosby. Mother had turned our phonograph on in the living room, and the upbeat tune flowed into my ears as I held my warm mug of delicious chocolate between my palms.

Bing Crosby! Oh, how I loved the man and would for many, many years to come.

I squealed, just as a newly turned eleven-year-old was wont to do, and plopped my mug onto the countertop with a small *thud*, sending some of the dark liquid spurting from the top to stain the counter with tiny, yet thick droplets. I grabbed Barbara by the hand and pulled her toward the middle of the kitchen, where I proceeded to fling my arms around her shoulders and sway my hips from side to side. I wore an enormous grin, and my elation only intensified as I spied my parents from the corner of my eye through the doorway to the living room. They were dancing, hands entwined, legs moving swiftly, and their smiles... Those smiles I will never forget. Father was wearing clothes that needed mending, and Mother hadn't been to a stylist for quite some time, but there they were, hand in hand, dancing merrily as if nobody were watching.

Oh, but I watched. I continued to shimmy with Barbara, but I watched.

The other girls joined in the fun, and soon, my small house was filled with raucous, merry laughter. At one point, Barbara and I even slid to the floor in a fit of giggles.

I wasn't ready for my friends to leave, but they eventually did until only Barbara was left. Later, even she had to head home, though she expressed a wish to stay with me.

"Can't you?" I asked, and Barbara shook her head.

"Not tonight. We're leaving in the morning, and my mother wants me home."

"Where are you going?"

"I don't know."

"You don't know? But why?"

"I didn't ask. But I'll find out tomorrow, won't I?"

"I suppose," I said. "But I wish you could stay."

"Maybe next time," Barbara said.

"Yes," I agreed. "Next time."

"I had fun."

I beamed. "So did I. I'm happy you came."

"Me too."

"You're my bestest friend. My birthday wouldn't have been the same without you."

"I feel the same way," Barabara said.

"That my birthday wouldn't have been the same without you?" I teased.

Barbara swatted my arm and laughed. "You know what I meant."

"I know," I said. "Will I see you tomorrow?"

"Don't know," Barbara said. "'Cause I don't know where we're going. But on Monday, you will."

"Meet me in my driveway?" I asked, hopefully.

"That's a silly thing to say," Barbara said with a smile. "I always do."

I kissed her cheek, and she exited through the front door. I shivered in the frigid January air as I watched my friend go. Once she arrived at her doorstep, she turned back and waved. I returned the gesture then poked my head back into my warm house and closed the door.

...

A few weeks passed, and I found myself sitting beside my mother on our couch in the living room on a Saturday afternoon. We were knitting a pair of mittens from the wool of a sweater that had been my father's. The sweater had seen the worst of its days, and so my mother thought it best that we unravel it and reuse the wool. She had recently taught me to knit, and I found that I rather enjoyed it, though I wasn't sure if it was the actual knitting I enjoyed or the extra time spent with my mother.

A frenzied knock sounded on our front door, and I turned to Mother with surprise in my eyes. She returned my gaze momentarily and then stood, placed her knitting on the couch, and walked to answer the door.

Barbara rushed inside, looked around frantically, and then hastened to my side, not even removing her snowy boots. She wasn't wearing a jacket, or any cold-weather clothes, for that matter. I didn't know how she had kept warm in the late January chill, but perhaps in her rush to my home, she hadn't been thinking of a jacket. Her eyes were red-rimmed and her cheeks puffy. I leaped from the couch, and my knitting project fell to the floor.

"What's wrong?" I asked.

"We're moving," Barbara said without preamble, her voice high and panicked.

"What?"

"We're moving," Barbara repeated. "Papa and Robbie aren't making enough, and Papa was even threatened. He might lose his job. And... and..."

"Shh..." my mother said soothingly. "You girls sit down now. I'll get you a glass of water, Barbara." She exited the room, and Barbara and I sat side by side on the couch, our knees touching. I clutched my best friend's hands in my own.

"You're moving?"

She nodded.

"Where?"

"In with my grandparents," Barbara said.

"Where's that?"

"The other end of town."

The pain that had constricted my heart just moments before subsided the slightest bit. "The other end?"

Barbara nodded again.

"Not... not another town or another state?"

"No."

"But not next door anymore?"

"No." A fat tear dribbled down Barbara's swollen cheek.

"Who's gonna live next door?"

36

"I don't know," Barbara said. "But not us. Not anymore."

My mother returned with a glass of water, which she offered to Barbara. Barbara removed one of her hands from mine and accepted the glass, though she brought it to rest against her thigh instead of bringing it up to her lips to take a sip.

"When do you have to move?" I asked.

"Tomorrow."

I gasped. "Tomorrow?"

"Yes. Tomorrow. We're packing our things now. We'll come back for more, Mother says. But tomorrow we leave."

"But…" I couldn't wrap my head around the news she'd just imparted. "But… I don't understand. Tomorrow?"

Barbara nodded. "They knew. They knew, and they didn't tell me."

"What?"

"Papa and Mother. They knew we had to move, and they didn't tell me until now."

"But… why?"

"I don't know. But they said it was so I didn't"—she hiccoughed a sob—"so I didn't get sad." I watched as my mother sat in a chair opposite the couch, her concern clear in her countenance. Her beautiful gray eyes misted over with unshed tears.

"But I *am* sad. Really, really sad. I…" Barbara held back another sob. "I'm leaving. I can't believe I'm leaving. And I won't… I won't be able to come here anymore."

"Oh, you'll come back," my mother assured her. "You are welcome here anytime, Barbara. You always will be. You might not be next door, but that does not mean that you and Martha are no longer friends. It only means that it might be a bit harder for you to get here. But we'll come and pick you up anytime you want, I assure you. Anytime."

Barbara swiped the tears from under her eyes. "Really?"

Mother leaned forward. "Of course."

"Maybe… maybe you can live here," I suggested. "With me."

Barbara's eyes widened with hope, but Mother said, "I do not think that's possible, my dear. Barbara's parents will want her with them." And I watched as Barbara's hopeful expression disappeared entirely.

"They will," she agreed.

"But… what about school? Barbara," I said, a new wave of panic setting in, "will you have to leave school?"

"No," she said. "But there's a different school I need to go to."

"No!" I cried. First, my best friend was leaving her home, and now she was also leaving our school. When would I see her? My heart felt like it was shattering right there at that very moment. I grasped my best friend's hand even tighter. "Tell me it's not true!"

"It is," Barbara said, and her hand trembled within my own. Mother reached over, took the glass from the precarious clutch of Barbara's opposite hand, and placed it on a tabletop by the chair. I swooped in and claimed Barbara's hand with mine.

"Promise me you'll come and see me tomorrow morning before I leave," Barbara said.

"I promise." I was crying now, giant droplets coursing down my cheeks. I lunged forward and flung my arms around my best friend's shoulders. We both shook in each other's embrace as our sorrow poured out, my misery a scourge that I felt to my very core.

I didn't sleep well that night. My slight, eleven-year-old

body tossed and turned, finding comfort impossible when my mind was so addled. I wept, soaking the pillow that rested against my cheek. I had never known a friend like Barbara. She was more of a sister to me. We were enmeshed, she and I. Our souls had recognized each other's kindred natures from the start—the days, the weeks, the years that followed only intensified our love for one another. My young heart was breaking.

As promised, I walked to Barbara's house the following morning. It was still the weekend, so I wasn't expected at school. I knocked hesitantly on the Browns' front door, and her mother answered. As soon as the door slowly opened to reveal her face, I saw the large bruise that marked not only her eye but a portion of her cheek as well. I said nothing, made no sound. I lacked the ability to form the right words and merely stood there on the front stoop in the cold, feeling lost and useless.

Mrs. Brown held the door open and stepped back to let me enter. I obliged, though unease roiled in my stomach. The door closed behind me, and Robert emerged from the back of the house. At almost fifteen years old, his already stocky body had filled out even further. He wasn't very tall, maybe five foot eight if I had to guess, and my guesses lacked accuracy at that age, to say the least, but his presence was foreboding. His aura pervaded the room as soon as he set foot into it, and my unease intensified.

But I was here for my best friend, so I planted my feet stubbornly and glared his way. Robert scowled at me. "What you doin' here?"

My hands instinctively flew to my hips, which they often did in Robert Brown's presence. "Visiting my best friend," I said with furrowed brows and a frown. Mrs. Brown paid no heed. She merely turned on a bare heel and left the room, shoulders rounded, head down.

"Go away," Robert said, pointing at the door that was now at my back.

"No," I replied defiantly.

"This is my home, and I'm tellin' ya to leave."

"No," I repeated. "Anyway, it's not your home anymore." I didn't know what compelled such words to exit my mouth, but exit they did, and I immediately pressed my lips together, shocked that I had the audacity to speak such an utterance at a time like this.

Robert's eyes narrowed, and his chin dipped almost imperceptibly as he trained his gaze on me. My hands were still planted on my hips, but I no longer felt so sure of myself.

But, as fate would have it, Barbara ran into the room at that very moment, fortunately breaking the silence that filled the space between her brother and me, a silence more deafening than any audible scream could have been.

"You're here!" She hugged me tenderly and forcefully. I felt her relief seep from her core and into mine.

"'Course I'm here," I said. "I promised."

"I just didn't know if you could come," Barbara said. "But I'm so glad you're here. Most of my stuff is packed, and we're leaving soon. My grandparents are coming and then... then..." No further words were necessary. I knew what she meant. Then she'd be taken away. Away from here. Away from me. She might only be moving to the other end of town, but to me, it felt as if she was moving to another country.

We embraced again, our still small arms wrapped around each other with such a fierceness that no one who saw us could mistake our immense feelings toward one another.

"Come here," Barbara said, and she pulled me to her side and up the narrow stairs, where she led me into her room and shut the door behind us. She plopped down on her mattress—the sheets and blankets, I assumed, were packed away—and I followed her. We clasped hands.

"I have something for you," Barbara said.

"For me?" My breath caught in my throat.

"Yes. To say goodbye. To make a promise too."

"A promise?" Despite loving books and the written word dearly, I must have come across as inarticulate just then. I simply couldn't find the words.

"A promise," Barbara confirmed. She reached behind her and to a single nightstand against her wall. She opened a drawer, and when she turned back to me, I saw that she held a single photo in her hand. I immediately knew what it was. I had given it to her after my mother took it on our first day of school.

"But that's your favorite picture!" I exclaimed. "You can't give that to me."

"I can," Barbara replied. "And I will. I want you to remember me."

"How can I forget you? Plus, we'll still see each other."

"But it won't be the same."

"No," I agreed forlornly.

"You'll make new friends," Barbara said. "And I'm afraid."

"Afraid?"

"That someone will take my place."

I hugged my best friend. When I let go, I looked into her beautiful brown eyes. "Nobody will take your place," I promised. "That can't happen."

"But how do you know?"

"Because," I said, "it just won't." Oh, the conviction of the young.

"Here," Barbara said, offering me the photo once again. "Please take it."

"You need it more than me. You're the one moving. And," I reminded her, "it's your favorite."

"And I want you to have it. *Because* it's my favorite. That way, you know how much I love you."

"I love you too!"

"I know," Barbara said, eyes moving to the photo held reverently between her fingers. "Here. Take it."

I hesitated, but only a moment later, I accepted her generous gift. I looked down at the photo, the black-and-white shot that my mother had taken just before Robbie and Eugene had exited their house on my first day of school. When Barbara and I were alone in my driveway, our hopes portrayed by our facial expressions: wide grins and twinkling eyes. Our arms were comfortably wrapped around each other's shoulders, lunch pails in hand. Edith, Barbara's favorite doll, was hanging at her side.

Snap.

"I'll keep it safe," I promised.

"I know," Barbara replied.

No more words were said. We merely sat in each other's presence for a time, tears streaking our cheeks, emotions eliciting a sense of exhaustion.

I don't know how long we sat there, looking down at the photo and into each other's eyes, conveying the love we had for each other; it could have been twenty minutes or two. But before I was ready for it, Mrs. Brown entered Barbara's sparse room and told her it was time to go, that her grandparents had come to get her.

I instinctively flung myself at my best friend and grabbed the sleeve of her worn sweater with incredible desperation. "Don't go," I whispered. I could feel my face heat up even further and a new set of tears well in my eyes.

"I have to," she whispered back. But she hugged me then, and in that hug, I felt all the love she possessed for me pour forth, which somehow, somehow, allowed me to eventually pull back and follow her out of her bedroom and down the stairs. In the living room, Mr. Brown was scolding Robert and Eugene. For what I didn't know, and right then, neither did I care. All my attention was on my best friend.

One last embrace, and I turned around and slowly, miserably, walked out the door and onto the icy stoop. I began my trudge back to my house, the home with vibrant red panels that always welcomed me with its warmth and eased any discomfort I had accumulated throughout my days. But today, my home seemed a million miles away, and it wasn't the destination I desired.

My booted feet crunched on the packed snow in Barbara's driveway. When I approached my front door, I looked back and noticed Barbara lingering in her doorway, her arms wrapped around her chest, shivering. Robert suddenly appeared from behind, flung his beefy arm around my best friend's neck, and tugged her back inside forcefully before slamming the door closed.

I wanted to run over to them, to hasten to my best friend and tell her bully of a brother to let her be. I didn't like that boy one bit, oh no! And now that they were moving clear across town, I have even less opportunity to offer Barbara comfort when her brother wasn't kind.

Who would do that for her now?

And for the first time, the gravity of Barbara's words

rang in my ear. What if I found another best friend? What if someone took her place?

What if someone took *my* place?

I had other friends, true. But nobody compared to Barbara Brown. I might have been young, but youth didn't hinder me from feeling such unadulterated love for another human being, another girl like myself, who was such an integral part of my life. Even at the age of eleven, I told Barbara everything. We confided in each other. Even then, before our interest in boys would develop, I had learned that nothing in this world compared to the love one woman could possess for another. Not a romantic love, no. But a love that burns just as bright.

Both of my parents tucked me into bed later that night. Usually, it was just my mother. My father might have been unconventional for the time, but he left certain aspects of coddling to my mother.

This night, I think he knew that I needed him.

They took turns kissing me on my forehead and then walked out of my room and down the stairs. Time passed. Slowly and torturously. It was the first night since she and I had met that my beloved Barbara was not in the house next door, so close by my side, only steps away whenever we needed each other.

I tossed. I turned. I wasn't even aware that tears were leaking from the corners of my eyes until I turned my cheek on my pillow and discovered the cool wetness against my skin.

And then I heard it: a sound seeping from the living room, up the stairs, and into my bedroom.

Bing Crosby. "Love Me Tonight."

The familiarity of his voice soothed and comforted me. And while I normally would have remained in my room, I was somehow compelled to follow that voice, so down the stairs I crept, careful on the balls of my feet so as not to alert my parents to my wakeful state. I peeked my head around the wall and into the living room and saw something that made my heart flutter, even through the sorrow. I silently sat on the bottom stair and watched as my parents held each other in their arms, my mother's cheek against my father's broad chest and his chin resting against the top of her head. And the look on my father's face: Oh, I didn't know what romantic love was at the time—not how it felt, anyway—but that look spoke nothing of love and adoration, and a child knows, don't they? A child can intuit when they are in the presence of something truly remarkable. And I think it was then that my heart swelled and my endearment toward my father only intensified. I knew a lot of men, even then. I saw my uncles, my grandparents, my parents' friends. And there was Mr. Brown. But nobody exuded an aura like my father's. No other man could compare. I felt it. Inside. I couldn't fully identify it back then, but I felt it all the same. Pride. Contentment. Love. Adoration. Safety.

I slowly stood and walked into the living room. My mother startled when I approached her side, but my father smiled down at me.

"Martha," my mother said, her face soft. "Darling, why in the world are you still awake?"

"I couldn't sleep," I said. I swiped at my eye. There were no tears any longer, but my eyes were puffy, and my skin still felt hot and clammy to the touch.

"Oh, darling," my mother said. She broke from my father's embrace and ran her fingers through my hair.

Then my father bent his knees, placed his large hands under my arms, and lifted me. I wrapped my legs around his waist—even though I thought myself mature at eleven years old—as he held me with one arm, grabbed my mother with his other, and pulled the two of us closer to his chest. "My girls," he said. After a slight pause, he looked down at me, his face so close I could detect every small pore in his skin and the dark stubble on his chin. "We're sorry about Barbara, Martha Moo." His voice, though deep, was soft when he spoke to me.

I rested my head against his shoulder, and together we swayed to Bing Crosby's melodic crooning.

I didn't know it then, but as I sit here nearing the end of my days, as I think back upon that moment, I know it now. My parents were hurting that night too. When they saw me so affected, it inevitably affected them.

I wish all were as fortunate as I was to have such loving parents.

And oh, how I regret that I didn't have more time with them.

MERLE

*I*t proved less difficult than I expected for me to see Barbara after her move. True, I didn't see her nearly as often as I would have liked, but my parents were supportive of our relationship and knew how desperately I wanted to spend every possible moment of my free time with my best friend. So they drove me to the other end of town for me to visit in her home. More often than not, though, one of my parents would drive to Barbara's to pick her up and take her back to our house, where she would often spend the weekends with us. She frequently expressed a desire to be anywhere but with her family, which I understood. I often found myself uncomfortable when at her house, so I could only imagine how she must have felt living with Robert and Mr. Brown.

At times, we would get funny looks if it was my mother who drove me to Barbara's. I didn't realize it then, but at the time, not many women in our town had their licenses, relying instead on the men in their lives to drive them from place to place. Add the fact that our town was rather walkable, and many women would simply trudge by foot to their destination. Oh, it couldn't have helped that my mother often drove with the windows wide open, the wind tousling her hair, her posture erect, assured. I believe my mother had a reputation around town, though that was never a topic of conversation in our home. I merely saw it on the faces of some other folks with whom our paths crossed.

Out she would step, my mother, in her heels and beautiful dresses. Even then, when many of us were still reeling from the Great Depression, and my mother's dresses were well-worn, I thought them beautiful. Perhaps I was biased because of the woman who was wearing them. But no matter. There she was, garnering stares with her attire and her shoulder-length brown hair, which she curled so expertly, her head always held high as if she had not a care in the world.

And her eyes. Oh, her eyes. I swore they shone, and one could see them twinkling even from a great distance. I wanted to be just like my mother then.

The most difficult transition for me without Barbara was school. I still walked to the small one-room schoolhouse where I spent my days. But I was obliged to do so without my best friend. She attended another school clear on the other side of town, and I lamented my time without her. If it wasn't for Mrs. Maccomb, I'm not sure I would have persevered in those early days without Barbara, even with my love of learning. There were two girls with whom I'd struck up friendships: Annabelle, with her red hair and freckled pale skin; and Mary Lou, with her circular black-rimmed glasses and frizzy brown hair. I adored them both, and the three of us had become an entity after Barbara had left. We were never seen without one another during school hours, especially at recess, when one girl would push

48

another on the wooden swing, or the three of us could easily be found giggling by the corner of the schoolhouse. And by golly, did we girls love it when Mrs. Maccomb took us walking to one of the many local farms, where we would spend time with the horses, cows, goats, and pigs as Mrs. Maccomb inserted a lesson into the excursion.

But through it all, even with Annabelle and Mary Lou by my side, I still desperately missed my best friend.

Time passed. The economy eventually recovered, at least enough for me to notice a difference in not only my home but the homes of others, although I still knew several kids whose fathers were unemployed, or whose mothers had entered the workforce—not by choice as I am sure some did but out of necessity to keep their families afloat.

In 1936, when I was fourteen, something miraculous happened in our town. Our schools consolidated! Though many one-room schoolhouses still existed at the time, a small minority of which would run until even the early 1960s, some one-room schoolhouses throughout the state had closed as early as the 1920s. More families owned vehicles as their primary means of transportation, and I suppose even our little town in southern New Hampshire wanted to keep up with the times, especially men who found themselves traveling a bit farther for employment. I didn't know the reasoning behind consolidating schools back then, and at fourteen, I didn't care. But oh, was I thrilled, for with the consolidation, Barbara and I were once again together during the day. Barbara was already acquainted with both Annabelle and Mary Lou and them with her, since we had all attended school together prior to Barbara's departure, but we hadn't traversed the line between acquaintance and friend then. When we were reunited, we became a foursome of sorts, though it would always be Barbara and I that gravitated toward each other instinctually, especially when passing time outside of the school environment.

And it was Barbara in whom I confided my feelings immediately after a new boy started at our school.

A boy that irked me something great, don't you know.

A boy that would change my life irrevocably.

He walked into my classroom on a fall day toward the beginning of the school year of 1937, when I was fifteen and a half years old. I remember the day well. My desk was by a window, and I was looking out this window when the interruption occurred. The leaves were vibrantly beautiful, and I was marveling at the natural progression of plant life, lost in my own reverie, when Annabelle leaned over her desk from behind me and tapped vigorously on my shoulder. I turned to look at her with a frown and saw her staring at the door to our classroom with an expression I would never forget: a slight softening to her features, her lips pressed together, and her eyes almost hungry. I was quite confused. I followed her gaze and noticed a tall boy about my age, standing just within the doorway.

"Class," our teacher announced—although this teacher was kind, and I liked her well enough, she wasn't Mrs. Maccomb. No teacher ever did measure up to dear Mrs. Maccomb—"We have a new student. This is Merle Mayhew come to us from Massachusetts, am I correct?" She looked at Merle, who nodded. "Class, please help me in welcoming our new student."

A collective murmuring sounded around me, and when I looked back over my shoulder at Annabelle, I noticed a pink tinge on her freckled cheeks. Instead of feeling pleased that my friend had a sudden crush, I became inexplicably annoyed. She had experienced crushes before, and I had heeded her constant mooning over the boys, much to my chagrin. I would have much rather spoken about schooling or books or what we four friends were going to do together the following weekend. And now, here was this boy—attractive, yes, but standing there with his sudden unappreciated presence, already stealing my friend away from me.

I loathed him instantly.

"And what brings you to our town?" our teacher asked.

"My father's job," Merle answered. I watched him standing there beside our teacher, posture erect—did I detect a cockiness or was I already biased? His voice was deep, and it surprised me, to tell you the truth. I hadn't expected it. Not from one so young. I assumed, like myself, that he was fifteen years old. Most of the other boys' voices had changed, but those alterations had been more minute. I rolled my eyes at the thoughts that Annabelle was probably conjuring, and I knew that I, along with Barbara and Mary Lou, would hear about this new boy, this Merle, come lunchtime. I dreaded it.

"Very good," our teacher replied. "We are happy you are here with us. Please have a seat. Any open seat will do."

Since there were only two open seats, I watched as Merle walked closer and closer toward me. My stomach dropped when he chose the vacant seat directly at my side. Our eyes caught, and he smiled. It almost seemed genuine, even though I didn't want to believe it. And even then, through my annoyance, I noticed his eyes: green, like the leaves in a forest after a fresh rain. They were beautiful, which only proved to further annoy me.

I heard a shuffling of feet behind my chair and knew that Annabelle was either uncomfortable or eager because of this new boy's proximity.

Merle sat, placing his brown Oxford-clad feet squarely

on the ground, his knees in their long brown trousers practically hitting the top of his desk. I startled momentarily at the sight, for my father owned a pair of those very shoes. I looked up and into this new boy's face and caught him looking right back at me with a sort of smirk the likes of which I couldn't decipher. His expression just irritated me further, so I lifted my chin in defiance, grimaced at him, and turned my head to look back out the window. And do you know what that boy did? He chuckled. I heard him right and clear, so I leaned back in my chair and wrapped my arms in a huff across my chest.

I couldn't concentrate for the rest of the class, sensing this boy's presence beside me. He didn't do anything further to infringe on my comfort, but it didn't matter in the least. His presence was bother enough.

We were eventually dismissed, and the morning progressed until it was time to break for lunch.

Blessedly, all the students in the same grade shared their lunch with one another, so I hastened to the cafeteria from the classroom to seek out Barbara, who often arrived before I did.

She spotted me before my eyes caught her long-legged figure, and she approached my side, lunch pail held in one hand, the same one she had been using since our very first day of school when we were both a mere six years old. Her smile was wide, as it often was when we were together and at school.

"Are we eating outside today?" she asked. "It's beautiful."

Then she must have seen the look on my face because she asked me what in the world was wrong.

I sighed. "There's a new boy in school."

"Okay," she said, side-eyeing me with her brows furrowed.

I sighed again. "And Annabelle has a crush."

Barbara laughed. "Another one?"

"It's not funny," I lightly scolded her. "Now she's going to be talking about this new boy, and well... Why does she have to always—" I wasn't able to finish my sentence as Barbara tapped me on the arm, her gaze set beyond my shoulder. I knew that Annabelle was near.

"Hi," Annabelle said breathily when she approached, a smile on her pink lips.

"Hi," Barbara replied amiably as I gazed at the floor and mumbled a half-hearted hello.

"Where's Mary Lou?"

"Not here yet," Barbara said. "Want to eat outside?"

"Yes," Annabelle said, but then I noticed she was looking around the cafeteria. I knew, of course, that she wasn't looking for our friend but rather Merle Mayhew.

I stiffened, turned on a heel, and headed for the door, desiring the outdoors, where I could inhale a fresh breath of crisp autumn air. Barbara and Annabelle followed my lead, and together, we found a desirable patch of limp grass where we sat and began to eat. Mary Lou found us there mere minutes later.

"What are we talking about?" she asked, crossing her legs and tucking the dress of her skirt under her thighs modestly. She pressed her finger to the middle of her glasses and slipped them back into place.

"How amazing my mom is at making cake," I answered hastily, not giving Annabelle a chance to change the subject to a more undesirable topic.

"She is that," Mary Lou agreed. "Every time I go to your house, she has something else for us to eat, and it doesn't matter what it is. I always eat it. My mother, on the other hand—you would think for all the time she spends cooking and baking that she'd be able to make something that doesn't taste like I'm eating paper." She chuckled, her voice low.

"I think—" I began, but Annabelle interrupted me with a thwack on my arm.

"There he is," she hissed.

Oh, here we go, I thought. But I said nothing.

"Who?" Mary Lou asked, turning to search the area where Annabelle was looking.

Annabelle leaned forward conspiratorially, and both Barbara and Mary Lou joined her at the center of our self-made circle. Barbara was clutching a half-eaten sandwich, which rested on her thighs, the thought of eating quickly discarded. I had warned her about this new boy, but it didn't matter. No. My Barbara did like a little bit of gossip from time to time.

"There's a new boy in town," Annabelle explained. "And to our school. His name is Merle Mayhew and... oh," she sighed. "He's dreamy."

"Dreamy?" I said, rolling my eyes. I found I had become quite adept at doing so that day.

"Yes," Annabelle confirmed. "Don't you think so, Martha?"

"I do not," I replied with conviction. I stuffed my mouth with a large bite of my mother's homemade cake.

"Well, I do," Annabelle said, turning back to Barbara and Mary Lou. "He's from Massachusetts, and he has a look about him... How can I explain... He looks like he's kind."

Yes, that's it, I thought sarcastically.

"I'm sure he is," Barbara said. "Sometimes you can just

tell." Then she turned to me. "Can't you, Martha?" She was challenging me, I knew. Leave it to my best friend to do such a thing. "You are always the one telling us that you can tell right from the start whether someone is a good person or not. You said you did that with me, even though we were just little girls, and you told me that you knew with both Annabelle and Mary Lou, too. So…" She eyed me, her brows lifting. "What do you say? Does this Merle Mayhew seem like a good person?" She brought her sandwich to her mouth and took a bite, the glint in her eyes teasing me.

I would get her for this!

I sighed dramatically and then said, "I suppose so. He did seem kind of nice when he was talking to the class."

"And when he sat down next to you," Annabelle added. "He smiled at you, Martha. And what a smile it was." She sat back. "I wish he'd have smiled at me like that."

"Don't be ridiculous, Annabelle," I said. "He's just a boy."

Annabelle frowned at my scolding, and I had the heart to feel slightly abashed at my harsh tone.

After a moment's silence, I said, "I'm sorry. I shouldn't have said that."

"It's okay," Annabelle replied. "But thank you."

"I'll give it to you," I said by means of conciliation. "He does have a kind face."

Annabelle smiled. And then, her smile transformed, growing wider and wider. "He's so handsome!"

I frowned, but both Barbara and Mary Lou laughed.

"Where is he?" Barbara whispered, turning her head from side to side.

"Over there. Just by the door. He's talking to a teacher."

Barbara and Mary Lou gazed toward the indicated

direction, but I had already seen. I didn't need to look at Merle Mayhew again, thank you very much.

"Ooh," Mary Lou said in her soft voice, "he is handsome."

Annabelle beamed.

I stuffed my mouth with the last bite of cake.

We girls chatted for a while longer, and then it was time to head back indoors and to our respective classes. Much to my chagrin, Merle shared my next class with me too.

He spotted me almost immediately, and his lips turned up in a grin. He found a vacant seat in front of me, turned around, and said, "Hey ya."

My brows creased in response.

"So," he tried again. "What's your name? I remember you from this morning. I'm Merle."

"I know," I said but didn't offer him my name.

Merle smirked. How insufferable!

"Making me guess, then?" he asked.

"I don't care what you do," I said. I was not going to give him the satisfaction of my name. Oh no!

And then my classmate Gloria Birthwright approached my side. "Hi, Martha." She plonked herself down in her chair. I inhaled deeply and sat more erect in mine.

"Martha, is it?" Merle said, flashing that incorrigible grin of his.

I said nothing, merely looked ahead at the teacher writing on the chalkboard.

I heard a deep chuckle before the teacher began to speak and Merle turned back in his seat.

Oh, for the love of God!

At the end of class, I couldn't exit the room fast enough. That night, I had trouble getting to sleep, though I didn't know why, and my stomach ached when the thought of seeing Merle Mayhew the following morning crept into my mind.

Annabelle blushed profusely when she saw him in class and he said good morning to her. He then turned to me with a greeting as well, but I ignored him, right and good. He seemed unfazed, which annoyed me further. Merle Mayhew had that effect on me.

Several weeks passed in which Merle attempted to speak with me, I indicated quite blatantly that I didn't appreciate his efforts, and he grinned in response, almost relishing the challenge.

We girls sat in the school's cafeteria one day in early November when Annabelle announced that she had met a boy in church and that her sights had homed in on him instead of Merle. I was not surprised. This was so very like Annabelle in those days, but she was my friend, and I loved her dearly. Even when she couldn't make up her mind and her heart went aflutter at any attractive boy who crossed her path.

"Anyway," Annabelle told us then, "I think Merle likes *you*, Martha."

"Oh, don't be ridiculous, Annabelle," I retorted.

"I do think he likes you. I see the way he looks at you sometimes. Maybe I was interested in him, but that doesn't mean I'm blind."

I scoffed. "Merle Mayhew does not like me."

"I believe he does."

"Oh, rubbish! And it makes no difference, does it? I don't like him."

"And I don't pretend to know why," Annabelle said. "He's really nice, Martha. He's talked to me a few times. I think… I really think he's a good guy."

"He's talked to me too," Mary Lou said in that shy,

demure way of hers. She smoothed her brown frizz from her forehead. "He doesn't make me feel uncomfortable like some boys do."

"That's right," Annabelle said. "How about you, Barbara? Have you talked to Merle?"

"No," Barbara replied. "Not really. We haven't had the opportunity."

"Well, I'm certain you will," Annabelle said. "And girls, I have news."

"What?" Mary Lou asked, her eyes widening eagerly beneath her black-rimmed glasses.

"My church is putting on a dance!" Annabelle said.

"Ooh," Mary Lou squealed. "Really?"

"Yes, really. And we can invite people that don't attend. So you all are welcome. Promise me you'll come."

"When is it?" Barbara asked.

"Next weekend. My mother has already given me permission to go and to invite you all too. And she said that you could spend the night if you'd like."

"Ooh," Mary Lou squealed again. "That sounds fabulous!"

"I know!" Annabelle agreed. "So tell me you'll come."

"I will," Barbara said.

"I need to ask my parents," Mary Lou replied.

"And how about you?" Annabelle said, turning to me.

"I'm sure my parents will let me go."

"Oh, how wonderful!" Annabelle clasped her hands in front of her with delight. "I can introduce you to Fred."

"He'll be there?" Mary Lou asked. "This new crush of yours?"

"Yes. He already said he would come when he asked me if I was going."

"He asked you?" Mary Lou said, eyes widening again.

Annabelle smiled. "He did ask me. And I said that I would be there. And then he told me…"

"What?" Mary Lou asked, leaning forward.

"He asked me if I would dance with him."

"He did?" Mary Lou whispered.

"He did." Annabelle's freckled pale cheeks tinged pink with pleasure.

"Oh, Annabelle!" Mary Lou exclaimed.

"I know," Annabelle said. She folded her hands in her lap and placed them atop her dress. Her shoulders arched, and her chin lifted slightly. Her expression bespoke her bliss.

I asked my parents that night if I could attend the church's dance event. They happily gave their assent. The following day at school, I found out that all four of us girls had permission to attend and that we would all spend the night at Annabelle's home, which brought me a great sense of anticipated glee. What a fun-filled weekend we were bound to have together!

And then my elation was ruined when Merle Mayhew spotted me as I began my walk home. He ran to catch up and smiled down at me. "Hi ya, Martha."

Hi ya? Why in the world did this boy say such a ridiculous thing?

"Hi," I begrudgingly replied.

"Where you off to?"

I looked up at him with a frown. Didn't he know where I was going? I would have thought, with it being the end of the day and all, that that was rather evident. "Home," I supplied.

"Me too. Where is it that you live?"

"Not far away."

"Me neither," he said. "Maybe I could walk with you."

"I don't think we're going in the same direction," I said.

"But I think we are," Merle replied with a grin. "See, I've noticed that we go in the same direction until Pine and then split off."

I halted and turned to look into those green eyes of his. Their piercing beauty caught me off guard for a moment, but I shook it off and said, "You've been following me, Merle Mayhew?" I stuck my hands on my hips just as I used to do when I was a stubborn, sprightly six-year-old.

"No," he said. "Not following. Just walking myself, you see. And we go in the same direction until Pine."

I huffed and then started walking again, lunch pail in one hand and books slung together on my back between the leather of my book straps.

"So," Merle said, "want to walk together?"

"Not really."

Merle wasn't deterred, though I had no idea why not. I wasn't being very kind.

I continued my pace and Merle slowed his so he could walk by my side. We proceeded in silence for a few minutes until I tripped suddenly on a tree root that was jutting out of the earth. I stumbled forward, my lunch pail clanking in front of me and my books tumbling to the ground. One slipped out of the straps, and Merle bent down and picked it up. He crouched, bottom touching the heels of his oxfords. "*Gone with the Wind*," he said, handing my book back to me.

"Yes," I said. I grasped the book and tucked it under my arm in my haste to get home. I was back to walking when I heard Merle's voice carry from behind me.

"That Scarlett O'Hara is quite a piece of work," he said. I turned and saw him stand from his squatted position.

I halted momentarily before pivoting back and resuming my pace. Before I knew it, Merle was beside me again.

"What do you know of Scarlett O'Hara?" I asked, annoyed.

"Oh, quite a lot," Merle said. "I've read the book, you see."

"You have not."

"But I have."

My head facing forward, I caught him in my peripheral vision.

"She's coquettish, don't you think? Mooning over all the boys, especially that Ashley. And then she—"

I twirled on the pebbled street and looked him full on. "Coquettish?" I demanded.

"Yes. And selfish."

"How could you say such a thing? There was a war going on."

"And?"

I was so taken aback by his opinion that I didn't know how to respond. "The ending," I said, walking once again, though my pace had slowed. "The ending says it all, don't you think?"

"Says what? That she finally realized what a turkey she'd been?"

"Turkey?"

Merle shook his head with a smile. "My dad says it. Thinks they're kind of stupid." He shrugged. "The saying kind of stuck."

"But the ending. She… she does learn. And it speaks to… evolution."

He raised a brow, a grin playing on his lips. "Evolution? Not sure I'd use that word. You think she really learned?

Even after all that time with the amount of people she hurt with her selfish ways?"

"We will have to agree to disagree," I said rather haughtily.

"Suppose we will."

"I just… You've really read it?" My voice lowered.

"Think a boy can't read?" Merle asked playfully.

"No," I said, taken aback again, this time by my slight abashment. "I know you can read. I just didn't think you'd *want* to."

"That's where you're wrong," he said. "It's something we have in common, reading. I've seen you with your books."

"You have?"

Merle nodded, comfortable at my side. "You read sometimes when you're walking home after school. A lot, actually. Watched you almost get hit by a car the other day. And sometimes I see you peeking at a book under your desk instead of listening to the teacher." I felt a blush spread on my cheeks, something that didn't often occur. The sensation was unwelcome.

Much to my surprise, I found I wanted to speak to this boy more. "What else have you read?"

"Other than for school?" He laughed, and again, I surprised myself by smiling slightly in return.

"Yes."

"Let's see, then…" He looked up into the sky before saying, "I like Fitzgerald and Hemingway."

"You do?"

"Mmm-hmm. And have you read Virginia Woolf?"

"Of course I have." I then turned my eyes to him. "*You* have?"

Merle nodded.

"I... I'm surprised," I admitted.

"That a boy like me would like Virginia Woolf?"

"That a boy would *want* to read her."

"There you go again. Don't think too highly of us, do you?"

"No, that's not it," I said. I was pleased to notice the hint of a smile on Merle's lips.

"Not all boys are turkeys, you know."

"No," I said softly, thoughtfully. "I suppose not."

When I noticed Merle had stopped walking, I turned back and looked at him. "What's wrong?"

"Pine," he said, motioning with his chin to the street sign. I hadn't even realized we had come this far. And so quickly.

"Oh, Pine," I said unnecessarily.

"See you tomorrow?" Merle asked.

"Yes."

He took a step away from me, headed in the opposite direction. "Bye for now."

"Bye," I said quietly.

Merle waved before turning his back and sauntering down the road.

Feeling utterly confused and conflicted, I walked the rest of the way to my house with only my thoughts for company.

. . .

The day of the dance arrived, and we four girls couldn't have been more delighted. It was a Saturday, and we had decided to all meet at Annabelle's home before the affair to dress and primp ourselves as best we could. We had been wearing our hair in the style of our time, emulating our mothers' technique as opposed to the bobs, bangs, and ponytails of our youth. When Barbara had been over at my house just months prior, Mother had allowed us to try her wave device, which was an unruly mechanism, to say the least. Mother had instructed us on its usage and even demonstrated it, so once she had left my bedroom, Barbara and I were certain we knew what we were doing. Much to my chagrin and complete and utter shock, the iron was entirely too hot and even scorched off a chunk of my hair! Oh, how I was mortified, let me tell you! Luckily, the tendril had been severed toward the bottom, and my hair was rather thick, so, with some further instruction from my mother, I hid the mistake well enough. By the night of the church dance, that tendril of hair had grown out to its normal length. Because of this mishap, though, I arrived at Annabelle's house with my own iron, a newer contraption that Barbara and I had tried together, an endeavor that had fortunately been successful. It hadn't scorched our hair, and that was good enough for me.

During a typical school day, I wore no makeup. I just couldn't be bothered. Neither did Barbara, though not because of a lack of desire. Her mother had given her permission and even offered Barbara the use of her own supply, but Barbara's father had refused, offering a few choice names of his own for young teen girls who, in his own words, "painted their faces like whores."

Oh, my... No, that isn't good at all now, is it? Mr. Brown was a character with whom I never did like to associate. I never wondered why Barbara preferred my home over her own.

Although I had met them on several occasions, I didn't know Annabelle's parents very well, but I found them to be pleasant enough. They offered us our privacy, and so we got ready for the dance in the room that Annabelle shared with her older sister, who happened to be out that evening. She was not going to the dance, instead preferring to spend her time with a girlfriend. She was not due back home until the following day, so we girls would have Annabelle's room to ourselves.

"How excited are you, Annabelle?" Mary Lou asked. "With your boy going to be there and all?"

"Fred," Annabelle said dreamily as she held a hairbrush to her chest, her eyes rolling upward. She giggled and then brought the brush down on Barbara's golden hair. Barbara, who was sitting on a boxy wooden chair in front of a well-used writing desk, looked into the small mirror in front of her and grinned.

"I can't wait to meet him," Mary Lou told Annabelle.

"Neither can I," Barbara agreed.

Not to be left behind and most certainly not wanting to come across as uncouth, I told Annabelle that I, too, was looking forward to meeting her potential beau. I might have thought Annabelle's numerous crushes to be a little exaggerated, and I might not have understood them, but she was still my good friend, and I could easily sense that she was happy and quite eager to see Fred that night. I was truly pleased for her.

"Maybe you'll meet somebody, too" Annabelle said as she ran the brush one last time through Barbara's hair and then picked up the heated curling iron. Annabelle was clearly speaking to us all.

"Maybe," Mary Lou said, a twinkle in her eye.

"Maybe," Barbara agreed. "Though I'm not sure what

would come of it. There's no way my father would allow a boy in our house." She paused. Then, almost as an afterthought, said, "Or for me to even date."

"Who says he needs to go to your house?" Annabelle asked. "Can't you take him somewhere else? And your father doesn't need to know."

"Annabelle!" Mary Lou chided. "She wouldn't dare be dishonest."

"Won't she?" Annabelle asked innocently. "I'm sorry, Barbara, but we know what your father's like. How will you ever meet anyone with him hovering over you the way he does? And that brother of yours…"

"Ugh. Robert," Mary Lou scoffed. "Don't get me started."

"Maybe we should talk about something else," I suggested. Although I held no love for either Robert or Mr. Brown, they were members of Barbara's family, and I didn't want her to feel like we were speaking ill of folks she had no control over. We don't choose our families, now, do we?

"Maybe *you'll* meet someone," Mary Lou said, looking directly at me.

"I don't think so," I replied.

"And how do you know?" Mary Lou raised her brow. "It could happen. Even to you, the one of us that doesn't care about boys." She laughed. "Maybe *because* you don't care, you'll be the one to meet someone."

"There might be some truth to that," Annabelle remarked.

From her seated position and with the iron nestled in her hair, Barbara quickly gazed at me, and our eyes met. She knew that conversations about boys never interested me. Bless her heart, she changed the subject.

"I'm not a very good dancer. Annabelle, maybe you could teach me?"

"Yes! I would love to! Let me finish your hair, and then we'll have a lesson. You're bound to be asked tonight, and you'll need to know what to do."

We chatted a bit more as Annabelle finished with Barbara. "Done," she announced and patted Barbara's shoulders. My, but my best friend did look beautiful. Her hair was set nicely in waves, tight against her head. Her makeup had already been applied—that was one thing her father certainly didn't need to know of and about which Barbara didn't need to feel guilt. Her ruby red lips accented the tone of her skin and even seemed to set off the golden hues of her shiny hair. She looked up at me with a smile. I gazed into her brown eyes with their speckles of green and smiled warmly back. Barbara walked to a larger mirror in Annabelle's room and grinned at her reflection.

"I look different," she said.

"Gorgeous," Annabelle said.

"Absolutely," Mary Lou agreed. "You should wear makeup more often."

Barbara caught my eye once again, this time through the mirror. No words were needed. That happened often between the two of us, my best friend and I. She knew my thoughts even before I vocalized them, and right then, she knew that I thought her to be beautiful. Makeup or no makeup, styled hair or not, my best friend was beautiful.

"Okay," Annabelle said. "Here." She grabbed Barbara by the arm and pulled her toward the center of the room. "I'll play the boy so you can practice." She placed one palm in Barbara's and then instructed Barbara to fling her leg out in a certain way. Twirls and giggles and rapid movements ensued as Annabelle taught Barbara the Lindy Hop, a dance that both Barbara and I already knew and of which Barbara feigned ignorance for my sake, bless her heart.

Annabelle and Barbara ended up in a heap on the floor, all squinted eyes, open mouths, and hands on bumbling, heartened bellies.

Mary Lou took my hand, and together, we began to dance. Further laughter ensued.

"Careful, careful," Barbara said as she giggled and lightly touched her hair. "You'll ruin it."

Our laughter eventually subsided, and Annabelle went to work on my hair as Barbara waved Mary Lou's. When through, Barbara, Mary Lou, and I took turns beautifying Annabelle. Before we knew it, we were ready, clad in our best dresses and shoes. Mine were a pair of off-white T-straps with a small heel that were perfect for walking around and, yes, dancing. Oh, how I loved those shoes. They were the first pair that truly made me feel like the young woman I was becoming.

We piled into Annabelle's family vehicle—such a tight fit that I had to sit on Barbara's lap. She wrapped her arms around my waist as her thigh pressed against Annabelle's. Despite my petite stature, my head nearly hit the roof of the car, so I leaned forward. Annabelle, from the middle seat, laced one arm through mine and the other through Mary Lou's, an enormous smile on her red lips. We four girls shared the same tube of lipstick that night, something in our giddy teen-girl camaraderie we felt brought us even closer together.

Annabelle's father parked the vehicle, and we exited. I stumbled and righted myself by palming the side of the car. Annabelle burst out into laughter, which only intensified my own. My, but we were happy that night.

There was a chill in the air—it was autumn, after all—

and the aroma of decaying leaves wafted my way in a slight breeze. I've always loved the smell of dying leaves. Nothing about that scent reminds me of demise. Quite the opposite, actually. For me, it holds a renewal, a sense of promise. A thrill.

I stepped forward, my arm linked with Barbara's, and my shoes, my wonderful, adored shoes, crunched on the leaves that littered the ground in the church's parking lot. When we entered the community room, my eyes took in the sights with wonder. The room was decorated so tastefully. Tables were filled with various drinks and snacks, all of which we girls could partake of. Lights twinkled on the ceiling, and some balloons floated about the room. In a corner, a full jazz band strummed and trumpeted. The fast-paced melody filled the room, reverberated from the walls, and entered my body, which sent a splendid thrill to mark the skin on my arms. I smiled. Already, a good number of people were on the floor, and to my utter delight, they were dancing the Lindy Hop.

"Have fun, now," Annabelle's mother told us. That was all the permission we girls needed to grab one another's hands and rush to the middle of the dance floor, immersing ourselves within the throng. We began to dance, Barbara with me and Annabelle with Mary Lou.

Oh, how I thrilled in those movements, my lithe body quick on my feet. I was quite the good dancer in my time, you know. Quite.

"Where's your beau?" I asked Annabelle as we shimmied on the dance floor, trying to raise my voice over the instruments playing their upbeat tune.

"I don't know," she shouted back. "I looked, but I don't see him yet."

And then she jumped as a hand spooked her from

behind. She turned, and immediately, I saw her face transform. She smiled demurely and looked at the floor. A blush crept over her cheeks. When she gazed back up, she grinned so widely it was a marvel her lips didn't crack. And much to my amusement, the grin on the boy before her was just as extensive.

I glanced over at Barbara and Mary Lou with my own smile of pleasure for our mutual friend. Then I saw both of their faces alter as they spotted something beyond my shoulder. Mary Lou smirked, and Barbara held her mouth partially open in surprise. I turned slowly and couldn't quite believe what—or who—I saw.

It was Merle Mayhew.

Merle Mayhew at the church dance. In the very same room. With us.

With me.

I wasn't sure why it surprised me so. Ours was a small town, after all. And although Fred lived in the next town over, I was sure many of our classmates attended this church. But surprise me it did. And very much. He must have sensed my confusion, for he looked at me with a soft smile and said, "Fred invited me."

I cocked my head as I looked at the boy in front of me, at his loose-fitting trousers held up by a pair of suspenders, with a white button-up shirt underneath. His tie looked as if it had been knotted hastily, but it fit him well. I asked, "How do you know Fred?" Again, I raised my voice to be heard over the music.

"He's a buddy of mine. Thought I might like to come tonight."

"Oh," I said, rather stupidly.

"Nice night for a dance," Merle said.

"What?" I held my hand over my ear, indicating that I couldn't hear well over the band's playing.

He leaned in closer toward me, and this time, I heard him. "Nice night for a dance."

"Yes," I said. "It is."

"You're pretty good," Merle remarked.

"What?"

"You," he said. "You're a pretty good dancer."

He had been watching me?

"Oh," I said. "Thank you?"

Merle laughed. Then the song ended, and the band immediately struck up a new tune. Mary Lou and Barbara both cheered at my side, grasped onto each other's hands, and began to dance. Fred offered his hand to Annabelle, and she happily accepted. Merle and I stood there in the center of the dance floor flanked all around by smiling, joyful, bouncing dancers.

"Shall we?" he asked.

I nodded uncomfortably. What else was I to do?

He took my hand, and I was immediately surprised at how warm and soft his skin felt on my own. I wasn't sure what I was expecting, but softness was not it. The sheer size of his hand startled me too. It dwarfed my own.

Merle grinned and then spun me on the dance floor. I tipped onto the ball of my shoe, my dress billowing around my calves with the momentum of the fast-paced, sudden move. And then I laughed, caught up in the moment. We spun. We kicked. We danced. I looked up into Merle's face and spotted that smile of his, and I did believe that it was genuine. I thought about the first day of school, not that long ago, and how he had grinned down at me while taking his seat beside me in what would become a classroom that we shared. That day I had assumed he was cocky, hadn't I?

71

But this—the Merle before me now? No. At that moment, I questioned the way I had treated him, the assumptions I had so readily allowed myself to conjure.

I chastised myself as he spun me again. But, for some reason that I couldn't quite explain at the time, I wasn't entirely ready to let all my inhibitions go.

The song ended, and we friends dropped our arms to our sides, sweat dripping from brows and foreheads. Annabelle's cheeks were flushed, and Mary Lou's red lipstick had marked a minute portion of a front tooth from the breadth of her smile that I quickly indicated surreptitiously she should wipe away. Fred led Annabelle off to the refreshment table while Mary Lou grabbed Barbara's hand and tugged her forward, presumably to head outside for a bit of fresh air or to see something in the distance that had caught her eye. I didn't know. But my best friend held back momentarily, looked me directly in the eye, and creased her brows questioningly. I gave a minute nod that was enough to let her know that I was okay. Appeased, Barbara let Mary Lou lead her off the dance floor.

Another song struck up, but instead of Merle asking me to dance again, he leaned in close and offered me something to drink.

I shook my head.

"Something to eat, then?"

I shook my head again. Merle chuckled with amusement.

"A walk? It's a bit hot in here, dontcha think?"

I frowned slightly, pondering, but then acquiesced and let Merle lead the way outdoors. As soon as I set one foot over the threshold of the church's community room, I was startled by the chill that encircled my body. I wrapped my arms around my chest and brought my knees closer together.

Merle held up a finger and jogged back into the building. Before I had time to wonder what in the world he was doing, he was back at my side, offering me a brown sweater. "Took it off," he explained.

I shook my head. "I'm all right."

Merle grinned and arched his brows. "You're shivering," he said. "And I see goose flesh."

I looked down at my arms and noticed that Merle was right. I frowned, and that was permission enough for Merle. He gently laid the sweater over the wide, puffed shoulders of my dress, and I tugged it closed around my collarbone. It smelled of soap. "Thank you," I said. I had to admit to myself that it was rather kind of him to think of me in such a way. Most boys our age were too busy fooling around to care.

"Welcome," he replied.

"But," I said, "won't you be cold?"

Merle shook his head. "No. I don't get cold easy."

"Oh." I looked out into the night and then up at the stars in the sky, a proliferation of sparkles. Their beauty was never lost on me, not even in my youth.

"That's the north star," Merle said. He squinted and pointed with his arm outstretched.

"I know," I said.

"Do you now? I'm not surprised." He grinned as he looked at me and then turned his attention back to the sky.

"And that one there. See that? That's Cassiopeia. Looks kind of like a W, doesn't she?"

"Yes," I said. "I know."

Merle raised a brow. "And next to her are Andromeda

and Perseus. Also Lacerta and Cepheus. And one other, but I don't remember the name right now."

It was my turn to raise my brow. "How do you know that?"

Merle shrugged. "Kind of into astronomy."

"I can see that," I said, amazed at his memorization.

Merle grinned again and pointed. "That there, that one is Perseus. It's huge, really. Cassiopeia is part of it with her W. See that, there? And there? You go through the North Star and down. And then, to the right of Cassiopeia. Do you see it?" He was moving his pointed finger, and I tried to follow but got lost.

"No," I admitted. "I know the North Star, and I know Cassiopeia because she's easy. And I know the Little Dipper. Sometimes I can see the Big Dipper, but it's harder for me to find."

"It's tough to explain just by looking," Merle said. "I've got a book. It's easier to look at that first, familiarize yourself with it, then go back to the sky, you see. Maybe I'll show you sometime."

I pressed my lips together, paused, then nodded slightly.

"Martha!" I turned at the sound of my name and saw Annabelle as she lingered in the doorway and motioned for me. "Come on! This is a good song!"

I looked up at Merle then let his sweater drop from my shoulders. I handed it back to him. "Thanks again," I said.

"You're welcome." He motioned toward the doorway, and together, we walked into the building's warmth as the band played their tune, and the dancers spun merrily on the dance floor.

Merle hung his sweater on a hook by the door beside several coats, sweaters, and scarves, and we joined our friends. He and I began to dance, and my feet found their

74

bounce again, my shoes clicking and clanking on the floor.

And then I was caught off guard when murmurings followed by a bit of chaos ensued. The band stopped playing, and I watched as several partygoers gathered around a prone figure on the dance floor. My fingers found my painted lips as my eyes widened in surprise. It was a middle-aged woman, her eyes closed, hair splayed around her face, in apparent distress. My immediate instinct was to stand there like a fool, looking on as others rushed to her side. I didn't know what to do, how to help. I was pushed as something whirled past me, and I lost my balance. I righted myself and noticed that a tall boy was kneeling beside the woman, hovering, turning her over, placing his ear over her mouth. He was nodding, saying something to the others who had gathered around. One man rushed off one way and another in the opposite direction. The boy placed the woman's head in his lap, and only then, as I looked from the woman's face and up the boy's trousers to the white shirt beneath his suspenders and then to his controlled expression, did I realize that it was Merle cradling the woman's head in his lap. Merle. How had he gotten there and so fast?

And then the woman's eyes blessedly opened, and I released a breath I did not know I'd been holding until then. My heart pounded less fiercely in my chest, and I held my hand to my stomach as my body attempted to cease its quaking.

I watched as Merle helped the woman sit up, his palm on her upper back to steady her. She swiped her hair off her cheek and smiled wanly at Merle. The smile he returned made my heartbeat quicken again, though this time for an entirely different reason.

75

Merle and another man helped the woman to her feet. I looked at Barbara, who stood at my side with her hand over her heart. She mirrored my gaze, and when I looked deeply into her brown eyes, I knew we shared the same thoughts, the same sense of relief and bewilderment. But instead of offering appeasement, I found myself ever more confused at the emotions coursing within me. They were sensations I had never felt before, and I wasn't entirely sure what to do with them.

As an adult and especially as an elderly woman, I have heard it said time and time again to the younger generations, "You have time." Time to fall in love, time to wait out a marriage, time to truly find yourself. Many of us older folks, people who have lived a lifetime and more, feel wizened and have experienced so very much that we look upon the younger generations with a sense of aged superiority. Who meets another when they are fifteen, falls in love, and has that love last through the ages?

Not many of us, I'll admit. I have seen entirely too many marriages fold, too many relationships fail, to harbor naïveté.

And yet, I knew. Oh, I knew.

When I think back upon my time with Merle, when I think of all we've been through and all we've done, I realize it was this very moment, at that church dance, in that stuffy room with its sweaty, jovial inhabitants, that I knew. I knew that Merle was someone special. And I know now what I didn't understand back then: I was in love.

So sometimes fortune smiles upon you at a mere fifteen years old, you fall in love, and you are blessed in life to have that love last.

Even when someone's heart has expired.

...

Merle and I began walking home together from that day forward. He'd offer to hold my books, and instead of keeping them close to me, stubbornly refusing to relinquish my hold, I let him. And when we arrived at Pine Street, we did not part ways. Instead, Merle walked me to my doorstep, saw me in—often chatting a bit with my mother if she was home while my father was still at work—then retreated down the road and to his own house.

We never did declare ourselves a couple. It was just a natural progression. I think each of us knew what was in the other's heart. Our eyes spoke. Our expressions spoke. Our postures spoke. And that was all we needed, even then. We could read each other.

He kissed me for the first time on one of those walks home. It was an afternoon in late November, and the chill in the air bit my cheeks and left its mark. As usual, Merle was carrying my books for me. I wrapped my jacket more snugly against my chest and tugged my rounded felt hat farther over my ears, though it didn't cover them completely. That was the fashion of the time, I suppose. Not like the hats of today, with which I can cover the scalp of my aged head in its entirety, along with my ears and, golly, even my chin if I so wish.

I bought a particular monstrosity of a hat for myself a few years ago; by look alone, I thought it would keep the heat from escaping my head and dissipating in the frigid winter air. I need all the heat I can muster up, you know. This old body of mine has trouble regulating temperatures these days. And jackets. Can I just touch on those for a moment? When Merle walked me home that day, so many years ago, I was wearing a woolen blue wrap-coat, tied at its center with a knot. Now, my mother owned a fur jacket at that time, and it did have a rather bulky fit; it was nothing like the coats you find on the shelves these days, I assure you. The jacket I bought recently makes my slight figure look immeasurably comical, all puffiness and bulk. But it is warm, and at this stage of my aged life, warmth is what matters. And if I walk down the street, slow though I am, and make someone smile because of the ridiculous sight they behold, well... that makes me smile too. But I digress...

We were walking home from school that day, Merle and I, and he suddenly stopped and stood there in the middle of the vacant road, staring down at me. I couldn't fully decipher his expression, but it made me blush nonetheless, a sensation that the skin of my cheeks had not been used to feeling until Merle entered my life. It was as if he was searching, grasping, discovering. My stomach began to tingle, and I pulled my jacket even closer to my body as I dared myself to return his gaze and fall into his striking green eyes.

And then he bent down. Slowly, slowly, until his warm lips touched mine, and oh... I will never forget it. It was seventy-six years ago, but when I close my eyes and think of that day, when I remember the feeling of his lips on mine— my, how it makes my heart smile. The world paused for me right then. I no longer felt the frigid wind upon my cheeks, could no longer hear the banging of an ax from the house next to us, or even the lone bird that had been chirping from a tree not far away. Nothing. Time stopped, allowing me to marvel at these new sensations: the feeling of his lips; the taste; his breath upon my cheek when he pulled back;

his smile. The way his lids sat heavy over his eyes. The softening of his face. The whooshing of my own heart beating.

Don't you wish we were afforded our first kiss all over again? If it wasn't a pleasant experience for you, then the moment could be erased, and you could start from scratch, knowing what you do now, allowing yourself to be immersed in the novel sensations. But, if like me, your first kiss was a priceless experience, you could rewind to that moment time and time again, feel what you felt inside, linger there. Relish it. But, because that's not possible, I am thankful for my memories. I am thankful that I can still close my wrinkly lids over my milky eyes and conjure this image of Merle in my mind as he looked down at me. That I can dip back in time, plunge into the past, and remember.

Sometimes Merle comes to me in sleep. I dream about him, the man I have lost. Sometimes I yearn to sleep so that he'll be there with me, that we will be together. For always. But I am lucky. I have all my faculties about me. I might not have full control over this body of mine, oh no. But my mind is still as sharp as a hawk's talon. Well, mostly...

He took my hand after that kiss, not uttering a single word. He merely looked down at me and I up at him. And we walked. Slowly. We were in no rush. It was just the two of us. Even when we passed by other people walking, even when a neighbor's dog approached us, tail wagging enthusiastically to say hello, it was just us. When I stooped down to pet that dog's head then watched him rumble away, I felt Merle at my side, a constant desired presence, a promise. The two of us.

Even at fifteen years old.

...

79

．．．

Time passed, as it always does. I think back upon those years at the end of the 1930s and into the '40s, years of turmoil for our country, yes, but also for me personally. Time passes quickly. Too quickly.

Until it doesn't, and you wish it would.

In the summer of 1941, I was nineteen years old and working for a kind old man in his attorney's office. Merle was still in school, his desire to become a doctor necessitating many more years of study. Luckily, we still saw each other often, though not as often as I would have liked. Though I enjoyed my work, my days felt long, and the time I got to spend with Merle felt short, always ending when I wasn't yet ready to say goodbye.

I took after my mother, I suppose, since I was a rather independent, nonconforming young woman for the time. My mother, in fact, still volunteered on a regular basis, wore those heels of hers, and held her head high when around town. She was the type of woman that drove with all the windows down, not caring a lick about mussed hair. She loved to feel the wind upon her face and the freedom of movement.

And golly, I recall more than one occasion when my mother suddenly halted her vehicle, leaving me stupefied in the passenger's seat, and stepped out into traffic to rescue an animal that she had spotted in turmoil. Once, it was a raccoon lumbering across the road in broad daylight. My father had not been happy about that one, let me tell you. *What were you thinking, Ruth? You know I love your good heart, but you could have been killed. It was probably rabid!* I chuckle to myself now, thinking of my father's expression and replaying my mental image of my mother, heels clicking, cars honking as they swerved to pass her by, as she ushered a raccoon that should not have been there in the first place across the street.

Another time, I was with my mother when we had parked downtown to do a little shopping, and we heard a whine coming from a short distance away. She caught my eye and then scurried over, again in heels, to investigate, with me trailing behind. And wouldn't you know, a young pup had gotten herself stuck between a garbage can and a concrete wall. She was clearly petrified as we approached her, eyes wide, squirming all about. The poor thing was bleeding, the red liquid spotting her mangy brown fur. My mother knelt and spoke to the little dog, her voice low, soft, and soothing. It took ages for that pup to calm, but calm she did, and my mother and I could eventually move the hefty garbage can just enough for the dog to wriggle out of her predicament and into my mother's waiting arms. My mother drove with that little bundle on her lap all the way to the shelter, one hand on the wheel and the other petting the girl's small head. We later learned that the shelter bathed her, cared for her wounds, and found her a family with whom to live. My mother and I continued our shopping that day despite my mother's scuffed shoes and the unsightly tears in her stockings. In fact, I think she was rather proud of her disheveled appearance. The smile on her still-red lips bespoke the pleasure she had received in helping the stray, and I know she carried that with her as people stared at her walking by.

My mother...

After we had completed our schooling, Barbara and I had acquired our own apartment in town and moved in together. Managing the rent was much easier with Barbara splitting the cost, and I would have felt very lonely, indeed, if I was living by myself. I was used to the lively presence of both my mother and my father and to sharing my dinners with them as well. I relished the company of others. And although many young women of my time resided with their parents until they were married, that was not something I wanted to do. Miss them I did. But I also yearned to experience more of what life had to offer, and I had their blessing to do so. It helped immensely that I still lived in the same town and saw my parents often.

Annabelle, Mary Lou, and I spoke frequently. Annabelle and Fred married when they were both eighteen and resided one town over. Mary Lou was living with her parents and was working in a factory sewing various uniforms. I was abysmal at sewing back then. And who am I kidding? Sewing never has been a particular talent of mine. I'm still terrible at it! I often found myself looking to Mary Lou when I needed some work to be done, and my friend was happy to oblige.

One day melded into another.

Until the day that changed everything.

I was walking home from work on that summer day— my apartment stood about a mile from the office— marveling at the beauty that surrounded me. I was fortunate to live next to a park that boasted a playground for children, an abundance of tree-lined trails to hike, and a small pond where we could enjoy a light jaunt or a picnic lunch. Summertime in New Hampshire, in all its glory, has always thrilled me. The scent of blossoms in the air, the chirping of birds in their trees, the lushness of color appealing to the eye. And this day was no different as I walked next to the park, mere steps away from my apartment. The sun shone down on my face, and I lifted my chin to the sky, closing my eyes, and breathing it in, letting it soak into my skin. Merle was going to meet me soon—though I should have time enough to freshen up before he arrived—and I was very much looking forward to my time with him.

I walked ever so slowly by a thick line of trees, enjoying the beauty of the day, as the sound of children playing enveloped me. I couldn't see those joyful children through the thick mass of bushes and trees, but I smiled at the calls of youthful joy lingering in the air. The street was rather barren, for which I felt thankful, since it offered me more peace in my walk. I felt the earth beneath my shoes—flats, for by that time I had realized, unlike my mother, that I detested walking in heels—and the slight breeze on my shins' exposed skin.

And then a tug, forceful enough to make me stumble and fall. I was being dragged, my dress catching on pebbles, my thigh scraping against dirt and then branches, pricking my skin, a pain radiating outward, enough to make me cry out.

A hand on my mouth.

In my hair.

Pulling.

An aggressive jerk on my dress. A rip, the sound accosting my ears, fear flooding from my extremities right to my very core.

"Think you're so good." A male's voice. Grunting. Hostile. Filled with loathing.

I knew that voice.

I kicked, flailed, tried anything I could to get away from him. I couldn't scream, though I wanted so desperately to do so. His hand was still on my mouth, pushing hard.

I bit down. He yelped, and his hand retreated.

I tried to scream now that I could, but my voice was stuck inside me. I grasped at the ground, at anything.

It was no use.

Another rip.

I was panicking. Crying. Desperate. In pain.

And then relief.

He was no longer on me, no longer tugging, probing. The moment his weight lifted, I felt a blessed release.

The sound of skin on skin. *Oof.* A body dropped to the ground.

I scrambled to sit up. My heart was pounding. My entire body was shaking profusely. My leg was bleeding, and my dress was in ruins. One shoe had fallen off, but I wasn't aware of my appearance at the time. My mind was elsewhere.

I was lifted into someone's arms. I dazedly looked up.

Merle.

How had he found me?

He ran. Faster and faster, with me limp in his arms.

I laid my head on his chest and forgot myself, forget everything. Gave myself over to oblivion.

But not before catching sight of my attacker, bloody and wreathing on the ground.

Robert Brown.

...

"I can't believe he did this."

Barbara had arrived home to find Merle gently cleaning my wounds with a warm cloth as I lay on the couch. Her eyes went wide, and she rushed to my side and asked me what had happened. When I told her, she placed her hand over her heart and fell into a chair. She was now pacing the room—back and forth, back and forth—and starting to drive me mad.

"Believe it," Merle said, his deep voice barely audible.

"What has gotten into him?"

"He has always," I managed to croak, "been... troubled."

"Troubled?" Barbara said incredulously. "This is more than troubled, Martha. He was trying to... He was trying to..." She didn't need to finish her sentence. We all knew what he was trying to do to me.

Merle ran the cloth down my thigh, wiping the blood from a rather deep gash in my skin. It would leave a scar, right and good. A scar that I have even today. A scar that reminds me daily of what occurred and of what *could* have occurred had Merle not been there.

"How..." My eyes fluttered.

"You need to rest," Merle said. "Don't talk."

But I needed to know. "How were you there? How did you know?"

"I got here early," Merle said. "I was waiting outside the building. I saw you walking down the street, by the park. And then I saw... One second you were walking toward me, oblivious. The next, you were on the ground. Then... gone. I ran. Don't think I've ever run so fast in my life. Lost my hat." He let out a soft chuckle, striving to lighten the situation. I appreciated the attempt.

"You love that hat." I tried to smile, though it hurt to do so.

"I have to go to my parents," Barbara said. "I just have to! I know Robbie hasn't been happy in a while. I know he's had a difficult time. I know he's been angry. I know he's rather jealous of you and me, Martha, that we have this apartment together, that I like my job. But I never... I just never thought..." She shook her head ever so slowly while clenching her eyes shut. When she opened them, she repeated, "I have to go to my parents."

Merle turned on her. "And what is your father going to do about it?" he asked. I had never heard him sound so upset, so full of abhorrence, my Merle. He was typically a jovial sort of person, slow to anger. But that day, I saw a completely different side of him. "From what you've told me and what I hear, he's just as bad."

Barbara stumbled backward, but she didn't refute Merle's statement. She knew it was true.

"My mother, then," she ventured.

"Won't do anything," Merle said. Again, that was true. Mrs. Brown never could step up to her husband.

Merle looked at me, bloodied cloth in hand. "We have to tell *your* parents, though."

I shook my head, shame and embarrassment radiating within me. A few tears dripped from my eyes, stinging the scrapes on my cheeks. I swiped them away. "Please don't tell them," I begged. "I don't know what my father will do. Please, Merle, tell me you won't say anything to them. It will crush my mother."

"I'm sorry, Martha," Merle said softly. "They need to know. They care for you. They love you."

"And I them," I said. "That's why they can't ever know." My voice was pleading.

Merle sighed. For a moment, I thought it was out of resignation, but I was wrong. "We have to tell them," he insisted gently.

I laid my head back and closed my eyes. I knew he was

right. Oh, how I wished circumstances were different, but they weren't. What had happened to me happened; there was no way of denying that. I was marked, scarred.

I didn't know then that most of my scars would be internal.

Merle agreed to let me heal for a time before we told my parents. A few days later, on a Saturday evening, we arrived at my parents' home, having set prior dinner plans that we adhered to, despite my wishes to cancel.

My mother opened the door, a wide smile on her painted lips. When she saw me, her smile vanished. "Martha! What happened?" She ushered me inside and insisted I sit on the couch. I obliged, having no desire or energy to resist.

"She was attacked," Merle explained. "A few days ago. On her way home from work."

My mother's hand flew to her mouth. "Attacked?" she whispered. "By whom?"

Merle opened his mouth to reply but was interrupted by my father, who had just entered the area. "Hello!" he boomed, not immediately reading the room. Then he looked from Merle to me, and his eyes narrowed darkly. "What's going on?"

"Martha was attacked," my mother said. Her eyes welled, and her lower lip trembled. "A few days ago on her way home from work."

"Attacked?" my father asked, looking directly at me. I feared he could sense my shame, and a blush crept onto my wounded cheeks. I averted his gaze. That didn't deter him, though. He walked to my side, knelt, and looked me in the eye. "Tell me," he said. And although I was fighting many concurrent feelings within, my father, there by my side, attentive, his body so large in contrast to my own, was a welcome presence that seemed to comfort me in a way. I believe, even if it was just for a moment, I regressed back to childhood as I looked into my father's eyes, back to a time when I ran to him for solace.

The tears that had welled were unbidden but insistent. They spilled onto my cheeks. My chest began to heave. My father immediately wrapped his massive hand around the back of my head and pulled me to his broad chest. I wept into his shirt, clutching onto the front of it as my emotions poured forth.

Merle spoke over my sobbing. "Robert Brown," he said. "It was Robert Brown."

Mother gasped, and I felt my father's hand grip my head a bit more tightly.

"How do you know?" my mother asked.

"I saw."

"I don't understand," my mother said. "What do you mean, you saw?"

"I saw him grab her," Merle said, and a sob broke from my mother, audible even over my own. "I ran, Ruth. As fast as I could. I... didn't know who it was until I had Martha. I've only met him once, but that was enough. I punched him several times, left him there."

"Where is he now?" my mother asked.

"I don't know."

"We have to find him," she said. "Something must be done!"

"No," I cried into my father's chest. I lifted my head, blinking rapidly in an attempt to correct my blurred vision. "Please don't. He'll only... Maybe he'll hurt me more?"

"But Martha," my mother protested, "this boy cannot be allowed to do this to another. Certainly, you see..."

"No!" I cried. "I'm… I'm scared." I grabbed at my father's shirt again and looked him in the eye, imploring.

He returned my gaze, intent. I could see his inner angst. And then he spoke. "I'm going to the police," he said.

"No, Daddy, please. No."

He stood, leaving me grappling from the couch.

"Merle," my father said. "You coming?"

"Yes, sir." Merle looked at me, and in his expression, I saw him pleading with me to understand. Of course, now, after all this time, I do. But then, in 1941, after the scariest experience of my life had occurred, and my body throbbed with scrapes, cuts, and bruises—it was hard for me to understand. It was a different time then, not only for women but overall, compared to how things play out today. And all I wanted to do was weep, to let my torment free. To sleep. To heal.

To forget about everything that had happened.

But what I didn't know then was that such an experience, such trauma, would never and could never be forgotten.

I watched my father and Merle walk out the front door of my childhood home, taking my youth with them.

…

A slap on the wrist: that was essentially what Robert Brown was given as punishment for attacking me. The police questioned him, questioned Merle. Questioned me. They saw the physical marks that had been left on my body, saw Merle's scraped knuckles, and saw Robert's black eye and beaten-up cheek. But even with the physical evidence in front of them, the police claimed that it was his word against ours, that clearly I had been attacked, but it couldn't be proven Robert Brown had done the deed. Yes, his face was a distorted mess, and yes, Merle's knuckles were scraped, but that only proved that both Merle and Robert had been in a fight. It was one man's word against another. Apparently, my word counted for nothing. There were no other witnesses, they said. Nothing could be done. They were sorry.

Sorry.

...

My physical wounds healed, but the internal trauma proved much more difficult to contend with.

For her part, Barbara stuck by my side, ever the supportive friend. Not once did she question the validity of what I claimed, and for that, I was truly grateful. Perhaps it was easy for her to believe because of the childhood she had led, watching her father's fists upon her mother's face, hearing her brother's words, privy to the way Robert interacted with his family, especially Eugene. Eugene had dropped out of school. Living under that roof had become too much for him. Leaving must have been difficult for him, what with his inhibited personality and all. All I knew of Eugene at the time was a frightened little boy, cowering under his older brother's wrath.

But we all find strength when it is most needed, I suppose. Perhaps leaving wasn't difficult in the least.

Barbara and he spoke about once a month at the time of my assault, though their parents didn't know that. Eugene had made Barbara promise that she would never reveal his whereabouts to their family, and it was an easy agreement between the two siblings. One day, when we had first moved in with each other, Barbara even confided in me that she wished she, too, had broken relations with her father and Robert. Fear and a sense of unwarranted loyalty had kept her tethered to them, she supposed. She did not, however, desire estrangement from her mother.

Barbara's strength came after Robert attacked me.

She never spoke to Robert again after that day. She attempted to converse with their father, to reason with him, but he wasn't having any of it. Some people are set in their ways, refusing to believe the truth even when it's staring them straight in the face.

Barbara didn't fully break contact with her mother, though the pair didn't connect regularly, and whenever they did, Barbara was left with a deep feeling of depression for a day or two afterward. It was difficult for my friend to see the bruises lining her mother's jaw or the way she cowered at a fast-moving object or a loud noise. But, even with Barbara's coaxing, Mrs. Brown was just that: Mrs. Brown. Mr. Brown's wife. The submissive role of a wife unto her husband had been ingrained in her from an early age before the turn of the century, and she held to it. I don't think she ever possessed the mental capacity to break from her bonds. I watched my best friend struggle with this dynamic for many, many years until her mother passed at the age of seventy-two. For my dear friend, her mother's death was one of sorrow but also one of release. Her mother was finally free, though Barbara's sorrow stemmed not from the loss of life in death but from the loss of life when her mother was actually living it.

The hot days of summer waned, and the leaves began to change. First, a single leaf on an abundant tree would turn yellow, and then the transformations would proliferate until every last leaf had turned, wilted, and slowly descended to the ground.

Thanksgiving arrived in the midst of this seasonal alteration, and with it came a visit to my paternal grandparents' home with Merle. Everyone was there, just as they had come throughout my childhood: aunts, uncles, cousins. We were a large family, on both sides, and my father and mother were the only adults that had just one child. Though we grew up together, my extended family and I, many of us lost touch throughout the years, as families sometimes do. Times changed, and people moved on. My grandparents remained where they set their roots until the days in which they perished. Most of my aunts and uncles did, too, but my cousins—in time, many of them sought enjoyment elsewhere, building their lives around jobs, spouses, or in the case of one female cousin, a climate change.

Thanksgiving was a boisterous affair, and I found myself enjoying the festivities immensely with Merle by my side. It helped, I'll admit, that my physical wounds had healed by then, and nobody in my extended family had been apprised of my attack. Although my father and Merle had sought the aid of the police—what good that did us!— my father and mother had promised, for my sake, to keep the news just between us.

Oh my, but the Thanksgiving feasts of my youth were unparalleled. We ate much as we do today, but there was such a comforting sense of camaraderie at the time and within my family that I remember them well even to this day. We had no pressing engagements to keep us apart, and most of the extended family at the time of my youth lived within half an hour of us at the time. That's not to say we had no drama. Oh my goodness, no. We most certainly did. But it was whispered behind hands, spoken behind backs. I'm not sure if that's any better than getting it right out and into the open like I have learned to do. At my age, you don't keep secrets. If you want to know something about me, you just need to ask. I'm not ashamed of my life. Yes, I have made mistakes, as we all tend to do. But I have grown to believe that those mistakes only proved to mold me, to shape me. We all strive for self-actualization. We never do fully achieve that goal, no. Not perfectly. But we strive nonetheless, and each step toward self-actualization only proves to make us stronger, more empowered.

The elation I felt after that Thanksgiving feast of 1941 didn't last long. There was a war going on in Europe, a war that I had been sheltered from in my small New Hampshire town and within my even smaller community of friends and family. A war that was so very far from home and my nineteen-year-old mind. But with the bombing of Pearl Harbor, the United States entered that war, and it petrified me. My darling Merle was only twenty. What would happen to him? Even my father was just middle-aged and still quite strong and able-bodied. I feared for them both. That fear might have been exaggerated, but war does that to you, does it not? My mind was reeling, racing. My emotions were affected by what I saw and heard around me, and that proved to only frighten me further.

But as luck would have it, neither of them had to fight. And yet, as I think upon those days, was it luck, really? What about those young men that *did* have to go overseas?

What about the men that left wives and children, mothers and fathers, at home to fight, whether it was by choice or conscription? It is said that ten million United States men fought in World War Two. Ten million. Fifty million were required to sign up for the draft. I close my eyes even now and think about that number. It is so gargantuan that I cannot comprehend the sheer quantity of men, merely from this country alone, that fought. And of the ten million, neither Merle nor my father was among them.

I had several cousins who were shipped overseas and several other former schoolmates and acquaintances that volunteered, were conscripted for duty, or found work here at home that directly impacted our war efforts. Two of my cousins didn't make it home alive. One uncle, on my father's side, flew home in a casket as well. This particular uncle had joined the war effort even before the bombing of Pearl Harbor, and his body was flown home a mere month after the United States declared war.

The agony on my father's face during his younger brother's funeral is something I am sure I will never forget. I sit here at one hundred and one, and I still see the wretchedness in his countenance when he saw his brother's casket for the first time. I was there. My strong, broad, hard-working, formidable father wore a look of such unabashed misery that his torture was palpable, projecting through the air and finding my heart with ease. I watched my father through blurry eyes and a feeling in the pit of my stomach I had never experienced before as he ran his hand down the length of the casket from which his brother would never rise. There had been no viewing. There wasn't enough body for that privilege.

While my father helped to bury his brother, and while we said our goodbyes to other loved ones lost in the war,

Merle continued his schooling. The war had somehow given him even further conviction that becoming a doctor was the correct path to pursue. He believed that if he could heal those that were afflicted physically and spare their loved ones the pain of their loss, then one very substantial objective of his life would be fulfilled day in and day out.

Shortly after that glorious Thanksgiving with my extended family but before the loss of my uncle, Merle told me another of his life's purposes was to be my husband, to walk this road beside me, to become a family.

Merle asked me to marry him soon after the bombing of Pearl Harbor, when our world was in the midst of entering the worst war it had ever encountered. When hope was lost and futures were uncertain, we clung to each other, finding light in the bleak depths of darkness. I was still only nineteen and Merle twenty. So young, I know. But as I've said before, sometimes you are one of the fortunate ones. Sometimes love finds you young, and you know, don't you? You just know that it's a love to last the ages. And oh, how Merle and I showed the world!

We weren't in a rush to marry, though. War rations were meager, and many of our friends and relatives were off fighting or otherwise preoccupied with various war efforts. Plus, no piece of paper was needed to prove the love we shared. No, people could see it in our faces, I was sure, from the way we looked at one another and the way we acted when we were together. No one could doubt that we had already pledged ourselves to each other, marriage certificate or not.

But oh, even though I knew a wedding wasn't necessary to express my love to Merle, I yearned for that wedding all the same. The dress, the cake, the groom. Our friends and family at our side in celebration…

I had to believe, you see. I had to believe that the accursed war would end. When you are living a nightmare, you need to grasp onto hope as tightly as you can, a saving grace, a way to keep yourself afloat so you don't plunge under murky waters never to resurface, fill up your lungs, and sustain your heart with life-saving air.

Had I known then what I was soon to find out, we would not have waited.

But we were young. Even despite the war and the losses we'd suffered, we thought we had all the time in the world.

Oh, if only I had known.

FATHER

*W*hen I think about my father, even now at my ancient age, I still find myself, upon occasion, mentally referring to him as Daddy. Fierce, loving, affectionate, a fighter. His love for my mother and his love for me were never questioned. He was not like a lot of other fathers that I had met during my childhood. Oh, I'm not saying that other girls didn't love their fathers just as much as I did, or that other fathers didn't show affection or care for their children. I'm just saying that my father, to me, was the best. Because he was mine. And when someone is yours, they hold a special place in your heart, sometimes even helping to fill it completely.

My first memory of my father was from when I was perhaps three. I had been playing outside with a doll, pushing her in a buggy, when I discarded the buggy entirely and bent down to scoot a toy truck across the grass. I lost my balance, and my hands sprang toward the ground to catch my fall, but my forehead hit the truck, and an immediate burning pain shot through the area. Of course, I began to cry. Mother ran to me straight away—the door had been left ajar, so I presume she was keeping an eye on me from inside the house. I never did wander far. She took one look at my forehead, and the expression on her face sent me into a new flurry of tears. I began to scream. I felt the blood dripping down my forehead and onto my cheek. Mother ushered me indoors and set about finding a cloth. She placed me on the kitchen counter and pressed the cloth to my head, shushing me. Even then I could intuit that she was scared, and I felt her fear inside of me.

And then my father entered the room. He was smiling, which confused me. Mother wasn't smiling. She was scared. My forehead was throbbing, a cloth placed upon it. I hurt. Why was he smiling?

But he approached me, winked down at my mother, and placed his hand over her shaking one as she held the cloth in place. She slipped her hand from under his and slowly retreated backward until she had fled to the living room. Daddy and I were alone. She must have been relieved that he had taken over, but I was still scared. Tears continued to course down my cheeks, and I was sobbing so forcefully that every few moments, my chest heaved as I attempted to catch my breath.

"Now, now, Martha Moo," my father said. "No need for that. Let me see." He lifted the cloth from my head, and I watched as his face inched closer to mine, his eyes on my wound. He inspected it, but his face betrayed no fear as my mother's had. Instead, he replaced the cloth and smiled down at me. "See? Nothing to worry about. Just a little scrape. Now, come here." He scooped me up from the counter, hand still on my forehead, and I wrapped my legs around his waist. His sheer size dwarfed my meager three-year-old body, and I suddenly felt very safe as he held me in his arms. My sobs subsided until only a hiccough remained, then I rested the unblemished side of my head right above his heart. I felt his warmth and imagined I could hear his heart beating, though I'm not entirely sure I did. But what I did do—and this I am certain of—was sing. In my head. A song that I made up at that very moment as my father cradled me in his arms.

I love you, Daddy.
I love you, Daddy.
I love you, Daddy.

And so on. Perhaps it was because of my limited vocabulary at the time that I couldn't think of anything more complex to sing, but honestly, nothing else really needed to be expressed. That was exactly what I thought and how I felt: I loved my father.

The blood eventually stopped its flow, but by that time, I had fallen asleep, still nestled within my father's strong arms. He must have laid me down to nap because I remember waking on the couch and looking around the living room, disoriented. I heard my mother humming from the kitchen, and the scent of spices tickled my nose. My father was in the room, and he stopped what he was doing, looked down at me, and said, "Well, she lives. How are you, Martha Moo?"

And I smiled. My head throbbed, and my stomach was still a bit unsettled from the entire ordeal, but I smiled. Just as my father was smiling at me.

Maybe I'm misremembering the details of that day.

That wouldn't surprise me after all these years. But what I do remember, fully, was how I felt in my father's arms and the tickling sensation that coursed within me when he smiled at me while I otherwise was full of fear. He allayed my misgivings. I felt his love, his strength.

That was simply who my father was.

And I loved him for it.

When I met Barbara, and she began coming around to our house more often, I think my love for my father grew, if that was even possible. I didn't understand then what I would later learn about Barbara and her family. But I intuited that her homelife wasn't a happy one, and my parents welcomed her into our house from the get-go with open arms, ready and willing to make her feel comfortable, appreciated, and an extension of our family.

This speaks to who my parents were, both as individuals and together.

That's not to say my parents didn't fight. Golly, did they fight. Not often, but when they did, it was always a doozy, I can tell you that. They fought brazenly and without restraint. My mother's face would contort, her painted lips pressed together in anger, then they'd open as she spat out some sort of retort at my father. And Daddy gave it right back. They'd fight in front of me too. But never did they name-call. And they always, always calmed rather quickly, tempers receding, and apologized. My father often made the first overture, the lines of his face softening, his shoulders rounding. He'd take a tentative step toward my mother, and as soon as he did, I would watch as my mother's posture relaxed, and her anger, too, slowly melted away. Words were spoken, and further apologies were made. I don't remember what my parents fought about, and I'm not really sure it mattered much. What I do remember is what happened after they fought: those apologies and my parents' ability to come together as two rational adults.

When Merle and I fought, I would often think of my parents. I never did learn how to push my anger aside as well as they did, let me tell you, and I'm thankful that Merle had a very unruffled personality. It kept us together, I'm sure. Unlike my parents, who could speak directly after throwing angered words w at each other, I often had to leave the room when Merle and I fought throughout our long-lived relationship. I had to process information on my own before I was ready to push my pride aside and admit any wrongdoing. But as I pondered, my thoughts always traveled to my parents. Their images would enter my mind, and the way they looked at each other after an argument—well, I can see those expressions even now when I close my eyes and search them out. And they helped me. They gave me the strength and reasoning to approach Merle after an argument and speak calmly.

So yes, my parents fought, mind you. But I believe that arguments are a natural part of any relationship. It's how you argue and the validity of the apology afterward that counts.

I remember my father on my first day of school as Barbara and I met at the end of my small driveway. Her brothers, Robert and Eugene, had joined us. Eugene I didn't mind, but Robert I didn't like. Oh no, not one bit. But you know that by now, surely, so it comes as no surprise. I remember how Robert took Barbara's doll. Goodness, I even remember her name, that doll of hers. Edith. Did I tell you that already? I'm sure I did. My mind is strong, acute. Especially for my age. But I do tend to repeat myself at times.

Robert—bully that he was—had taken Edith from my

best friend, and my father came out of the house to inquire about the ruckus being made. Don't you know, he fixed that situation right and good. That was my father for you. In my memory, I see Robert's face, dejected. That could just be a twisted remembrance for me, molded to my own devising. But I'll keep it as such.

Oh golly, do you know what my father did when he first met Merle? It was when Merle had first started walking me home from school. Those were early days. Oh, but I have the fondest memories of them. My mother was often home when I arrived from school if she wasn't off working with the Volunteers of America. What surprised me on this particular day, though, was my father's presence. Why was he home? My father was almost always at work during the week at that time of the day.

Merle had walked me to my doorstep, and as he was handing me my books, still wrapped in the leather strap that bundled them together, the front door opened, and there stood my father. Merle was a tall boy, but it appeared as if my father loomed over him, broad as he was. And the look on his face wasn't one I could quite decipher. He wasn't even looking at me. Instead, he looked directly at Merle. And oh, I've got to give it to Merle. That boy… He wore a smile and appeared entirely unfazed to encounter this imposing figure before him. "Hi, sir," he said. And he stuck his hand out. It hovered there, between him and my father. My father looked down at it then back up at Merle. Then he looked over at me for a moment before planting his eyes back on Merle. And then slowly, ever so slowly, he reached out his hand and accepted Merle's offering.

"Hi," my father mumbled.

I laugh when I remember that moment. My father had not been one to mumble.

"My name is Merle Mayhew, sir."

"Yes, all right," my father responded. And I must have looked at him with a confused expression because he shoved his hands in the pockets of his trousers and said, "Nice to meet you, Merle."

"It's nice to meet you, too, sir."

My father cleared his throat, his expression still unreadable. "And how do you know my daughter?" He didn't speak forcefully or with accusation. Rather, he sounded truly curious.

"She and I go to school together, sir," Merle said. "I moved to town not that long ago, you see. My family and I, that is. I met Martha on my first day at school."

"Is that so?"

"Yes, sir. She has been really nice to me."

Then I must have startled a bit at Merle's statement, for my father looked at me with a narrowed brow. And how could I not have startled at what Merle said? I most definitely had not been kind. Not in the beginning, mind you. But that was just Merle, I suppose…

"Is that so?" my father repeated.

"Yes, sir. I don't live too far away. We walk home together now."

"Is that so?" my father asked again as if he had no other replies in his repertoire.

"Yes, sir."

"Do you live on this street?"

"No, sir," Merle said. "Not on this street. On the other side of Pine."

"I see," my father said, tilting his head. "And you walk my daughter all the way here?"

Merle smiled and placed his hands in his pockets, just as my father had, though Merle's gesture was one of comfort rather than confusion. "Yes, sir. I like the walk. And the company."

My father looked at Merle then—really looked at him. My eyes darted from Merle to my father then back to Merle again. What in the world was going on?

Eventually, my father said, "Well, then. Thanks to you."

"Of course, sir," Merle said. "You're welcome. My pleasure. Martha's a good conversationalist."

I was?

My father cocked his head to the side once again, his face nearly expressionless but for the slight furrowing of his brow. "Well, then," he said, "good to meet you, Merle Mayhew. We'll see you around, I'm sure." And with that, my father removed his hand from his pocket and offered it back to Merle.

His grin enormous, Merle shook my father's hand. "I'd like that, sir. Thank you." Then Merle turned to me and said goodbye, and with a merry wave, he jaunted down the driveway and out of sight.

My father held the door open for me, not saying a word. I heard my mother singing along with a Bing Crosby song in the kitchen. I wanted to ask my father why he was home. I wanted to ask him what had just happened and what he thought of Merle. I was confused. No boy had ever walked me home before, and I liked Merle. My father was often open with me, never one to hold back words, but right then, and with his silence, I felt a sensation in the pit of my stomach and found that I was not only confused but nervous.

My father walked out of the living room and into the kitchen, leaving me behind. Instead of following him and greeting my mother, I walked up the stairs and to my bedroom, where I deposited my belongings onto my bed, sat down with a thump, and attempted to sort through my feelings.

I didn't emerge until I was called down for dinner. My parents were already seated at the table and dishing themselves out some food when I approached. Slowly, I sat down, placed a napkin in my lap, and helped myself to portions of the meal my mother had prepared.

The table was silent. I looked over at my father, who was entirely too busy inspecting his food. Then I looked at my mother. Her eyes were downcast, but she had the shadow of an amused smirk on her lips. And then I noticed, much to my surprise, that she must have kicked my father under the table. I saw her upper body move in tune and my father drop his fork from his lips as he stared over at her. His eyes widened as he held her gaze, a pleading look on his face.

And that's when my mother laughed, the sound melodic and bright.

"What is going on?" I demanded. "You are both acting so weird!" My stomach flopped.

My mother's laughter only intensified, and she placed her fork down on her plate so it wouldn't slip from her fingers. I looked at my father and noticed a slight pink tinge on his cheeks. Blushing? Was my father actually blushing?

"Oh, get on with it, Ruth," he said, clearly uncomfortable with the situation playing out before him.

"It's just…" She was hunched over now, her shoulders shaking. "Oh, Arthur. You should see your face!"

"Don't know what's so wrong with my face," my father replied as his chin dropped even farther toward his chest.

My mother's laughter eventually diminished. She looked at me, and I must have appeared horrified because she said, "Not to worry, Martha. Your father here, he just doesn't know what to do now that his baby girl is growing up. Do you, Arthur?" She looked at my father with a very playful expression, and his blush intensified. Her gaze moved back to me, and she said, "He doesn't want to believe that another man has entered your life. He"—and here she chuckled—"your big ol' dad who always seems to have everything together, he's just realized that he doesn't know anything!"

"Wha—what do you mean?" I asked.

"Oh," she said as she patted his hand, "your father is just a big old sappy baby himself sometimes." But beyond the humor, I saw the look in her eyes. It held love and adoration.

My father lifted his gaze from his plate, his cheeks still tinged pink, though the color was fading. And he smiled. A big, goofy, uncomfortable smile. And it made my mother burst into another bout of laughter. And then, to my surprise, my father joined in, his chuckles deep and hearty. *What in the world?* I sat there at the dinner table, feeling utterly lost. But when they both looked at me, their eyes shining—my mother's tear-filled—because of her excessive laughter, I chimed in. I couldn't help it. I laughed too. I laughed until my stomach ached and tears coursed down my cheeks. We laughed until our food cooled, and when we finally got to eating, even though it was no longer hot, it tasted heavenly.

Although I didn't understand it then, when I think back on that day after experiencing so many disparate reactions from my girlfriends' families when the girls introduced boys to their parents, I'm thankful for my father and mother both. But especially my father. I'd known some fathers to stand looming over a young man who'd arrived to take their daughters on a date, glaring at the boy with malice, judging him even before the boy had a chance to open his mouth in self-defense. By golly, I even had one girlfriend who told me about the time she introduced her date to her father one evening before the boy took her to see a movie. She had been so eager to go out, and she adored this boy, truly. She hadn't the slightest inkling that anything would go awry. But, as the boy entered her home, one of the first sights he saw was his date's father shining his gun collection. That boy left the girl's house in such fear that he didn't touch her all evening, not even to hold her hand! He never did ask her out again, sadly.

So, when I think of instances such as these, I'm thankful that my father's initial reaction was one of utter surprise, not anger. He did not threaten Merle. He spoke no unkind words. He merely grappled with the realization that I, his daughter, was becoming a woman. His actions speak volumes to me, even all these years later. It wasn't anger I had seen on his face that day. My father was uncomfortable. My blessed, wonderful, adoring father was uncomfortable. And not because he didn't want Merle there on his doorstep but because, perhaps, he had to come to terms in a mere unexpected moment with how fleeting time was.

I think if my father had reacted as some other fathers have, in a threatening manner, it would have made me feel not only anger at the way he treated Merle but anger at the way I would have felt he was treating me as well. His reaction would not have been directed at me, but it would have made me feel that it was nonetheless. If he had treated Merle in such a manner, that would have spoken to me about my father's lack of confidence in the choices I made for myself. But that was not the case. My father trusted me. I know that now. He trusted me. It was just hard for him to begin the process of letting go. And through his manner and the words he used with Merle, I believe that he was also expressing a sort of respect for the young man I chose to associate with.

And that spoke volumes too.

From that day forward, Merle was always welcome at our home, especially when my parents found out that our relationship had morphed from platonic to a budding romance. My father never expressed any doubts about Merle's intentions toward me, though I wasn't privy to the internal thoughts he chose to keep hidden.

My mother adored Merle, and it's no wonder why. Merle always had a smile on his face. That was just his way. And he was genuine. I believe those around him knew this to be true. A certain aura surrounded my Merle. Some people just pull you in. Some people, by their very presence, make you feel comfortable. Some even make you feel good about yourself.

A particular memory I have makes my heart smile fiercely. It was after Robert Brown attacked me and after the bombing of Pearl Harbor, when Barbara and I were living in that small apartment adjacent to the park, and I was working my first job as a secretary for a local attorney. My mother called me up one night and invited me over to the house for dinner. She told me to bring Merle and Barbara and, in an effort to be inclusive, I'm sure, any beau that Barbara might have had at the time. Since she hadn't one, it was just we three that showed up at my parent's door. I stepped right on in—even though I had moved out of the house, I still thought of it as my own, and my parents never indicated otherwise. We walked out of the frigid December air and into the warm living room, and an immediate sense of peace settled within me. Because it was nearly Christmas Day, the small space boasted a decorated tree with gifts already wrapped and placed underneath. Decorations abounded throughout the room, and the upbeat melody of a jazz rendition of "Santa Claus Is Coming to Town" was on the radio, a rectangular wooden contraption that my mother kept next to her record player near the stairwell. The air was fragrant with the scent of cranberry, apple, and cinnamon, and my stomach rumbled. Mother made the best pies, and I hoped that the aroma I detected was just that.

I shimmied out of my knee-length, woolen, wrap-around coat—a coat that I had had for a few years by that time—and hung it lazily over the stairwell banister. Merle removed his trench coat and placed it on top of mine, followed by Barbara with her jacket.

"Welcome, welcome!" Mother entered the room, a printed apron tied around her waist and resting against her dress. I smiled when I spotted the Santa Clauses that adorned it. The patten summoned memories of my child-hood. Her grin was wide, her lips were lined with bright red lipstick, and her cheeks were pink. Her blue-gray eyes shone as she walked my way, arms outstretched. When she embraced me, I felt crushed beneath the weight of it. Even my petite mother could assert her strength when she wanted to.

"Oh, how I've missed you! We're going to have a wonderful meal tonight." She held me at arm's length. "Good thing you're here, right? I'll feed you up."

"Feed me up?" I said, nearly rolling my eyes. "I do eat, you know. And you saw me last week. I don't think much has happened since then."

"Everything has happened since then," my mother said.

"Huh?" I cocked my head.

"Oh, nothing," she said dismissively before her eyes

quickly darted to Merle at my side. Her smile widened, though I'm not sure how she managed that without her painted lips cracking in the process.

"Hi, Merle," my mother said. She stood on tiptoe in her heeled shoes and pulled him down and toward her. Merle made an *oof* sound but chuckled and hugged her right back.

"Hi, Ruth."

When Merle first met my mother, he had respectfully referred to her as Mrs. Laplant. My mother had looked right at him, flung her hand in the air, and declared, "No Mrs. Laplant this and that. You call me Ruth, won't you?"

Merle had been taken aback but willingly obliged. In truth, I think this informality pleased him. It had taken my father quite a bit longer to suggest Merle stop calling him "sir," but he eventually did, and so by this particular Christmas dinner, Merle addressed my father as Arthur. I liked it so much better. So much less stifling, isn't it? Though I do believe wholeheartedly in addressing your elders with respect until they direct you to the less formal title.

My mother greeted Barbara, and then I watched as my father entered the room, taking up nearly the entire doorway, with a smile on his handsome face. His dark hair was slicked back, and he wore a shirt and tie. "Daddy," I said with a pleased smile of my own, happy to see him. "You're dressed up."

"Have to dress up to see my Martha Moo," he said.

"And you're still calling me that." It wasn't a question, of course. And truth be told, the term of endearment I'd heard since my earliest days only intensified my pleasure at being in the company of the people surrounding me then, the people I loved most dearly in the world.

"You bet," my father replied. He wrapped his big arms around me and leaned down for a hug. Having inherited my mother's height, I stood on tiptoe to reciprocate. He smelled of pine and pomade, and I drank in the scent, letting it fill my soul.

And then my father grabbed my hand and began to dance to the jazz tune still playing in the background. I laughed then kicked my leg and let him spin me around. Merle grabbed my mother, and they began to dance as well, Mother in her apron and all, her melodic laugh reverberating throughout the room. Though Barbara was smiling, she had been left alone, so I dropped my father's hand and motioned toward my dearest friend. Leave it to my father; he wasted no time in shimmying toward Barbara, grabbing her hand, and giving her a spin. She laughed with delight, and I thought my heart was close to bursting.

We danced and even began to sing along to the radio when Glen Miller and his Orchestra played their rendition of "Jingle Bells." Such a quintessential Christmas song, is it not?

Oh, how we relished that time together, my loved ones and I. Robert's attack had only occurred months before and was still on my mind daily, but in that moment, it was forgotten. I held no wounds, physical or emotional. Only love existed. Comfort and caring and family. The wonderful family I had been born into as well as the family I had chosen.

How had I gotten so lucky?

Eventually, we stopped dancing. I noticed that a sheen of sweat covered my father's forehead. Barbara was nearly panting from her exertions, and my mother was fanning herself with her hand. Merle stood in the center of the room with his hands in his trouser pockets, the bow tie he

111

was wearing cocked askew, and his woolen newsboy hat on the floor, where it had landed as we danced. He picked up the hat and planted it on top of our jackets on the banister. His brown hair was slightly tousled, which I found endearing.

We sat down to a splendid dinner of scrumptious turkey —Mother always knew how to cook it just right—along with giblet gravy, homemade cranberry sauce—which she always made with cinnamon, nutmeg, and cloves—bread rolls, and roasted sweet potatoes. Although I felt completely stuffed after that meal, I ate a slice of my mother's apple cranberry pie nonetheless. Oh, that pie! Despite all my efforts through the years at recreating her exact recipe, I never have been able to do it. That pie belongs to Mother and Mother alone. Golly, do I miss it.

We sat at the table for a while after eating, simply talking amiably and listening to the radio's Christmas tunes. My heart swelled that day. Not only because of my time with my parents, Merle, and Barbara but because of what happened afterward as well.

We said our goodbyes later that evening when the waxing crescent moon was high in the sky, though it was such a small sliver that it was hardly noticeable. Merle and I smiled as we stepped out into the frigid night air and immediately spotted a very bright, twinkling North Star. By that time, Merle had shared his book of constellations with me —many times over, in fact—and I was a bit more adept at identifying them, though I would never be as good as Merle.

After climbing into Merle's vehicle, he set off for the apartment I shared with Barbara. I was blessedly content in the passenger seat of his car, languidly sitting with my head against the headrest, while Barbara occupied the seat behind me. When Merle veered off in a different direction, I didn't immediately question it. I figured he was just taking an alternate route home. But when we pulled up next to Annabelle and Fred's place, and Barbara exited the car, I was surprised, to say the least. Annabelle was hanging out of the doorway, peeking into the night as Merle's car idled in her driveway, with Mary Lou next to her! And then Fred, taller than either woman, appeared behind them and smiled. Barbara rushed toward our friends, and they ushered her inside but not before all four of them turned to the car and waved. When the front door closed, I looked at Merle.

"What?" I asked. "Why didn't I know that Barbara was coming here?"

Merle grinned, and beneath his expression, I detected a conspiracy. "Said she was gonna spend some time with them, is all."

He drove me home that night and kissed me goodnight from his parking spot along the street. "Goodnight," I replied, and I was sure in that single word, he could detect my confusion. But, since there was nothing to be done, I pushed the car door open and stepped into the cold. I wrapped my jacket more tightly against me and hurried to the main entrance of my apartment building. I glanced over my shoulder before I pulled the door open. Merle sat in the driver's seat and smiled my way. I waved. He waved back. And then I went inside.

When I arrived at my door, I pulled out my keys and unlocked it. I pushed the door open and stepped inside.

And my mouth fell open in surprise.

I glanced around the room. A gentle glow came from a light that had somehow been left on, and red silk lay draped over the lampshade. Rose petals lined the floor, and someone had left a vase filled with flowers on our small kitchen table, which I could clearly see because the kitchen was open to the room I stood in, my feet planted on the floor. Music played. Bing Crosby.

And then I startled as I felt a presence at my back. I turned, and there stood Merle, a silly, pleased expression on his face.

"Merle Mayhew," I said breathily. "What is going on?"

Merle closed the door behind us and took my hand. He led me to the couch, where we both sat, our legs bent, our knees touching. "Mary Lou, Annabelle, and Fred came over when we were at your folks'," he said.

"They did?" My voice was soft, filled with awe but still confused.

"They did," he confirmed. "You've got some good friends there."

I nodded, swallowed. "Yes," I managed to say. "But why…" I looked around me. "This?"

Merle smiled. I watched as he got down on one knee before me. "So I could ask you to marry me."

Just like that, it was out. That was my Merle. To the point. But always still managing, with his words and actions, to make me feel like the only woman on the face of the Earth.

I swallowed again. "What?" I began to tremble, and Merle took my hand.

"Marry me," he said.

"I…"

Merle lifted a brow. "I hope you're not saying no." His voice was playful. He knew I wasn't about to say no to his proposal. How could I have?

"No," I said then cleared my throat. "I mean, no, I'm not going to say no."

"No?" He was teasing me more now, I could tell. And it made me laugh.

I was crying. I swiped under my eyes. "No," I said. "My answer is yes."

"That's a bit confusing," Merle said, and it made me laugh again. And then Merle leaned in, closer toward me. His smile faded, and more seriously, he said, "So that's a yes?"

I nodded. "It's a yes."

Merle sat on the couch and gently touched his forehead to mine. "I love you, Martha Laplant."

I sniffed then said, "I love you, too, Merle Mayhew."

And then Merle lifted his head, looked directly into my eyes, moved in closer, and kissed me. And oh, how that kiss felt different somehow. New. A beginning. And an end. A promise amidst a world in turmoil.

After we celebrated our new engagement at Annabelle and Fred's home, Merle drove us back to my apartment, while Barbara stayed the night with our friends. Merle spent that night with me, though I won't go into detail. But, if you could see this aged face of mine now, you'd realize that even ancient people still blush.

...

I celebrated my twentieth birthday the following month with my parents, Merle, Barbara, Mary Lou, Annabelle, and her husband, Fred. We all piled into the apartment Barbara and I shared, and oh, it brought me nothing but joy. I might have been only twenty years old, but I knew how blessed in life I had been.

We were all sitting in the small living area, Annabelle and Mary Lou admiring the ring that Merle had given me, when the telephone trilled. We were quite fortunate to have a telephone in our apartment; not many people did at that time, you know. Barbara smiled and nodded my way, indicating that she'd answer it. I watched her walk away, but only when I heard the loud *clang* of the receiver bang against the wall did I realize something was amiss.

I stood from the couch and walked toward my best friend. I smoothed her golden hair off her forehead and caught her gaze, willing her to tell me what she had heard. She looked back at me, and I noticed that her beautiful light brown eyes were misting over. She offered me a wan smile and then softly said, "That was my mother."

I nodded, placed the telephone's receiver back on its cradle, and urged her to continue.

"You know my brother."

I nodded, though my stomach roiled. I somehow knew she was not speaking of Eugene.

"He's dead."

The news hit me so suddenly that I didn't know what to say, or even how to feel. I should not have been surprised. I loathed Robert Brown with every fiber of my being for who he was and what he had done to me, but he was still Barbara's brother. Even though she had broken ties with him, he was still her brother. They shared history, and I was sure she must have been fighting through a plethora of emotions.

After a few moments, I still was not entirely sure of what to say. I lifted my chin and kissed my best friend on the temple. A single tear dripped from her eye and onto her check. When it met the corner of her lip, she offered a drained attempt at a smile, turned, and walked into her bedroom, shutting the door behind her.

I wrapped my arms around my stomach and rejoined our guests, who were all looking at me expectantly. "Barbara's brother is dead," I told them bluntly. And then after a pause, I clarified by saying, "Robert."

Annabelle just stared at me. Fred bowed his head. Mary Lou nodded but otherwise lacked expression.

When Merle wrapped his arm around my shoulder, I looked at my mother. "Good," she said, and even I found myself letting out a gasp.

"Ruth," my father warned.

"What, Arthur?" she demanded. "That boy was nothing but trouble. What he did to Barbara... what he did to our daughter."

I closed my eyes with resignation. Up until that point, nobody but my parents, Merle, and Barbara knew what Robert had done to me. I knew now that there might be an uncomfortable conversation in the near future with the rest of the small group gathered in my apartment, though I knew none of them would ask for clarification outright.

"That may be," my father countered, "but he was still a boy."

"A boy that did nothing but harm," my mother said. "If we know of these actions, what else has he done and to whom? Would you like to answer me that? Come now. Out it comes. I'm waiting."

"I'm not getting into this with you right now and not with Barbara in the other room."

My mother shook her head and then looked directly at me. "You might think I'm cruel," she said. "But just you wait. You'll be a mother one day, and you'll understand.

That is, if you don't already, after what he did to you. What he"—she choked on a sob—"*could* have done to you."

Although I understood where my mother was coming from and though I was still struggling to heal from the wounds Robert had inflicted upon me, I wasn't sure he deserved to die for them. I tended to sway toward the side of forgiveness back then. Goodness, I still do, to tell the truth. And if I wasn't forgiving, then at least I lacked the desire for outright retribution. Yes, I wanted Robert held accountable for his actions when my father and Merle had gone to the police after the attack, but did I want him to die? No, though I didn't know everything there was to know about Robert Brown, I didn't think he deserved to die.

I looked toward Barbara's closed bedroom door. My heart ached for her. I didn't pretend to know how my best friend was feeling. Perhaps she mourned her brother's death. Perhaps she mourned not his death but the life he had led. Or maybe she had just mourned what he could have become, her hope for a future in which he could have proven himself to be anything but a monster.

My party ended shortly thereafter. Annabelle and Fred took Mary Lou home. My parents left, and it was only Merle and I for a time, since Barbara was still in her room. He didn't ask me how I was feeling, and I was grateful to him for letting me sort through my thoughts on my own. Even then, he knew how I processed. Eventually, he, too, left the apartment.

I later found out the cause of Robert's death was some sort of fight that broke out between him and another boy in the middle of the night. Alcohol was involved, and so was a knife. But I didn't know any of these details the night of my birthday, and I didn't need to.

After a time, I knocked on Barbara's door. She made no sound, but I slowly turned the knob and poked my head inside. She was sitting on her expertly made bed and gazing out the window and into the park across the street, the park where I had been attacked. I sat beside her and placed my hand on her shoulder. She turned, and when I searched her face, her eyes, I knew that my best friend, like me, needed time to process her feelings. She placed her head on my shoulder, and we sat there, the two of us. Two women who loved each other dearly.

Even between best friends, sometimes feelings are spoken more acutely in silence than they are in words.

...

It was one year later, in February of 1943, while I was preparing for my early-June wedding, when I learned that one person's death elicited a sorrow within me for the person they could have been but an almost apathetic reaction to their actual passing, while the death of another I mourned with immense ferocity.

Some losses are insurmountable, and sadly, this would not be my first.

The telephone rang while I was at work at the attorney's office on a Monday morning. I remember the day well. Even now it creeps into my mind, the memory surfacing unsolicited when I least expect it. On the other end was a sob and then another.

"I'm sorry," I said to the person who had rung. "But I can't understand you."

A whimper and then a wail, and then I recognized it: my mother's voice.

"Your father..." She was gasping for air.

"My father," I said. "Mom? What's happened?"

"He... I... Oh, God!" Another wail.

"Mom!" I screamed into the phone. "You're scaring me."

"Heart... his heart... hospital... now..." And that was all I needed to hear. There was only one hospital near town.

"I'm coming," I called. I slammed the phone down on its receiver, grabbed my coat, and hastily explained to my boss what had happened. I ran out the door and only then realized that I had no car. What a silly thing to forget, but in my fearful state, how I would get to the hospital hadn't crossed my mind. I just knew that I needed to be there.

Feeling utterly helpless, I spun in circles on the icy sidewalk. I rushed back into the office and told my employer that I had no way to get to the hospital. I asked to use the telephone to try to call Merle, though I wasn't sure that would even remedy my precarious situation, since Merle was in school, and I was unsure how they would find him if I called the main campus office.

I panicked. My employer looked at me with such paternal concern that I almost wept. "I will take you," he said. He grabbed his coat, and we set off. The dear man didn't drive to his office, since he lived close by, but we rushed to his apartment, at which his old vehicle was parked. We climbed in, and I wrung my fingers together in my lap for the duration of the short drive, not knowing what to do and feeling utterly out of control.

We blessedly arrived at the hospital, and I rushed to the front desk, leaving poor Mr. Morris behind. "Arthur

Laplant," I said. "I think he's here. Something about his heart, maybe? I don't know. Is he here?"

After what felt like ages, I was directed on where to go, and I ran. Down the hall, up the stairs. I found my father's ward and then his room. My mother sobbed at his bedside, surrounded on either side by other hospital beds, not affording us much, if any, privacy. I hastened to her, and we embraced. I looked at my father lying supine on a hospital bed that couldn't even fit his entire frame. He had a blanket pulled to his chest, his hands open, and his palms resting at his sides. He was breathing, thank God. I saw his chest rise and fall. I don't remember many more details than this, though he was hooked up to some sort of machine. I smelled something stringent in the room, a smell that I would associate with hospitals even into old age. A smell that would inevitably bring me back to this very day as time passed.

I turned to my mother. "What happened?"

"Heart attack," she said. "I got a call this morning. It must have happened just after he got to work. They called me at home. They got him here. Thank God, they got him here!" I could tell she was trying to hold her emotions back for my sake.

"Heart attack?" I looked at my father again.

"Yes."

"He's breathing."

"Yes," she replied.

"Is he... Will he be okay?" I touched my father's hand and was surprised when he didn't flinch. I had almost expected him to open his eyes, dart up in bed, and tell me that he had been fooling around the entire time, playing a cruel joke.

"I don't know," my mother answered honestly. "They

said… Oh God, Martha, they said they weren't sure if he'd come out of this alive."

"What?" My lips trembled, and my knees felt jellied. I feared they would give out on me at any moment. I wobbled to a chair beside my mother and managed, in a daze, to lower myself into it.

"He… he might die?" My voice croaked, and I suddenly felt parched.

My mother merely nodded, her eyes bloodshot and her skin pallid.

I reached my hand toward my mother, and she took it within her own. We both stared at my father as he lay motionless in bed. Time passed, during which we didn't speak. There was only hope. Hope and fear.

Nurses came and went. A doctor too. I don't remember their words. Those just seemed to swim around the room. I felt like I was drowning, trying to breathe but unable to break the surface to do so.

My arm ached, but I paid no heed. I was not about to let go of my mother's hand.

Later, I used a telephone to reach Merle when I knew he'd be home. He insisted on joining us at the hospital, and of course, I wanted him there at my side. My paternal grandmother also joined us.

Night turned into morning. I found sleep somehow. I woke with my arms wrapped around my chest and my neck aching something terrible. I rubbed my eyes and leaped out of my chair to look more closely at my father. He was still in the same position, and blessedly, he was still breathing. My mother was awake, her eyes so red I was amazed she could see out of them. Merle stood beside her, looking disheveled with bags under his eyes and tousled hair. I wondered if he had slept at all.

I sat back down, and we endured another hour or two. A nurse tried to get us to eat, but not one of us had an appetite.

At one point, Merle sat on the cold, hard floor, his back against the wall. I followed. My body was already greatly sore and achy, but I wanted, needed, to be near Merle right then. He put his arm around my shoulder, and I rested my cheek against his chest. He held me tight, and I welcomed it.

And then it happened. My mother began to scream. "No, no, NO!" She was standing, hovering over my father, shaking profusely, grasping, trying to cling to his hospital gown. I leaped from the floor and saw immediately why my mother was inconsolable.

My father wasn't breathing.

I stood stark still. I couldn't move. I was rooted in place with fear.

A doctor and two nurses rushed to my father's bedside. I don't remember much of anything from there on in, I was in such a daze. But I remember when my mother collapsed to the floor. And I remember her words. "He's gone." And I remember Merle catching me.

Then darkness.

Merle took us to my parents' house that day. My mother and I both entered in a silent stupor. I'm not sure I even remember stepping inside. I was just somehow there. Merle stayed with us, comforted us. My grandmother was there to care for my mother, though she was also grieving fiercely for the loss of her son. Aunts and uncles came by the next couple of days. The funeral had to be planned, after all. But I was having none of it.

Merle slept on the couch. And my beautiful, generous best friend, Barbara, helped me immensely those first few days after the death of my father. She climbed beside me in my childhood bed, tucked the blankets around us, and wrapped her familiar arms around my back. She stroked my hair, embraced me, fed me soup even when I tried to refuse. I'm sure I was a mess, and I'm certain I smelled, since I couldn't bring myself to shower. But she made no complaints, said very little, in fact. She didn't have to. Just her presence there, her skin on mine, spoke volumes.

The morning of my beloved father's funeral dawned, and the sun taunted me; it shone brightly as it reflected off newly fallen snow. Barbara was awake beside me, and when she saw my eyes open, she placed her palm on my shoulder. I turned my head and looked into her eyes. Her caring, light brown eyes, still laced with a splattering of green. She peeled herself from the bed and made for my closet, from which she removed a black dress and hung it on the door.

I didn't want to move. I didn't feel I could. Not that day. I didn't want to have to say goodbye to my father. For always. Knowing that he'd never speak to me again, smile at me again. Never again hug me with his large, loving arms.

I began to cry, my eyes still caked over from tears I had shed in the night.

Barbara came to me then, smoothed my greasy hair off my wet cheeks. She gently prodded me with her hand, and I reluctantly sat up.

"I..." I looked at my best friend, tears coursing down my cheeks. "I can't... I..."

"I know," Barbara said with a nod. "I know." But she helped me to my feet anyway. I don't know how she managed it, but she led me to the bathroom and ran the faucet. She peeled the clothes from my body. She looked me in the eye almost the entire time as I continued to weep.

Then she helped me step into the tub. Barbara, God bless her soul, bathed me that morning, gently and with love.

And then somehow, it was time to go.

The church was packed full on the day of my father's funeral. He had been adored by both his family and the community in which we lived. I was only twenty-one years old, but I knew with certainty that the man in the casket at the head of the church had been my first love. Many women would say that the title belonged unequivocally to their mothers, and oh, I can see that. My mother and I shared a bond that only mothers and daughters could experience. But my father…

I have since come to think of death as a natural part of the progression of life. One has to think this way when they are one hundred and one years old, mind you. But then, when I was twenty-one and my father was lying in a casket, I thought otherwise. I was sitting in the front pew, my mother to my right and Merle on my left. Both were holding my hands. Love surrounded us, and yet, all I could think of was that my father was in that *thing*, and soon his body would be placed into the earth, where he would decompose, slowly, slowly, until nothing was left of him but a skeleton, clothes droopily draped over it. My father, as I knew him, would cease to exist. An echo left in his place.

My big, strong, broad, handsome, lively father.

He no longer existed in the way I had known him. Did he even exist at all? I didn't know the answer to that.

How had it come to this? That was all I could think.

And why?

I've grappled with a lot of deaths in my time, but even now, I have difficulty understanding my father's. When one loses a loved one at such a tender young age, one is bound to be affected in such a way, are they not?

My wedding to Merle that June of 1943 was a day filled with both joy and sorrow.

I prepared myself in a small room in the church in which my father had lain in his casket less than four months prior. By my side were my mother, my paternal grandmother—my mother's mother had passed when my mother was just nine years old—Merle's mother, Barbara, Annabelle, and Mary Lou. The rest of my family and friends were waiting in the church, since the wedding was about to begin.

My mother leaned in and embraced me. When she pulled back, I saw tears in her eyes. "I wish your father was here to see you today."

"I know." And I cried then, makeup be damned. The pain was still fresh. Even if I had married Merle years after my father's passing, I still would have cried. I'm sure of it. Some losses you never fully recover from.

I regretted then that Merle and I had waited to be married, even though that wait wasn't too long. We had thought we were doing the right thing, the reasonable, responsible thing, in waiting. And we had even pushed up the date. The war was not yet over, and we had initially assumed we'd wait until it was. We wanted all our loved ones there with us. Never did I imagine that an integral piece of me would be missing on such a momentous day.

But today was a time of celebration, and so I stood tall, wiped my tears away, and smiled. When one of my aunts knocked on the door to let us know that it was time, I grabbed my bouquet and exited the room. Merle's mother was escorted down the aisle. My beautiful bridesmaids followed her, and then Barbara, my maid of honor, smiled at me before she, too, proceeded to the altar.

And then it was my turn. The doors had closed behind

Barbara, and my mother and I stood together in the small lobby area of the church. She looked at me and I at her. She laced her arm through mine, and then the doors were opened once again. To melodic music, my mother led me down the aisle, my father's memory blanketing me with each step.

Soon, I was there, in front of a beaming Merle.

Oh, that smile of his.

He kissed my mother's cheek, and she sat, tears staining her skin. I chose to believe that they were tears of joy, that the sorrow had lifted from her heart while I said my vows to the man I loved. That love was so very different than the love I bore for my parents, though no less incredible. A love that made my heart flutter. A love that made me feel safe and secure. A love that I wanted to take with me into the unknown future.

Sappy? I suppose so. But when you're blessed to have had a love like mine, these are the memories, the feelings, you grasp at the end of your days.

Luckily, it wasn't raining on my wedding day, and thank goodness for that, since Merle and I had chosen to have our reception outdoors. It was held in a beautiful garden just down the street from the church, and there, we celebrated with loved, appreciated friends and family.

The evening came to an end—as all amazing evenings do—entirely too soon. But end it did. With the help of his parents, Merle had purchased a small home only a few miles from my mother, and he took me there. We stepped inside, and I immediately removed my shoes, collapsed onto the couch, and rubbed my feet. "Ah," I said. "What a night."

"Sure was," Merle said. "Mrs. Mayhew."

I grinned. "I like the sound of that."

"You'd better," Merle teased me.

And then I dropped my smile and took on a more serious expression. "I love you, Merle Mayhew," I said. "I love you very much."

Merle gave a lopsided smirked, and I knew that glint in his eye all too well. He scooped me up from the couch so suddenly that I giggled like a little girl. He carried me to the bedroom that we would share as a married couple, and it was there we began our life as man and wife.

And yes, this old woman is blushing again.

...

In October, just four months after our wedding, I discovered that I was pregnant. The birth of our son would teach me something entirely new in life, I can tell you that. A love like no other.

And a loss too.

MATTHEW

*M*erle, Martha, and Matthew. Perhaps we were silly with the naming of our son, three M's and all, but I think not. Matthew was perfect.

Everything about him was perfect.

I remember his birth well. How could I not? Not only because Matthew would become my first and only son but also because of the tumultuous climate of our country and world at the time. It was 1944, and World War Two was still raging. We people were exhausted, men and women both, and if I had learned anything from the atrocities of war and the loss of my beloved father, it was that I wasn't guaranteed to see tomorrow. My father had been young when he passed—only forty-eight years old. And yes, I happened to be much younger and healthy, as far as I knew, but we had also assumed that my father was the epitome of health, and our assumptions had been proven wrong. My father had been one of the integral people in my short life who had taught me about love—both how it felt to receive and to give that sustaining emotion we all crave. And he taught me about the importance of family. Merle and I agreed that we would live our lives to the fullest and to the best of our ability. We would embrace love. We would embrace family. So when I learned of my pregnancy with Matthew, Merle and I were overjoyed. We would be the first of our close-knit circle of friends to boast the title of parents, and I knew that my Matthew would be surrounded by a love that permeated the atmosphere around him, not only from Merle and me but from extended family and close friends, too.

And boy golly, did that make my heart smile.

I went into labor on July fifth, 1944, and to say I was nervous would be an understatement. I was young and hadn't spoken much about childbirth to anyone. My mother had offered up her own experiences, yes, but when she had given birth to me in 1922, she had endured a much different experience than most women did in 1944. Merle drove me to the hospital. Goodbyes were soon necessitated as I was taken to the maternity ward, while someone ushered him into a waiting room where he would meet my mother, who we had phoned prior to leaving the house. Oh, how she had screamed with excitement over the line, so even I heard her enthusiasm when Merle extended the receiver away from his ear. I was sure he didn't want to be deafened by my mother's outright elation.

My, but I was so scared. I was a young little thing, mind you—just twenty-two years old. And the pain I was feeling was acute, a sort of pain I had never experienced before. Fortunately, the hospital where I gave birth to my son no longer required women to undergo Twilight Sleep, the abhorred practice of placing women in a medically induced state somewhere between sleep and consciousness. Such horrific stories I have heard through the years about the unfortunate women who endured such a practice! They wreathed and moaned. It wasn't humane, I tell you. Not humane at all. And would you believe that this method was still in practice a couple of decades after I had Matthew? My hospital was an anomaly of sorts, I suppose, since many women who had children when I had Matthew—and many women afterward, too—were given the drugs to put them in this Twilight Sleep. We've come a long way since that time, and thank goodness for that!

I will never forget my nurse. No, never. She was an older, rather stout woman in a white cap and white nurse's garment. She had a frizzy mass of brown curls that poofed out and made me grin despite my pain. And her smile. My, hers was beautiful. And those eyes of hers... Have I told you that I can see someone's soul through their eyes? Yes, I'm sure I must have. And between her smile and those beautiful eyes, I knew. And I clung to her, I did. I was a young woman who had no clue what was going on within her body, and my nurse soothed me with such kind words. If not for my nurse, then I am convinced my experience would have been a negative one. I sadly do not remember her name, and seeing as I am one hundred and one years old now, this nurse no longer walks the Earth, and if she does, then she is most certainly some sort of divine being. But it makes you think, does it not? All these years later, and that one woman on that one day that we both happened to share with each other—her smile, her demeanor—affected my life. Enough that I still remember her now.

Sometimes life is a wonder...

I don't recall every moment of my labor with Matthew. It was so long ago. But I remember the very moment I could hold him in my exhausted arms. All the pain, all the fear, all the questions I had harbored simply disappeared. I had a son.

A son.

And right then, my entire existence was altered. I had been blessed to carry the title of daughter, best friend, wife. But now I was a mother. And it changed everything. As the days would pass, I would learn that Matthew's presence in my life would shape me in ways I had never anticipated, and the love I bore for him was like no other.

I held Matthew in my arms as I lay in that uncomfortable hospital bed, and he looked right at me. I know now that he was merely trying to acclimate to a brightness that he had not seen when in my womb, but right then, when his eyes found mine, I was convinced he was looking right into me. I could have sworn to you that he knew me, even then.

I stroked his soft cheek, his fuzzy brow. He had a full head of brown hair, but that was no surprise, since both Merle and I both had that color too.

I ran my fingers over his jaw and onto his tiny chin. I traced his pursed lips, so smooth and pink.

I found his shoulder, ran my finger down the skin of his arm, and placed it in his palm. He instinctively grasped my finger with his, and I sat there in wonder at this little being that was mine. At this beautiful boy that had grown inside me and now rested in my protective embrace.

My eyes blurred as tears welled then fell down my cheeks. One large drop plopped down and onto Matthew's nose, and my son startled, which made me laugh outright.

"He's beautiful," the nurse told me.

"He is," I agreed. "He really is."

When I watched my husband hold our son for the first time, I fell in love with him all over again. A love that was so intense with what we two had done that I was sure my heart would burst straight through my chest. A love that felt almost painful in its ferocity.

Merle was a tall man, though not large of girth. In his arms, our son looked like a mere doll, so small and fragile. I watched as Merle silently wept, my wonderful husband who never did have issue with expressing his emotions, even in a time where it was frowned upon for men to do so.

My mother was beside herself when she met her grandson. She had to sit down to cradle him in her arms, she was crying so hard. "I am so proud of you," she told me.

"Thanks, Mom." I was sore. Exhausted. Emotional. And yes, I was proud of me too.

I watched my mother as she gazed at my newborn son, and a wave of sorrow injected itself into my elated heart. My father was not there. I conjured an ethereal image of him. In it, he was sitting beside my mother, looking down upon their only grandchild. I saw the smile on his lips, the gleam in his eyes. I watched as he lifted my son from my mother's arms and held him cradled within his own, nestled against his massive chest. My son was small enough to fit on my father's forearm, and my father's palm dwarfed my son's head. And yet, he held him with such reverence in my mind's eye that I wept a fresh set of tears.

Oh, how I missed him! But I was also awash with a joy that I hadn't realized was possible with my father gone. I knew then that he had left such an enduring mark on my very soul that he would live on in my son. I was certain of that. He would live on when I held and comforted Matthew. He would live on when Merle and I played Bing Crosby and danced with our son between us. My father would live on when his grandson heard story after story about his granddad.

He would live on.

I wept openly and without shame as I looked up at my husband and then at my mother, who was affectionately cradling my son. A son who had been given the middle name of Arthur.

Oh, how life has a way of fitting into place, even when your heart is aching.

...

My mother was around to help a lot in those early days of Matthew's life, and I was devotedly thankful for that! I was not prepared for how difficult it would be with a newborn in the house. Golly, Matthew was not an easy child; he cried what felt like all the time. All the time! I was deprived of sleep. Merle, though he wanted to help more often, could not with his busy schedule. He was still in school, you see, and such a rigorous program he had. He worked part-time as well. My mother, on the other hand, had entered the workforce after Daddy passed but maintained the ability within her schedule to help me with Matthew. And, as much as I appreciated her help, I do believe it also saved *her*. The way she looked at my son, the way she spoke to him. She had been a shell of her former self since my father's death, and my son breathed new life into her.

Although I had enjoyed my time working as a secretary at Mr. Morris' attorney's office, I left my job when my son was born. Even though I was utterly exhausted, I tried to relish every moment I had with him.

Matthew grew from a gangly newborn to a robust, chubby six-month-old, who learned to sit on his own, drooled a lot, and cooed as if he couldn't hear the sound of his own voice often enough. When he'd lift those plump little arms of his, motioning for me to pick him up, my heart would soar. He'd look right at me, into my eyes. Me. His mother.

When I tickled him, his laughter erupted, filling the space around us. Needless to say, I tickled him a lot.

And Merle. Oh, how Merle adored his son. He'd arrive home drained from his busy day but would always, without fail, seek out his son straight away. Even before he kissed me hello. But I didn't mind. Quite the opposite, actually, for I understood.

Matthew would see his father, and his tubby little body would bounce in its seated position. Up and down, up and down. His eyes would go all wide, and his lips would curve into the most enormous smile. He'd babble exuberantly, a bit of drool lining his lips. His arms would flail at first and then extend out and upward toward his father.

Merle would rush over to our son and lift him straight into the air until Matthew was laughing hysterically. Merle would twirl him a couple of times, with Matthew held over his head. Merle would then place our son on his hip and ask him about his day. I'm not sure Matthew understood all the words his father used, but he'd look at Merle intently with eyes that had turned the most gorgeous shade of green, just like his daddy's, smiling the entire time. Our son, though a difficult, stubborn personality at times, often smiled at this age. Just like his father. And his granddad.

I recall with great clarity one night when I was preparing dinner in the kitchen. I was stirring the most fragrant sauce I ever did smell, a recipe handed down to me by my mother, whose culinary abilities I had devoured throughout my childhood. Though not nearly as good a cook as my mother, I did attempt to hold my own. I was often a clumsy mess in the kitchen, but this sauce was a specialty of mine. I felt I did just as well as my mother when preparing it, and boy, did Merle make the funniest expressions when he'd take his first bites after ladling an immense amount of steaming sauce over pasta.

On this day, I had an apron tied tightly around my waist, an apron that had once been my mother's. Because of my awkwardness in the kitchen, I found that aprons saved my clothes from ruin. I had just spooned a small portion of the steaming sauce from the pot on the stove when I heard a commotion from the living room, where Merle was playing with Matthew. I looked behind me and saw Barbara appear, out of breath, in the entryway to the kitchen, her arms extended and hands splayed, her palms pushing against the partitions as if they were all that held her in place.

"What's this?" I asked with an amused smile. Barbara was at our house often, but for her to appear in such a manner certainly made me wonder what she was about to impart.

"I..." she managed. "Oh, Martha!" And then she hastened my way and took my hands in her own. Since I was still holding the full spoon in one of them, the sauce spurted off and sprayed against my arm.

"Ouch!" I exclaimed. By golly, was it hot.

"Oh, I'm so sorry," Barbara said as she surveyed the damage she had caused in her haste.

"It's all right," I assured her. I put the ladle down, grabbed a kitchen towel, doused it in cold water, and gently wiped my scorched skin.

"I—"

I placed the towel on the counter. When I turned to

face my best friend, I put my hands on my hips and grinned with amusement. "You what?"

"It's gone and happened," she said.

I furrowed my brow. "What's gone and happened?"

"I've met him."

"Who?

"Well," Barbara said. "A man."

"All right," I said with a chuckle. "So you've met a man, have you?"

"Yes." Her voice was breathy and light and seemed to float in the air between us.

"And what sort of man is he, might I ask?" I was beginning to glean pleasure from our conversation, especially when I saw the look on Barbara's face.

"He's..." Her eyes rolled up and gazed toward the ceiling as she searched for the right words. "He's just... Oh, Martha! I know I just met him, but it's... Oh, Martha!"

I laughed. "Oh, Martha," I said. "Yes, that's me."

"Oh, you," Barbara said. She swatted me lightly on the arm.

"Careful there," I told her. "Because of you, I'm burned on that arm."

"Oh, that's right," Barbara said and then brought her fingers to her lips. She looked concerned for a fleeting moment and then removed her fingers and held my hands again.

"He's so different," she continued. "Martha, I felt so comfortable with him, and you know how I get with men sometimes. Well, everyone but Merle and Fred. Annabelle's husband doesn't make me feel uncomfortable. But I've always been a bit shy and timid, haven't I?"

A lopsided grin spread across my face. "I suppose."

"And I've never been good with men, and I certainly

haven't ever met a man that I wanted to spend more than a few minutes with, have I?"

"I suppose not," I agreed.

"But Joseph—"

"So his name is Joseph, is it?"

"Oh, stop that, Martha! You're teasing me!"

I squeezed her hand. "I am," I said. "But only because I love you. And I can see how flustered you are. Goodness, Barbara, I haven't ever seen you like this before."

"I haven't ever felt like this before."

"Okay," I said, pulling her toward the kitchen table, where we sat. "Tell me everything."

Merle appeared in the doorway with Matthew propped on his hip, our son tugging on his father's hair forcefully enough that Merle tilted his head to the side and winced. "All good in here?"

"Yes," I said as I shooed him away with my hand. "Leave us women to talk."

Merle held out a palm. "I got it, I got it." And then with a grin and an attempt to extricate our son's fingers from his hair, Merle retreated to the living room.

"So," I said, turning back to Barbara. I lifted a brow. "I'm listening."

"Okay," she said, straightening her back and shaking her head as if to gather her thoughts. "I met him just today, at the cafe of all places. You know how I go there sometimes when I get off work?"

I nodded.

"I was tired. It had been busy at the store, and I just wanted a coffee and a rest. I ordered my cup, and as I turned around to find a seat, a man bumped right into me, if you'd believe it. Just like that. He seemed to come out of nowhere. I don't think he was paying attention at all, and when he bumped into me, my coffee spilled all over my arm. Some even got on my dress because my jacket was open."

"That sounds familiar," I teased.

"Yes," Barbara said as she looked at my arm. "Sorry about that again."

I just laughed.

"There I was, all flustered, wasn't I? And I stood there like a ninny because I didn't know what to do. I had spilled coffee, and it was hot, and I still had the cup in my hands. I just froze. But Joseph excused himself again and again, and he really did seem genuine, so after a time, I relaxed. I let him take me to a table, and I sat down while he went to buy me another coffee. When he came back, he asked if he could join me, and won't you believe it, I said yes!"

I smiled. Her own pleasure radiated from her words and through her expression. "And then what happened?" I asked.

"We talked," Barbara replied. "And talked and talked and then talked some more. I don't think I've ever talked so much in my entire life! And I felt comfortable and good and warm inside the entire time, Martha. I really did. He has a pleasant smile and a mellowness about him. He's not the most handsome of men, I don't believe, but that doesn't matter. There was just something about him. And he looked dapper in his suit. He told me that he was also headed home from work. He said he didn't often stop at that café, but that day he just had an inkling, and so there we have it."

"Serendipitous," I said.

Barbara's eyes widened. "Yes!"

"How did you leave it?" I asked. "Surely you'll see him again?"

"Yes," she said with a grin. I watched as color rose to her cheeks. "He asked me if I would like to meet him at the cafe after work on Friday."

"And of course, you said yes."

"Of course I did."

I smiled and reached for her hands again. When she placed her own in mine, she squeezed.

"Martha," she said. "He told me that he had a wonderful time meeting me. He said that I was very easy to talk to and that he was very happy he had changed course to get a coffee. He shook my hand, but I think he might have let it linger a bit longer than necessary. I don't know." She shrugged. "Maybe I'm reading too much into it. Or maybe I'm reading what I want to read. But he was... He was wonderful, Martha. Just wonderful. He even took his hat off when he said goodbye and rested it over his chest. Wasn't that kind of him?"

I raised my brows. "Now you really are thinking too much!" I said, though my words were playful.

Her smile dropped. "Do you really think so?"

"No!" I laughed. "I don't really think so. I think that you might just have yourself a beau."

"My heart is beating too fast right now," Barbara said. "And I feel... It's like... I almost feel like I might float away."

"Let's not do that now," I told her. We were silent for a moment as we looked each other in the eye, our hands still clasped together, and then I said, "I am very happy for you. Truly, I am. He sounds like a wonderful man. As much as you know about him, that is."

"Yes," Barbara said. "That is true. I really don't know much about him at all, do I?"

I laughed again. "You certainly do not. But... I do

believe that sometimes things just fall into place, don't they? Sometimes... sometimes fate takes over, and you feel it inside."

"You believe that, don't you?"

"With all my heart."

Barbara met Joseph again for coffee that Friday afternoon. They talked at a little table in the corner of the room for hours. He asked her out again, this time for dinner, and she accepted. And thus began my best friend's courtship.

The following month, in February, Merle and I invited Barbara and Joseph over for dinner. Merle was playing on the floor with seven-month-old Matthew when I heard an expected knock on the front door. I nearly skipped to answer the call. I flung the door open wide, extended my arms to the side, and said exuberantly, "Welcome!"

The smile on my best friend's face as she stepped inside told me all I needed to know. She gave me a hug and then introduced me to Joseph. He kissed me lightly on the cheek and handed me a bottle of wine. Barbara glanced over at him with an expression that made her look about to burst.

Merle approached my side and gently placed his palm on my lower back. "Merle Mayhew," he said as he offered Joseph his free hand. Joseph smiled warmly, shook my husband's hand, and said, "Joseph Groggle." Groggle. Yes, the name was unfortunate, but it would bring us joy for years to come.

Merle and Joseph chatted in the living room while Matthew entertained himself on the floor with a rattle and a brightly painted wooden pull toy. The men seemed to hit it off immediately, so Barbara and I stepped into the kitchen, where she helped me finish the dinner preparations.

When dinner was done cooking, we all made ourselves

comfortable around the table, even little Matthew, who sat in his wooden high chair between Merle and me. I poured myself a second glass of the wine that Joseph had brought to share and sipped it with an ever-present smile glued to my face.

Oh, what a night that had been. I knew almost straight away what Barbara had been talking about when she rushed into my kitchen the month prior and told me how she felt about the man she had just met at a cafe. From the moment my eyes met his, I knew—just knew—that this man would be in my life for a while yet. You might call me silly, but I'm an old woman now, and I still believe that there are times in our lives when our intuition simply breaks the surface and tells us what we need to know.

Matthew, although often demanding of my attention when he was a baby, was the perfect angel that night. Perhaps I'm misremembering. Maybe he was glued to my hip. I am old, I suppose. But what I do know is that we finished those glasses of wine and forgot the dinner dishes on the table. We slipped into the living room and turned the phonograph on. Merle hadn't owned a phonograph when he bought the house, only a radio, but you can bet your buttons I wasn't having that. I had grown up listening to records with my parents, and I would continue that tradition throughout my marriage.

I set to work, and soon Bing Crosby's voice rang out through the living room. Oh, how I loved that man: handsome, well-dressed, charismatic, and he had such a wonderful voice. I listened to other artists, yes, but I often gravitated toward Bing Crosby, especially in those earlier days of my life. I even remember the song I played that evening: "Swinging on a Star." It had been in a movie that Merle had taken me to see at the theater. I loved going there. There was still a war on, mind you, so money was rather tight, and we didn't have the resources to do anything extravagant, not that I was ever much for extravagance anyway. But the theatre—we went often through the years. I loved movies! Yes, they were very different back in the forties but no less thrilling. I watch those old films still. They are timeless.

I began to sing, raising my voice. If you've never heard "Swinging on a Star," it's a funny one. Always made me giggle. With a wide smile, I sang and spun in my dress. The tendrils of hair I had curled that morning bobbed. Barbara laughed, and Merle bounced Matthew on his hip, which made our son squeal with pleasure. And then, much to my surprise, I heard a deep baritone voice ring out, and when I turned, I saw Joseph, arms slightly raised and palms up, looking back at me with a goofy sort of grin as he belted out the words. I stopped my singing, bent over, and placed my hands on my knees. I laughed with pleasure. Then I laughed some more. The song continued, and we all chimed in, Matthew's curious gaze darting from one of us to the other.

It might have been a modest evening with friends, but to me, it was nothing less than magical. These are the moments that stick out in my mind after all these years. These moments. Simple, hearty, joyous moments spent with the people I loved.

I didn't want the evening to end. But eventually, Joseph drove Barbara back to the apartment that we used to share with each other and in which she still resided, and Merle and I put Matthew to bed.

"Goodnight, my sweet boy," I said as I stroked my son's hair off his forehead. He always looked directly up at me and smiled when I did this, and on that day, at seven months, showed the single tooth protruding from his lower gum as well. "Mommy loves you."

He cooed and my heart swelled.

As I looked down at my son, I wished for him a life filled with wonderful friends like mine was. Filled with love.

...

Until I take my last breath, I will never forget a day just three months after that wonderful night on which we met Joseph. It was May 8, 1945, a day for the history books. V-E Day, Victory in Europe Day. Germany's surrender and the official end of World War Two. In Europe, at least. Japan would surrender later that year. Oh, how we celebrated. People crowded the streets that day, strangers hugged one another, and businesses had halted in jubilation.

I was in the kitchen with Matthew when I heard President Truman on the radio. I think my heart stopped beating for just a moment in time. Matthew, of course, knew nothing of war and didn't realize the enormousness of what we had just heard, but I scooped him up nonetheless and spun him in the air with elation. The telephone rang out from the living room, and I rushed to answer it with Matthew on my hip. I didn't want to let my son go. I wanted to hold him and shower him with kisses.

I lifted the receiver and placed it to my ear. "Hello?"

"It's over!" I knew the voice on the other end of the line. Of course, I knew.

"It's over!" I said. "Oh, Barbara, can you believe it? It's over!"

"Not completely, like Truman said," my best friend replied. "But almost. It's over, Martha. No more death, no more sorrow."

"We still have a lot of work to do," I said. "But yes, it's nearly over. And we can breathe again."

"Can I see you?"

"Aren't you at work?" I asked.

"Yes," she said. "I am. But they won't mind. Everyone over here is beside themselves."

"If you're sure they won't mind your absence, then yes, come over! Or… how about I come to you? I'd like to get out of the house. This news… It's just too big."

"All right," Barbara said. "Come here!"

And so I replaced the receiver and whisked Matthew to the car, the car my father used to drive and that my mother gave me when he passed. I placed Matthew in his car seat —a contraption that would make you wince if you saw how unsafe it was by today's standards—and set off down the road.

Barbara worked at a popular department store in the center of town. I parked the car on the side of the road, carefully dodging the joyous people celebrating in the street. I took Matthew out of his seat, propped him on my hip, and jogged into the building and up the stairs to Barbara's department. She was waiting for me by a glass display case with two champagne flutes in her hands. When she spotted me, she beamed and held the glasses aloft. As I approached her side, I flung my free arm—my other arm was occupied by my son—over her shoulder and hugged her with such might, some of the champagne spilled over the side of the glasses and dribbled down her wrists. But she only laughed.

I let her go and looked her in the eyes, those beautiful light brown eyes. I could have sworn those green specks sparkled under her lashes. "Here you go," she said and thrust a glass in front of me.

"It's morning!" I exclaimed with a hearty laugh.

"And?"

"Barbara Brown," I said with abundant tenderness, "I do believe you will be a bad influence on me."

"Nonsense," she replied. "On a day like today?"

"You do have a point." With a smile, I reached for the glass. Matthew lunged for it, and I had to extend my arm so it was out of his grasp. I turned my head, lifted the glass, and took a large gulp of the bubbling liquid. It fizzed on my tongue, and I swallowed, relishing the flavor as it slipped down my throat. Celebration, indeed!

We joined the buoyant customers and employees in their merriment. Matthew received quite a bit of attention, I must say, and it made my heart smile with such joy.

A woman in a wide-shouldered green dress with buttons down the front approached us. "Barbara, phone's for you."

Barbara swallowed a sip of champagne then said, "The telephone?"

"That's what I said. It's for you."

Barbara pressed her lips together in a grin, raised her brows, and said, "I wonder who that could be? I'll be right back."

A few minutes later, I saw my friend in the distance walking back toward me and Matthew, her gait light and with a little bounce to it. "Joseph rang," she explained. "He wants to see me."

I smiled. "Of course he does," I said. "Will you go to him?"

"No," she replied. "I'm here with you."

"Well, aren't you wonderful?" I said. "But maybe you can stay for just a moment longer, yes? Then you go and be with Joseph. Merle is probably wondering where I am, anyway. If he's looking for me."

"You didn't tell him?" Barbara let out a light chuckle.

I shook my head. "I didn't. It's hard to get in touch with him sometimes. I figured he was busy, even this morning. And I was in such a rush to see you."

I repositioned Matthew on my hip. "Oof," I said. "This boy of mine is getting mighty heavy."

"Here," Barbara said. She placed her champagne glass on the counter and motioned for me to hand over my son, which I gladly did. Once the weight left my hip, I felt much lighter.

"You are a big boy, aren't you?" Barbara crooned to Matthew. She bopped him on the nose with the tip of her finger. "So, so big." He looked up at my best friend with an enormous, drooly grin.

"I don't know, Barbara. I think Joseph needs to get on with it, doesn't he? My Matthew here needs a playmate."

"Oh, Martha, you big ol' goose!" Barbara exclaimed and swatted my arm. "We've only known each other for four months. That's barely time at all."

"Oh, I don't know," I countered. "You came running to me the very day you met him, do you remember? You knew it then. And he's clearly besotted with you. It's time."

Barbara laughed. "It's time?"

"Yes. It's time. I don't know why he's so slow."

My friend reached over with her free hand and pulled me toward her in an embrace. "I do love you, Martha," she whispered into my ear as the celebrations continued around us. Matthew grabbed a fistful of my hair and tugged.

"Ouch!" I said, pulling out of his grasp. "You little

147

monster!" I tickled him, and he squirmed with delight in Barbara's arms.

I touched my friend's shoulder. "I love you too," I said. "Very much. Forever and always."

"Forever and always," she promised.

We parted ways shortly thereafter, and I headed back home. When I entered through the front door, the radio was on, and Merle was sitting on the living room couch. What a surprise that was! He wasn't typically home during the day.

"What are you doing here?" I asked.

"A man can sit in his own house, can't he?" Merle asked, smiling.

Matthew reached out his chubby hands. His father stood and whisked him out of my arms. "Hey, bud," he said. "Exciting day, isn't it?"

"So you've heard?" I asked.

"How could I not have? The news is everywhere. The entire world must know by now."

"Yes," I said with a chuckle. "I suppose you're right."

My husband pulled me toward him and planted a giant kiss on my forehead. "Thank you, God," he mumbled into my hair. "Thank you, God."

I placed my cheek against his chest and closed my eyes. I drank in the scent of our laundry soap and felt his warmth. Matthew swatted me on the top of the head, but it only proved to intensify my pleasure and my relief. I was with my family. And we were safe.

Merle held me in his arms as we lay in bed that night. I had thought I had my emotions in check about this abhorred war that had been fought overseas, but when I awoke in the middle of the night and opened my eyes to a darkened room, the sliver of a moon the only source of illumination, my pillow was wet. I had been crying.

I curled my legs toward my chest and wrapped my arms around my shins. I wept anew. Not with relief this time but rather with an immense amount of sorrow. Sorrow for the young men who had sacrificed their lives in the war and sorrow for the loved ones that would never again have the opportunity that so many of us take for granted every day: holding those we love in our arms; feeling their skin upon ours. Hearing their voices. Breathing them in.

In my mind, I saw my father again in his casket. I could see his waxen face, feel his rubbery skin, and I thought of these young men anew. I envisioned mothers hovering over the bodies of their departed sons, weeping, sobbing, the torment within too intense to control.

And I thought of my son. I thought of Matthew.

I wept harder and woke Merle. He said nothing, merely left the warmth of his own bed to join me in mine—this was a time before bed-sharing was commonplace, mind you —and took me in his arms. I wept against his chest, and he stroked my hair.

And then I thought of the stories I had heard, the atrocities that had been done to people in Europe. Everyday people, like you and me. We heard such things from the newspapers we read and from radios that were often left on in homes and businesses, mine included. Even as early as 1935, I knew that something was amiss when the United States was contemplating a boycott of the 1936 Olympics. They were to take place in Germany, you see. Ultimately, our country attended. But even then, even earlier than the Olympics, really, we citizens had heard of the antisemitic ramblings of people in power in Germany. And it had only intensified from there. I had heard about Jewish businesses being obliterated, about Jewish people simply disappearing, if you will. Yes, we heard. But it wasn't until after the war, when I saw abundant photos, read articles, watched television broadcasts, and heard personal stories of the war, that things truly sank in for me as a person that lived so very far away from the fighting and persecution. Yes, I had been affected by this war. We all had. I had lost family and friends, but I had not witnessed the everyday life of people in Europe under Nazi control. Even now, seventy-seven years after the end of the war—seventy-seven!—my mind will suddenly conjure a particular image from a photo I've seen, or I will hear the particular cadence of a woman's voice over the radio. Then my heart stops beating, my chest feels heavy, and I struggle for breath.

It would take hours—days, even—for me to relay to you all of what I felt and thought back then, both during the war and directly afterward when more and more information came to light about the villainy set upon people in those times. Average people that just wanted to live their lives. People that had the *right* to live their lives. People with mothers and fathers, aunts and uncles. People with children such as Matthew that they cradled in their arms, that they tried with every fiber of their being to protect and ultimately failed through no fault of their own but because of another's inhumanity.

I thought of Matthew that night as my husband held me in his arms. I thought of my darling boy, so innocent, so wonderful. I thought of the future he might have, the hopes and promises I held for him. And then I thought of Matthew being yanked from my arms, screaming, his little chubby legs flailing, his back held tightly against a starched uniform. I envisioned him reaching out for me— and his cries, oh his cries. I hear them still, and it wasn't even my son that had been stolen from his mother's bosom.

I cannot do this. I cannot remember.

Some things, even after years upon years, never vanish, never fade.

Some pain never disappears.

When I woke in the morning, my entire body ached, and my head throbbed. Merle was still with me in my little bed. At some point in the night, I had brought Matthew in with us. I simply had to, and it was there, in between his father and me, that our son slept.

I stroked his soft, unblemished cheek. His eyes moved beneath their lids, back and forth, back and forth.

My heart ached. There had been so much hate in this world, hate that I had either borne witness to or had heard of.

But there was also beauty, and it lay beside me in the forms of my husband and our son.

And at that moment, through pain and sorrow, with a sense of defeat but also of renewal, as my heart bled but also beat strongly in my chest, I held great hope for my son's future with the end of that war.

...

Barbara Brown married Joseph Groggle the following May. The day was a bit cloudy but gorgeous, as I recall. I was the maid of honor, and Merle was a groomsman. He and Joseph had become quite close, having discovered that they had myriad interests in common. Our little Matthew was an integral part of the wedding, too, and at almost two years old, he was walking. Unsteady on his feet still, yes, but walking nonetheless, and he was adorable, swaying side to side, his legs still chunky, his feet crammed into a pair of small black shoes. He was to carry a little pillow down the aisle of the church, and on that pillow sat the wedding rings.

Oh, how my heart smiled when I spotted him off in the distance in the doorway as I stood at the altar. He wore an expression of unbridled confusion on that little plump face of his. My mother was squatting next to him, holding his hand. I was sure she was attempting to ease his discomfort, but a lot of people were there, and he was moving his head around, searching for something. When our eyes met, I could see his grin even with the distance between us. He let go of my mother's hand and raced down the aisle as fast as his little feet would carry him. At one point he tripped, the pillow tumbled down in front of him, and he fell on his hands and knees. But he giggled, the sound echoing in the church. He righted himself, squatted and picked up the pillow, then continued on his merry way.

The guests chuckled, and I was sure there were many smiles in the pews as my son made his way forward, but all my attention was on Matthew, and his was on me. Our eyes were locked, and he was grinning that beautiful, enormous grin of his. And then, with arms extended, the pillow held in his hands, my son bumped into my legs. He dropped the pillow, and I bent down and whisked him into my arms, planting several kisses on the top of his head. Oh, but my heart swelled.

Barbara eventually made her way down the aisle, looking radiant in her simple gown. When she approached a beaming Joseph, she turned and handed me her bouquet. She looked at Matthew in my arms and said hello.

"Hi, Baba," he replied.

And goodness, did my heart beat even faster at that sound.

The procession continued with Matthew planted on my hip and the pillow nestled under my opposite arm. When the priest called for the rings, I handed the pillow to him. And just like that, my best friend was married. And to a wonderful man, thank the stars!

Time moved on, too quickly, as it tends to do when you're in the midst of living it. Matthew grew from a chubby toddler into a robust and healthy little boy. By that time, Merle and I had been trying for another child, but for whatever reason, it hadn't happened. Barbara and Joseph welcomed their first—a girl—just a year after their wedding and their second—another girl—two years after that. By the time Matthew was six years old, I was worried that something was wrong with me. Conceiving Matthew had been so easy. Why hadn't I been able to conceive another child?

And thus began a time in our lives in which Merle and I fought. A lot. He was content with just Matthew and had a hard time understanding why I was not. And I had difficulty explaining to Merle that it wasn't that I was discontent with our son. It was that I was so very happy, so in love, that I was full to bursting. I wanted to experience motherhood again with another child. I wanted to provide Matthew with a sibling, be it a boy or a girl. I just had so much love to give.

Merle still didn't understand me. So he'd see me wallow from time to time and would get all huffy. He was happy. He wanted nothing more from life than what we already had, and truth be told, I think my husband thought I was a little selfish for wanting more, and he took it to heart that I wasn't satisfied with just him and Matthew.

And oh, it wasn't that, was it? Not entirely. I think I also felt—at the time, anyway—that I was failing as a woman and as a mother. I don't feel this way any longer, not at one hundred and one years old. Not after everything I've been through and the life that I have lived. But I was young then. I still felt like a new mother. Barbara had two children, and when Matthew was six years old, she was expecting her third. She was overwhelmed and exhausted. And I was envious of her position, of the boisterousness that surrounded her in her little home. Of all that love, all the promises of what the future had in store for her.

It's hard to explain, to put into words, but it was contentious between Merle and me in those days.

And then, in 1951, when Matthew was seven years old, and Barbara had a newborn daughter at home, my son fell gravely ill.

By that time, Merle was a practicing medical doctor, but even he didn't know what had befallen our son. Matthew complained of stomach ailments. His head hurt, his eyes drooped. He missed school at times because he didn't feel well, and then he missed more and more schooling until he was at home with me one day and fell to the floor, unconscious.

I was in such a panic that I didn't know what to do! My son hadn't been well, Merle didn't know what was going on, and no other doctor had been able to diagnose Matthew either. So we had harbored hope that his ailment would pass, but this was far from passing! The last person that I had seen unconscious was my father. My father, who hadn't made it out alive.

Oh, dear God!

I screamed and rushed to my son. I bent over his prone body and pushed him onto his back. I placed my ear against his chest, hoping to hear a heartbeat. Thank the Lord, it was there!

"Matthew!" I screamed, patting his cheek. "Matthew!"

I began to cry, shaking so profusely that it was a marvel I still had a semblance of control over my own body.

"Matthew!" I cried again.

I extricated myself from the floor and looked around the room, my eyes darting here and there. I didn't know where to focus. Eventually, I had enough wits about me that I was able to lift my son from the floor, a son that, at seven years old and boasting his father's taller genetic propensities, was much too big for my slight figure. But in times of panic, when a loved one is in trouble, we manage to do the unthinkable, don't we? I ran out the door and to my car. I placed Matthew in the passenger seat, and his limp body immediately slid down.

I continued to sob. My entire body shook. My chest heaved, up and down, up and down, as I tried to gasp, taking in sporadic bursts of air.

I had to breathe. I just had to! What would happen to Matthew if I lost control now?

I rushed to the hospital with Matthew limp beside me. His eyes were closed, and I assumed he was still unconscious, though I could detect that he was breathing, thank God!

When I arrived at the hospital, I came to a screeching halt at the front entrance and hit the curb with my tire. I didn't care. I flung my door open, didn't even bother to close it, and rushed to Matthew. I pulled him out of the car and somehow flung his body over my narrow shoulder. I held his legs close to my chest, and his stomach hit my back, his head lolling and his arms hanging down my legs. "Help me!" I screamed. "Help me!"

An orderly came rushing to my side and took Matthew from me, removing my son's weight. With it gone, I felt lighter, but it wasn't a relief. Instead, I felt a sudden sense of dread and yearned to feel his weight once again, his presence. His close proximity. I didn't want to let him go.

The rest of that day was a blur. I don't remember all of what happened or who said what and when. I'm not even sure how they got ahold of Merle, though I imagine they must have inquired about him at some point, and I must have told them that he had a practice there in town. However it happened, Merle was soon at my side. And we were alone.

Eventually, although I don't know how many minutes or hours had transpired, we were approached by a doctor. Some sort of doctor. I don't remember. The doctor told us that we could go see Matthew, but that no, he wasn't awake. And no, they didn't know what was wrong with him.

We said nothing. Merle took my hand in his, and we followed the doctor down the stark, bare hallway and to our son's room.

And there he was: our Matthew. In bed. A blanket pulled up to his chest, a machine beeping beside him.

Oh dear God, not again!

I tried very hard not to think of my father, but I was reminded of him immediately. And it frightened me. I forced the thought aside and rushed toward my son. I grasped his hand, larger now that he was seven years old and no longer a baby, but—even though his hand was nearly the size of my own—it still felt small. And, in his incapacitated state, diminutive.

I began to cry, of course. I am an emotional woman, after all, and this was my son. In a hospital bed. Unconscious.

We sat vigil next to Matthew. I watched his chest rise and fall with each breath he took. I placed my head on his chest and heard the rhythmic beating of his heart. I prayed a silent prayer of thanksgiving. Merle and I didn't say much to each other just then. Words weren't necessary. We each knew what the other was thinking, feeling. He took my hand in his and we sat vigil beside our son.

I read to Matthew, hoping beyond hope that he could hear my voice. Our favorite story: *Curious George,* which Barbara had dropped off at the hospital for us.

And then a miracle: Matthew's eyes fluttered open. Just a slit at first and then wider and wider. Slowly. So slowly. But then they were fully open, and he was looking around the room.

I gasped. It couldn't be helped. My son was awake!

I leaped out of my chair and to his side, and wouldn't you know it, Matthew smiled at me. Smiled! His lips were dry and cracked, but my son still managed a small smile. I wept anew, this time with relief and gratitude.

With each passing hour, Matthew improved. He was discharged from the hospital a few days later when his fever had subsided, and he displayed no further signs of illness.

We never discovered what had ailed Matthew, but we thanked our lucky stars each and every day for the miracle we had been given: more time with our son.

By the time we had arrived at our house, our blessed, wonderful, love-filled house, we were joking that Matthew had caught the Matthew Mayhew disease. We joked about this time in his life for many years to come, especially once we knew he would be all right.

The years passed, and Matthew grew. Entirely too fast, if you ask me. One moment he was an infant in my arms, and the next, it seemed, he was looking into attending the same medical school as his father. "No kid should have to go through what I did," he'd say with that smile of his. "I'm gonna eradicate the Matthew Mayhew disease once and for all!"

"Oh," I'd say, laughing. "Is that right? Even though you are the only child to have had it?"

"That's right," Matthew would respond. "'Cause I bet I wasn't the only kid. Just the only kid we know about."

And then he'd fling one long, lanky arm across my shoulder lackadaisically and lean into me. He was tall, my son. At seventeen, he was almost six feet, goodness help me. I was only five foot one! I'd look up into those emerald eyes of his, eyes so much like his father's, and my heart would swell. Matthew had been a typical teenager, distancing himself a bit from Merle and me, spending an abundance of time with his friends. He had even dated a couple of girls he went to high school with. But even through it all, I felt deeply blessed that we shared the relationship we did. He still spoke to me and still spent time with me. At times, he would openly share about his day. Other times, I had to pry, since he would be in one of his—what I deemed then—teenager moods.

Something had changed internally for me when Matthew fell sick at seven years old. The fear that we would lose him had been so strong that it consumed me. When he came out of it, when we knew our son was going to be okay, one might have thought my desire for another child would have increased, but the opposite happened. I'm not sure why, but when I cradled my little boy in my arms, when he looked up at me with that smile of his that I held so dear, I felt such an abundance of love and gratitude and such relief that we walked out of that hospital as a little family of three, and, well, it was enough. I'm not discounting others' experiences with infertility, gracious no. But for me, this is *my* story. This is how *I* felt. This is how *my* life played out.

Everything that Matthew did, everything that he learned, and every experience he had until he was almost eighteen years old and about to graduate from high school were all firsts for me. And lasts.

I experienced life anew through my son's eyes. When he jumped into Merle's arms, I was jumping into my father's, and I could hear his voice in my ear: *"Love you, Martha Moo."* When he fell and I consoled him, I thought of my parents as I had known them in my childhood. When I held his hand on his very first day of school and walked him to the front door, I thought about my time with Barbara. The day inevitably brought with it some unwanted memories, memories of Robert and his snatching of his sister's doll, Edith. And that led, of course, to words that had been spoken, deeds that had been done when we were children. And then the memory of that day, that dreadful day in the park…

But with the memories of Matthew's first day of school, as I held my son's hand and walked him ever closer to the building in which he would spend his weekdays, came a flurry of happy memories, too: looking into my best friend's eyes and golden hair as it swept her cheek; Annabelle and Mary Lou, two amazing friends that were blessedly still in my life. I thought about the church function that we girls had attended and my evening with Merle, dancing and gazing into the night sky. And I thought about how he rushed to the aid of the woman who had fainted. It all came back to me, in quick succession, in just the span of a few steps beside my son.

From that day forward, I knew that I didn't have full control over Matthew's life. I wouldn't choose his friends, and I wouldn't know all of what he was experiencing when we weren't together during the day. He was only six years old at the time. Six. Still so young, and yet, I felt as if that very day was the beginning of an end. Yes, I know I sound dramatic, but I had to learn to relinquish my tight hold on Matthew. I had to let him go, watch him walk the steps to the front entryway and disappear along with the throng of other students.

I don't know what was going through Matthew's mind that day. Not everything. He told me he was happy and excited to start his day. And he smiled that smile of his, yes. But I wished that I could reach into his head and extract the threads of thoughts that I was convinced lingered within and that he didn't divulge. But I didn't have that ability, did I? Or that right. I was a parent. I was his mom. And as much as I wanted to be an intricate part of his life, as much as I wanted to know all there was to know about my son, I never would. I might still be an important part of his life *because* I was his mother. But not in the way I hoped to be. My son, even at six years old, was growing up. And I needed to slowly let him go.

The loss proved quite difficult for me. A type of loss I had never really experienced before. Yes, Barbara had moved away when we were children. Yes, I had lost my father. And yes, I had lost others both during and after the war. But this loss was different. Matthew Mayhew disease had not yet hit our household on my son's first day of school, but to watch the son I had spent every day with until then walk up those school steps alone—how

160

does one explain this type of loss, this type of letting go? How do I explain the feelings that were coursing within me?

It was harder for me than for Matthew that day. We lingered on the sidewalk in front of the building, and he looked up at me. "Okay, bye, Mom."

I looked at him, wondering if it really was that easy.

"Bye?" The word came out sounding like a question, though I hadn't intended such.

And then my son, my beautiful boy, dropped his hand from mine, smiled at me, and waved animatedly as he walked away, merging into the crowd of children, his leather backpack bobbing in the middle of his back. The sack he wore was so very different than the straps that used to hold my schoolbooks together. When I had made friends. When I had shared my days with Barbara. When I had met Merle...

Before we had started this beautiful, complicated, nuanced life together.

I did rather well when Matthew left my side. I held my sobs in until I rounded a corner and was in the presence of only a couple of other people on an adjacent road. Then I let them out: all the feelings flooding within me. You might think me silly, yes. You might. It was only your son's first day of school, you might say. But for me—for me, it felt like so much more.

So yes, I sobbed as I walked back home. But that did not mean I was unhappy for my son to start school. On the contrary, I was proud. And I felt blessed that we were both given that day.

But I still missed his presence beside me.

The house felt quite lonely when I returned. Empty. Silent.

161

I turned the radio on. And then I called Barbara. "Can I come over?"

"Of course you can," my best friend said. "I knew you'd call me."

I chuckled. "Oh, is that right?"

"Yes," she said, and I could sense her smile on the other end of the receiver. "I know you as well as you know yourself."

"You might be right about that."

"Of course I'm right," she said. "Come over. But don't mind the house. These girls will be the end of me."

And so, I spent the rest of my day with my best friend and her girls. She had two at the time. Barbara neglected the house chores to be with me, and the girls played both outside and in while we sipped glasses of wine and reminisced about our own school experiences. We laughed that day. Golly, did we laugh. Side by side on her couch, my body pressed into hers, we laughed. And when I left her so that I could pick up Matthew from school, my heart felt light and free.

I spotted Matthew before he caught sight of me. I was standing with some other parents on the sidewalk in front of the school, and I watched as he exited the main doors, an enormous grin on his lips, and walked down the steps with another boy. Red hair, freckles, a bit taller than my six-year-old. They parted ways, and then I saw Matthew searching me out. I waved my hand, and when he saw me, he skipped over.

"Who was that?" I asked.

"Edward."

"Who is Edward?"

"A boy in my class." Matthew's answer was direct and airy.

"I see," I said. "And it looks like you have made friends with this boy Edward."

"Yep."

I smiled. I could not have asked for a better day for my son. I wasn't privy to the experiences he had had while we were apart, but that he had walked out with another boy with a grin on his face and a hop in his gait told me all I needed to know.

And my heart smiled.

Sending my son back to school the year after his bout with Matthew Mayhew disease when he was seven proved even harder for me than his very first day of school had been.

When you almost lose one that you love so dearly, that you hold so close, who encompasses your entire world— well, then, you cherish every single moment you are granted with them. Every moment. And those moments fill your heart with an immense sense of pleasure as well as fear. A fear, though perhaps irrational, that you might just lose them after all. And then you grasp even harder, more fiercely.

Try grasping so desperately when your son is searching for autonomy, when he wants you to let him go...

When Matthew graduated from the lower grades and entered high school, I didn't cry. I managed to hold back the pooling tears that blurred my vision. But golly, it was hard!

I spent my son's first day of high school with Barbara while Merle was at work. Thank goodness for my best friend. She was a stepping stone through life, always there when I needed her. We loved each other immensely, with no stipulations. We did not always agree, or see eye to eye, but we respected each other nonetheless. Always. And as we each experienced life through the lens of motherhood, we only grew closer. And, I can admit to you, in each other we found common ground to occasionally vent about our husbands. Oh, my Merle was the most amazing man, truly. Amazing. But I believe with my entire being that two women share something between them that cannot be compared to the love a woman holds for a man. There is a special relationship between best female friends. I can attest to this love. For nearly ninety-eight years—ninety-eight!—I was blessed to have Barbara in my life. There are different types of love, aren't there? My love for Merle, my love for Matthew, my love for my parents. And then there is the love that Barbara and I shared.

She had four girls by the time my son started high school, and all but one were also now in school. On this particular day, her youngest daughter was over at a neighbor's home, so Barbara and I had her house to ourselves. I had grown accustomed to quiet and solitude through the years, with Matthew off at school and my husband working long hours in his practice. I had taken to volunteering, much like my mother had done and still did. I volunteered at our local church, which provided aid to impoverished families. I felt fulfilled in my work, but still, something was missing in my life. I had told Barbara as such through the years, but it wasn't until my son's first day of high school as we sat together at her kitchen table, sipping steaming mugs of coffee, that she suggested something that had eluded me, though I didn't know why in the world I hadn't thought of it myself.

"Why don't you go work for Mr. Morris again?" Mr. Morris was the lawyer who had hired me as his secretary after I had graduated from high school.

"Mr. Morris?"

"Yes, Mr. Morris," Barbara replied. "You were happy working for him. He's a nice man."

"He's an extremely nice man." I nodded and took a sip of coffee. "I hadn't thought about going back to work. Not with my time at the church and still needing to be home for Matthew."

Barbara smiled. "You don't need to be home for Matthew. He's a big kid now. He can take care of himself."

"Yes, true," I said. "But I *want* to be home for Matthew. The years are going by so fast, Barbara. Pretty soon he'll..." I didn't want to finish my sentence.

"Yes," she said gently as she laid her hand on mine. "I know. But you're not entirely happy."

"And I don't know why," I said with exasperation. "I have everything I could ever want. I have a wonderful husband, a great son. I have you." I smiled wanly. "What do I have to be sad about?"

"I think," Barbara said as she leaned back in her chair, contemplating, "we women are expected to do it all. We need to care for our families. We need to have it all held together. And we are expected to be happy doing it. But look at me." She flung her arm out with a flourish. "My house is a disaster. I can't ever seem to keep up with all the housework that needs to be done. I make breakfast. I prepare lunches. I make dinner. I have four growing girls that I am trying to raise to be good people while also attempting to be a good, supportive wife. I love my life, but sometimes it's exhausting, isn't it?"

I nodded.

"I think I'm beginning to believe that things don't need to be so cut-and-dry, do they? I think... Well, maybe it's okay for us to want a little something more." And then my best friend's features transformed. She looked distraught.

"Does that make me a terrible wife and mother?" she asked.

"Not at all."

"I'm tired, Martha. I'm just tired. All the time. And when I look at you, when we're together… I see you. I *see* you. Merle is supportive. Go and talk to Mr. Morris."

I thought for a moment and then said, "Merle is supportive, yes, but it's not just that. When would I do it? With the volunteering at the church and with me wanting to be home for my family—when would I work for Mr. Morris?"

"Stop volunteering."

"But I like it."

"Then maybe you have a choice to make," she said.

I sighed. "Maybe."

"It's just…" Barbara leaned forward. "Like I have said: I know you're not happy. Not entirely."

"And again, what is wrong with me? I have nothing to be unhappy about!" I threw my arms into the air.

"Maybe 'unhappy' isn't the right word. I think maybe… maybe there's just something missing? Something that isn't there any longer? Maybe just a small piece of the puzzle that needs to find where it fits?"

"Maybe," I conceded.

"Talk to him, Martha. It won't hurt. I know how you loved working for Mr. Morris."

"I suppose," I said. "But I can't imagine he'd have anything for me after all this time."

"And yet, he might."

I nodded. "He might."

"And if you could work part-time, be home for Matthew and Merle…"

"Yes," I said, letting the thought sink in.

"You've got a great support system at home, Martha. Merle will understand. I think this could be good for you."

"Yes," I agreed. "Perhaps."

"So... you'll talk to Mr. Morris?" Barbara asked.

I sighed but smiled. "Yes," I said. "I'll talk to Mr. Morris."

"Okay," my friend said. "Then off with you."

"What?" I looked at Barbara incredulously.

"I know you," she said. "You have it set in your head right now that you'll do this, but then you'll rethink it all when you get home. You'll see Merle off to work and Mathew off to school, and then you'll go back to the church. Just to get home and do it all over again. When something is missing. Go. Now," she urged again. "Go visit Mr. Morris at his office."

"But," I protested, "I'm with you."

"Yes," she said. "And we have all the time in the world to be with each other. Come and see me once you've gotten your answer from Mr. Morris."

I laughed. "You are incorrigible."

Barbara took a sip of her coffee and lowered her mug. "And you love me," she said with a smile.

"Dearly," I agreed.

I left my best friend's house ten minutes later.

...

Mr. Morris's office was still the same: a small room with a mahogany desk, a young secretary seated behind it; a window emitting the sun's rays, painting the walls in color.

167

A bookcase with an abundance of literary works as well as legal paraphernalia lined the wall.

"Can I help you?" the young woman asked me as I walked in.

"Yes," I said as I swallowed. "I'd like to see Mr. Morris. Is he in?"

I needed to say no more because, at that very moment, a slight, elderly man hobbled out of his office and into the small lobby, leaning on a cane. "Thought I heard a familiar voice," he said. His words were scratchy, and I smiled immediately at the sight of my old employer, my dear friend. Now in his early seventies, Mr. Morris had aged since the first time we had met. He was past the age of retirement, but I knew Mr. Morris. I didn't think he'd retire until he lost control of his faculties. If he lost them at all, that was. The man lived and breathed for two things: his work and his beloved wife, whom he had met in his teenage years. His hair had gone completely white, and his brows looked even bushier, if that was possible. He wore a pair of circular spectacles. He stood slightly stooped, and though he was still a small man, I could clearly see a slight paunch of a belly rolling over his tightened belt. He walked toward me.

"So good to see you, my girl. So good." He reached an arm out and patted me on the shoulder. "Why do I have this pleasure? Been a while since you've seen me at work, hasn't it?"

"I was hoping to speak with you."

"Yes, yes. Of course, of course. Come to my office."

I nodded to the secretary and thanked her as I followed my past employer into his office. His desk was strewn with papers, and I noticed the same framed black-and-white photo of his wife that had adorned it when I had first started working for Mr. Morris, fresh out of high school. The familiar sights made me smile and sent a tingling sensation up my spine. The feeling spread, and goose flesh prickled the skin on my arms.

"What can I do you for?" Mr. Morris motioned to the chair. I sat, and he leaned against his desk.

"This might come as a surprise, but I was hoping... Well, I was hoping that you might have a position for me."

Mr. Morris raised one thick brow, and his eyes widened. "A position? My girl, you want to come back and work for me? All okay at home?"

I laughed, feeling lighthearted at his concerned expression. "Yes," I assured him. "Everything is just wonderful at home. But now that my son is in high school, I'm just feeling... Well, I'd like to come back to work. Part-time if you have it. I know I might be pushing my luck, but I thought it wouldn't hurt to ask."

Mr. Morris eyed me for a time and then said, "Sylvia works for me. Don't really need another secretary, do I?" And then he scratched his head, leaving wisps of thinning white hair that stood in place. "But as luck would have it, I've got a lot of work on my plate, can't quite keep up. Slowing down these days, aren't I? Need someone I can trust to help me out, go through papers, do some research. Sound good?" He repositioned the glasses framing his soft, narrow brown eyes.

"Does it sound good?" I asked, feeling my jubilation about to burst forth. "Do you really need someone to help you?"

Mr. Morris eyed me again. "Mmm-hmm."

"Then, yes!" I exclaimed. "Yes! As long as it's part-time and I can still be home in the afternoons and evenings for my family, well, then, Mr. Morris, that would thrill me. If you really do have a position available."

"Guess I was waitin' on the right person to fill the shoes."

"Oh, Mr. Morris!" I leaped out of my seat and clasped my hands in front of me. I was happier than I had thought I would be. "This is such wonderful news. So wonderful! Oh, this is wonderful."

Mr. Morris chuckled. "Yes. You said that."

I grinned. "I suppose I did. I am thrilled."

His lips creased into a smile. "Welcome aboard, Martha. Glad to have you back." He held out his hand, and I shook it with enthusiasm and gratitude.

And thus began my days working as Mr. Morris's personal assistant.

MR. MORRIS

I first met Philip Morris when I was fresh out of high school and looking for my first job. I happened upon his office coincidentally, simply walking down the street with Barbara one day. A sign in a window announced his search for an employee. "Look at that," I said. "Do you mind if we step on in?"

We entered the building and found a placard adhered to the wall in front of us that pointed the way for us to find Mr. Morris's office. Down the hallway we went and soon saw his name printed on the blurry glass of a wooden door. I held the doorknob in the palm of my hand, took a deep breath, and entered the room. We walked into a small lobby, and I was taken aback by the state of disarray I beheld. A large mahogany desk stood in the center of the room, in front of a spacious window that overlooked the street from which we had just come. I noticed several bookshelves lining the white walls and a chair in the corner of the room. And on that chair, to my utter delight, slept a little dog, though I didn't know what kind. A mutt, perhaps.

An immense amount of brown fluff curled up in comfort. The animal opened one eye and looked directly at me. Apparently, it was unbothered, because it closed its eye once again and slumbered off to dreamland.

"Oh, oh, hello." I looked up and saw a slight man nestled in the narrow doorway of, based on what I could see from my position, was a very small room directly adjacent to the disorganized lobby in which Barbara and I currently stood. He had short yet disheveled hair, more gray than brown, and a small pair of circular spectacles lining his brown eyes, beneath the most enormous, bushiest brown brows I had ever seen. He was clean-shaven and wore a pair of trousers cinched with a belt. A suit jacket had been thrown over a button-down shirt, the top two buttons left open, and the collar jagged, as if he had just haphazardly slipped the shirt on. I perceived an air of discombobulation, but the smile on his face and the gleam in his eye comforted me. I couldn't entirely place his age, though if I had to guess, he was in his late fifties.

"Didn't know anyone was here," he said.

"Sorry," I said. "I was… I saw the sign in your window. You're looking for help?"

"Ah, yes, yes," he said. "That I am. Philip Morris is the name." He held out his rather slight hand, and I shook it. I was pleased by its warmth. Pleased, also, by the amount of pressure he supplied while my hand was in his: not too hard, not too soft. By golly, don't some people just shake your hand, and you feel as if it might fall off at any moment? Why must some people do that? I know it's a mark of respect to squeeze tight, to look one in the eye, but must they squeeze *that* tight? I might have been young then, but I'm an old woman now. No, you do not have to break my brittle bones, thank you. And while I'm at it, why do some people offer you a hand so limp you simply don't know what to do with it? Do I merely touch my fingertips to theirs? Do I even attempt a shake when I feel incredibly awkward? But of course, I digress…

He dropped his hand to his side and welcomed us with the flourishing of an arm. "Please, have a seat." Then he looked around the small lobby and furrowed his brow. "Just got the one seat, haven't I? Huh. Think I might need to remedy that."

"That is perfectly all right," I said. "I don't mind standing. Barbara can take the chair."

"And I presume you are Barbara." Mr. Morris looked at my best friend with a slight grin.

"I am, yes. Nice to meet you, Mr. Morris." She held out her hand, which Mr. Morris shook. Barbara then walked to the chair in the corner of the room, lifted the dog from its comfortable position, and sat. She crossed her legs at the ankle and placed the little dog in her lap before patting it on the head. The dog didn't have a care in the world. It simply went back to sleep.

"Oh," Mr. Morris said. "Clown that I am. You can sit over there." He motioned to a chair behind the desk.

"I'm really all right," I assured him. "I don't mind standing in the least."

"Suit yourself." Mr. Morris shrugged his narrow shoulders. "That there's Poppy," he said, motioning with his chin to the small dog on Barbara's lap.

"She's beautiful," Barbara said, scratching under Poppy's ear.

"My wife's dog," he replied. "Or both of ours, I guess. But the wife's busy, always out. So Poppy stays here with me. Old, she is. Just sleeps the day away. Likes it here."

"Yes," Barbara said. "I can see that she does."

After a lull in the conversation, I said, "So…" to get back on topic. "You need help?"

"Yes, rightly so."

"With what, might I ask?"

"I need"—Mr. Morris extended his arms and looked around the room—"a secretary. Had one, don't you know. She left. Wife helped out for a bit, but she does her own thing. Doesn't like my practice much, though she supports it." He ran the tip of his finger along his chin.

"Yes," he said conclusively. "I need a secretary." Then he turned to me and said, "When can you start?"

I laughed. I couldn't help it, and I immediately berated myself for my behavior. But I had to laugh. "You don't know the first thing about me," I said.

I saw his eyes squint behind his spectacles. "Need to know all I need to know," he said. His voice was a bit scratchy, and that endeared him to me even more. "You want a job. I need help. Not much more to it."

"But," I said, almost stammering. I could hear Barbara holding back a giggle beside me.

Mr. Morris looked at me and lifted a brow. "Want the job or no?"

"Well… yes," I admitted. "I think I do."

"When can you start?"

"I suppose I can start straight away."

"Good. Tomorrow, then. Eight o'clock. Paperwork to sign, but that's straightforward."

"All—all right," I stammered.

"Good. See you tomorrow, then."

Barbara stood from the chair with Poppy in her arms and looked at me, her lips pressed together, as she clearly attempted not to explode with laughter. She placed Poppy in the chair then led the way out of the small room. I followed, feeling utterly flummoxed. Only once we stepped onto the sidewalk did I realize I had never given Mr. Morris my name, and he hadn't asked.

What had I gotten myself into?

And with whom?

...

I started working for Philip Morris the following day. My parents had been thrilled that I had acquired this position and wished me the best of luck in my endeavors. My father, God bless him, looked at me with pride, and my mother nearly cried, which confused me then, though I understand her emotional reaction now.

I entered the office that morning already convinced that Mr. Morris was a quirky man. I left that afternoon assured of my conviction.

He was nowhere to be seen when I walked through the door and into the small lobby space, though it might not have been appropriate to even call it a lobby; it was simply a small room with bookcases, a chair, and a desk that had papers strewn across it. "Mr. Morris?" I called. There was no answer. Poppy, the very fluffy brown dog, lay in the chair in the corner of the room, where I had found her the day prior. Her ears perked up at the sound of my voice, and she opened her eyes, but she made no move to engage with me.

I wasn't entirely sure what to do, so I walked to the window and looked out and onto the street. Minutes passed. Then the lobby door opened, and in walked Mr. Morris from the hallway. "Ah," he said. "Hello, my girl."

He slipped his spectacles up farther onto the bridge of his nose and offered me a slight, close-lipped smile.

"Good morning, Mr. Morris."

"Ready to start the day?"

"Yes, sir."

"Let's get to it, then," he said. He walked to the desk. "This here's all the paperwork that needs to be filed. Never was good at that. Not very organized, you see, but I'm a damn good lawyer."

I nodded.

"Don't have a specific way I want things done. Just want to be able to tell you what to get me and have you know where you've gone and put it."

"Yes, sir."

"And no 'sir'," he said. "Too formal. Leave that for my colleagues."

"What am I to call you?"

"Philip is just fine."

I swallowed. "Yes, Mr..." I just couldn't bring myself to do it. "Mr. Morris."

My new employer looked at me from under his spectacles and raised his bushy brows. I would get used to this motion, since I would soon learn that Mr. Morris did it often. "Suppose Mr. Morris will do," he said. "And—" He stopped himself so abruptly that I was caught off guard. "Clown. I'm a clown. My girl, I don't know your name."

I smiled, and I felt the muscles in my abdomen constrict, holding my giddiness inside. I had known this man for mere minutes between our previous encounter and that morning, and he already made my heart smile. Though he was a man that seemed quite flustered and disoriented, I sensed great goodness within him and found it truly serendipitous that I had seen the sign in his window just the day prior.

"Martha," I told him. "Martha Laplant."

"Well, Martha Laplant," he said. "Got a big job ahead of you. But I know you're up for the challenge."

How he could have known such a thing when we hadn't spoken many words to each other, I hadn't a clue. But that was Mr. Morris for you, I supposed.

I smiled again and looked deeply into his brown eyes. And there I saw it. I've told you, haven't I, that I can see right into someone's soul? Yes, you might think me a silly old woman, but when you're my age, you cease to care what others think of you. I can tell. And with Mr. Morris, I saw it: his goodness.

"I am most definitely up for the challenge," I told him.

"Good, good. That's good." Mr. Morris looked around the room. "Better you than me." And then he slowly turned on a heel and stepped into his office, a space even smaller than the lobby in which I was to begin my work.

When he closed the narrow door behind him, I laughed. Out loud, too, though I didn't think he heard. I had walked into this room and felt an aura around me, something surrounding me in the air that felt welcoming, and I went with it. I accepted it. I trusted it.

I looked from the desk to the bookcases to the chair and then to the window that emitted the brilliant rays of the morning sun. I chuckled to myself. Where was I to start? What did Mr. Morris expect me to do? I didn't want to knock on his office door and ask, so I walked to the desk, sat in the chair, and riffled through the papers strewn across it, prolific for sure. There were piles of them! I set them all in a few bunches and pushed them to the side of the desk. I removed one sheet of paper from the top of the pile closest to me and looked at it. I took another. Soon, I had created several small piles with some semblance of order. I opened the desk drawers but saw nothing that would be of use to me there. I walked over to a bookcase. Nothing. Another bookcase, and there I found some file folders. Perfect! I set to the task of filing papers, and that was how my morning progressed. I was so engaged in my work that I didn't know how much time had passed. Then I heard the door opening, and I looked up. A woman who appeared about the same age as Mr. Morris stepped inside, holding a small paper bag. Her hair was thin, light brown, and curly. She looked to be a bit taller than I was—and plump. I liked her face immediately, since she wore a warm smile.

"Oh my," she said when she saw me sitting behind the desk. "How lovely. You must be Philip's new secretary. What a welcome sight. He needs help, you know. Never could figure this stuff out for himself. 'Philip,' I said, 'you must get help.' And here he's gone and done it. Good for him. And good for you. How are you liking it so far, dear?"

I felt my eyes go wide, and then I smiled. "You must be Mrs. Morris." Mr. Morris had mentioned that he had a wife the day prior, so I made the assumption and hoped I was right.

"That I am, dear. And what may I call you?"

I stood from the chair and offered my hand. "My name is Martha Laplant." She accepted my hand with her own, her shake weak but warm. "And yes, I am happy to be here."

"Well, that's some great news right there," Mrs. Morris said. "I've come to bring Philip his lunch. He loves these meatball subs from down the street. Every once in a while, I'll treat him to them. The man would forget to eat if it wasn't for me, I tell you. He'd just forget to eat. Skinny enough as it is. I'll just go and give this to him."

"Of course," I said and sat back down.

She walked into Mr. Morris's office and said, "Got your sub today, Philip. Don't you love me? All steamy, still. Almost ate it myself on my walk over. Don't know why I didn't. Smells so good. Maybe… maybe I'll just have—"

I smiled to myself as I watched the door close behind her.

I got back to work and was immersed in it by the time Mrs. Morris walked out of her husband's office. "That man," she said to me. "What would he do without me? Calls himself a clown, and that's just what he is. Asked me for extra napkins. Maybe you can be sure he's always got some on hand?" When I smiled, she said, "That's a dear. We'll get along, you and I. I just know it. Don't you mind Philip. Doesn't know his right foot from his left sometimes, but he'll treat you good. Been with the man since my teenage years, believe it or not, so I know I speak the truth. He's a good one, my Philip. Okay." She hurried to the door. "Got to go. I'll see you soon, Martha."

"Yes," I said. "Goodbye, Mrs. Morris."

She smiled and waved, and was out the door.

. . .

I had been working for Mr. Morris for two weeks when Mrs. Morris walked back into the office late one morning, a familiar paper bag held in one hand. I had seen her on several occasions by that time and enjoyed each encounter, some brief and some in which we chatted for a while before she departed.

"Meatball sub time," she declared as she held the bag aloft, the door softly closing behind her.

"Mr. Morris will be pleased," I remarked.

"That he will be. Now, let's hope he doesn't come home with a sauce stain on his collar like the other day." She winked.

I chuckled. "Did it come out?"

"Oh, I got it out," she said. "I've gotten pretty good at that. Have to with Philip for a husband."

I smiled, and she walked into Mr. Morris's office without bothering to knock on the door. "Philip, I brought your sub," she said. "You'd better——" And then the door closed behind her.

I had since learned that Mr. and Mrs. Morris had no children. They lived just down the street from the office, their apartment situated on the first floor of a three-story brick building, and Mr. Morris walked to work each morning. He lived and breathed this job. He loved it. But not as much as he loved his wife. I had seen the way they interacted with each other, Mrs. Morris fussing over her husband in a teasing manner and Mr. Morris merely taking it in without complaint. But I saw the way he looked at her. Oh, that I did. And it made me appreciate my employer all the more for it.

Mrs. Morris left rather quickly that day. We said our goodbyes, and then, as soon as she was gone, Mr. Morris walked out of his office, wrapped sub in hand. "Hi, Martha," he said.

"Hello, Mr. Morris," I said with a smile. "I see Mrs. Morris brought you your favorite sandwich."

"That she did," he said, looking down at it. He walked

to the chair in the corner of the room, laid the sub on its armrest, and picked up Poppy. Mr. Morris sat. "Thanks for keeping it warm for me, Poppy." With his hands still holding Poppy under her little legs, the dog stood—front paws on Mr. Morris's chest—and licked her beloved owner on the cheek then moved in circles on his lap until she was satisfied. She lay down, closed her eyes, and rested. Mr. Morris lifted his sub from the armrest and unwrapped it, holding it aloft so as not to disturb Poppy.

"Did you bring a lunch or do you need to go out and get one?"

"I brought lunch," I told him.

"Want to eat with me?"

"Oh," I said, rather surprised. He hadn't asked me to share our lunch break before. Mr. Morris usually worked through lunch, eating at the same time. "I would love to, yes." I grabbed my sack from under the desk and opened it. I hadn't packed anything special that day, just a sandwich and an apple. I bit into my sandwich as Mr. Morris took his first bite of the sub. A small glob of sauce trickled down his chin and onto the collar of his shirt. I immediately smiled, knowing how Mrs. Morris would react when she saw her husband's stained shirt that evening.

"Doggone it," he said, wiping at his shirt with a finger, eyes squinted beneath his spectacles. "Can't ever seem to stay clean."

"I imagine it's difficult with those subs," I said.

"For me, yes. For any normal person, no."

I chuckled.

"Think it's funny, do you?" Mr. Morris lifted his gaze and looked directly at me. For a moment, I wasn't sure how to answer. And then I saw his playful expression.

"I admit that I do," I said.

"Wife's not gonna think it's funny."

"Oh," I said. "I'm sure she won't mind. Not so much."

"Try living with her."

"Oh?" I lifted a brow.

Mr. Morris frowned, though I still detected a rascally gleam in his eye. "You married?" he asked.

"I'm not, no," I replied.

"Is there a man in your life? Ah," Mr. Morris said. "I see by that blush that there is. Good for you, good for you. It's nice to have a companion, my girl."

Again, I wasn't sure how to answer, so I merely nodded and took another bite of my sandwich.

"Met Elizabeth when I was seventeen," Mr. Morris supplied. He scrutinized something in his sub and then pushed a meatball with his fingertip farther into the bun. "She didn't like me at first. She tell you that?"

"Really?" I asked. "That surprises me."

Mr. Morris nodded. "Thought I was pretentious."

I laughed at that. "You?"

"Yes, me," he said. "She learned that I wasn't pretentious, just odd." He bit into his sub, and a small portion of a meatball tumbled out the side and onto Poppy. The small dog lifted her head, affronted.

"Doggone it," Mr. Morris said, though his voice was not raised. He said it as if he was surprised, which sent me into a fit of internal giggles. Mr. Morris lifted the piece of meat and placed it into his mouth. He began to chew and then grimaced. He reached into his mouth and pulled out what appeared to be one of Poppy's long hairs. He was about to swipe it onto the knee of his trousers before he thought otherwise and instead wiped his finger on a napkin. In my mind, I was already formulating my next topic of conversation with Mrs. Morris when I saw her again.

"So, when did she come to that conclusion?" I asked.

"A couple of years later," he said.

"A couple of years!" My voice rose in surprise.

"Yes. I was nineteen when she asked me one day to go to dinner, and the rest is history. Don't know how, though. I'm sure I spilled on myself that night."

I laughed. After a moment, I asked. "Do you have family in town? Siblings? Nieces or nephews?"

Mr. Morris nodded, taking a small bite of his half-eaten sub, careful not to spill another drop of sauce. He succeeded in keeping the sauce off his shirt, though a small glob landed on his chin. He wiped it off with the napkin. "We do. Both of us. No kids of our own, though. I'm sure Elizabeth told you that."

"Yes," I said. "Mrs. Morris did tell me."

"Never was in the cards, I guess. Elizabeth wanted kids. Me too. But it never did happen."

"I see," I said. I wasn't sure how to reply respectfully but knew the information warranted a response from me, nonetheless.

"It's okay, though," Mr. Morris said. "Elizabeth spoils her grandniece and grandnephew. I've got my work, and I do good in society because of it. We've got Poppy here." He patted the small dog's head with a care I wasn't sure I'd seen until that point. "We've got friends, get together often too. We lead good lives."

"I'm sure you do," I said. "I can see that you are very happy here with your work."

He looked at me then. "And what about you? Are you happy here?"

"I am," I answered honestly.

"Glad to hear it." Mr. Morris nodded and resumed patting Poppy with one hand, his other hand still holding his sub aloft. "It's been nice having you around. You're doing a good job."

"Thank you," I said. "That's wonderful to hear."

"It's true. And Elizabeth talks about you."

My eyes widened. "Does she really?"

"Yes. You've made a good impression."

I couldn't help but smile.

"Come to dinner," he said.

"Excuse me?"

"Come to dinner. This weekend. Are you free? Elizabeth and I will host. Bring along the man that you are seeing, or bring the friend that was here with you the day you asked about the job. Or both."

"You want to have me over for dinner?" I asked, pleased but surprised.

"Yes." Mr. Morris shoveled the last bit of sub into his mouth and chewed, his thin cheeks bulging. He licked a finger, wiped it on the napkin, and resumed petting Poppy.

"That's very... That's very kind of you."

"Would be our pleasure. Say, Saturday? Six o'clock?"

"Yes," I said. "All right. Saturday at six."

Mr. Morris stood, holding Poppy in his arms. He pressed his nose against the fur on her head then placed her back down in the chair. He crumbled the sub wrapper and threw it in the trash receptacle next to the desk on the way to his office. When the door closed behind him, I held my mouth open in surprise. Another smile crept onto my lips.

Poppy leaped from the chair and sauntered over to my side. She stood on her hind legs and placed her front paws on my knee. I pushed the chair back. "What is it, Poppy?" I asked. "You don't usually do this."

The dog pawed at the chair and then lowered to the floor. She bent then jumped into my lap. "Oh!" I

184

exclaimed. I hadn't expected it. I watched as Poppy circled twice then lay down on my skirt and made herself comfortable. I sighed contentedly, pushed in my chair, and got back to work.

...

Dinner at the Morrises' went splendidly that Saturday evening. Both Merle and Barbara joined me. Conversation flowed with ease, and I found my cheeks aching from the breadth of my smiles.

As time passed, my relationship with both Mr. and Mrs. Morris intensified. I felt close to them, as close as a young woman could feel to a couple in their late fifties.

Shortly after Robert Brown attacked me in the park in the summer of 1941 when I was nineteen years old, I called Mr. Morris to request a few days off from work. I heard the questioning tone of his voice on the opposite end of the receiver, but he didn't complain. I had never asked for a day off from work and hadn't been sick, either, so I was sure he was confused, especially since I offered no explanation.

When I went back to work, and Mr. Morris noticed the fading yellow bruises on my face, he looked at me from under his round spectacles and lifted his bushy brown eyebrows but said nothing. He stared at me for a time, and I stared back. He asked no questions. I was thankful for his silence. I felt awkward enough and was struggling with an immense sense of fear and unease. I knew I couldn't go into detail about my attack, even to a kind older man like Mr.

Morris. I would have broken down, I am sure of it. I wasn't ready. Not then.

So Mr. Morris bade me a good morning, told me about the past few days both at the office and at home, and I got to work. Sitting behind the desk and occupying my mind helped me considerably.

When Merle proposed to me, Mr. and Mrs. Morris were two of the first people I told. Mr. Morris looked pleased as punch, even though he wasn't one to smile wide, tending instead to offer his pleasure through closed lips. I often sensed his delight in his eyes and body language. Mrs. Morris gave an exuberant squeal when she learned of my engagement. "Oh, such a wonderful young man you've got there," she said. "We just love that Merle, don't we, Philip?"

Mr. Morris nodded.

I was in the office that day in February 1943 when I received the frantic phone call from my mother informing me that my father was in the hospital. By that time, Merle and I were finalizing our wedding plans. The news my mother imparted had never been something I thought I'd have to endure, and even if I had, I know I could never have prepared myself for the absolute torture the next few days brought with them. Mr. and Mrs. Morris were at my father's funeral, beautiful souls that they were. They were there. They lent their support to me in my time of need, two amazing people that had entered my life by a chance of fate. And they were there to celebrate with us four months later when I married Merle. I thought of Mr. and Mrs. Morris not as my employer and his wife but more like a beloved uncle and aunt. And if my intuition told me anything, it was that they thought of me not as an employee but as a dear friend.

One year folded into the other, time slipping by entirely

too fast. I left my job with Mr. Morris when Matthew was born, but our relationship did not cease to exist then. Mr. and Mrs. Morris invited us over for dinner quite frequently, and we reciprocated. Mrs. Morris and my mother had struck up a friendship and found themselves in each other's company at least a couple of times a month, shopping, enjoying a coffee, or sometimes going out to dinner. Mr. and Mrs. Morris even babysat little Matthew from time to time to give Merle and me a respite together. By the time of my son's birth, little Poppy was an ancient dog. She sadly passed away when my son was a year old. Hers was a difficult loss to take. For Mr. Morris, especially, who I knew was mourning her presence not only at home but at the office as well.

I never visited Mr. Morris's place of employment much once I left, though, which was why I was surprised to find a new secretary sitting at my old desk when I arrived on Matthew's first day of high school to inquire about part-time work. It had been a different woman the last time I had been there. I still saw Mr. Morris every couple of months, but as much as he adored his job, we didn't talk about it often. Mr. Morris was still the slight man that I had met eighteen years prior, though he now had a marginal paunch that hung over his tightly cinched belt, and his hair had gone entirely white. Even his huge, shaggy brows had turned snowy. His spectacles looked new, though they were the exact same type of spectacles he had worn since the day I had met him.

I had only been back to work for Mr. Morris for a week when I arrived home to an empty house. I turned the radio on and prepared myself a cup of tea. I was sitting at the kitchen table, relaxing after what felt like a rather long day, when Matthew walked through the front door. "Ma, you home?" he called.

"In here."

He clambered into the room wearing a large grin.

"Well, you look happy," I remarked.

"I am happy."

"School went well, then?"

"Yeah," he said. "It did."

"You've been there for a couple of weeks now," I said. "You're liking it?"

Matthew pulled out a chair and sat across the table from me. "I do."

I eyed him. "What's going on?" I asked. "I see that look on your face."

"Elections for student government today," Matthew said.

"Oh, yes?"

"Yeah. You're looking at the president of this year's freshman class."

"Matthew, no!" I exclaimed. "Really?"

"Yeah," Matthew said, running his fingers through his hair. His green eyes held mine, shining.

"Matthew, that's wonderful!" I leaped from my chair, spilling a bit of my tea in the process, and rushed to his side, where I flung my arms around his neck and squeezed.

"Ma, Ma," Matthew protested with a laugh. "Okay, okay. Go easy before you choke me to death!"

"Oh," I said. "I am just so happy for you, Matthew."

"I know," he said. "I'm happy for me too. I think it's gonna be a good year."

"That makes my heart smile," I told my son. And then my lower lip began to quiver.

"Aw, Ma," he said. "You're not gonna cry, are you?"

"No," I said. "Of course not." I managed to hold the tears within. Matthew knew that I was an emotional woman, but sometimes I could be a bit too emotional for him. How could I explain to him the feelings that coursed within me? How was I to explain that I had once almost lost him, and that experience lit a fire, and I had held on tighter, not wanting to take a single moment of our time together for granted? That each and every milestone he hit was cause for celebration and filled me with pride? How do you explain such things to one so young, to one that hadn't yet experienced adulthood, falling in love, becoming a parent? He'd understand in time, I was sure. But not then, and he saw me as a sentimental fool, I am sure.

Merle arrived home from work that evening as dinner was cooking. "Smells good," he said, plonking his briefcase on the counter.

"Thank you," I said. "Matthew has news."

"Oh?"

"Yes," I said.

"You're smiling," Merle remarked. He walked to me, placed his palms on my shoulders, and nudged my neck with his nose.

"I am."

"Well? Are you going to tell me this good news?"

"I'll leave it to Matthew."

We sat for dinner shortly thereafter, and Matthew relayed his appointment to his father. Merle was decidedly thrilled for our son, just as I knew he would be. Merle had proven to be an exceptional father, but I had never doubted he would be. Oh, there had been times when he and Matthew did not see eye to eye. They had thrown out some words that they had later regretted. But that's the way of life, of parenthood, is it not? And at the end of the day, Merle adored our son, and I knew Matthew felt it.

Matthew won the position of class president the following year as well then again in both his junior and senior years of high school. He dated a couple of girls, though neither relationship lasted very long. He made some close friends but none as close as Edward, the freckled, red-haired boy I had seen my son walking with on his very first day of school back when he was just a mere six years old. The two boys had been inseparable when they were younger. Now that graduation was upon them, they were still the best of friends, though I assumed that their paths had parted just a bit, since Matthew had told me he had made other friends in whom he found commonalities that he and Edward didn't share with each other. They had both chosen different paths to take after graduation: Matthew would head to medical school, while Edward would enter the workforce.

Graduation took place on a Friday night. I was sitting at my desk in Mr. Morris's office that day, a diminutive desk, since there was minimal space in which to put it. Mr. Morris hadn't wanted me in the lobby with the secretary. He preferred me closer to him because my job often necessitated that we speak.

"Big day today, yes?" Mr. Morris said.

I sighed. "Yes."

"And tell me," my older friend said, "why so sullen?"

"Oh, I don't know. I suppose it's just..." I swiveled in my chair and faced him. "Mr. Morris, do you ever have the feeling that your life is slipping away from you?"

"How so?" He pushed his spectacles farther up the bridge of his nose. I noticed the pronounced veins lining the skin of his mottled hand, the prolific wrinkles on his face.

"We met many years ago, you and I," I said, attempting to sort through my thoughts to formulate an articulate response. How could I put into words what my heart had been feeling these past days—these past years, even?

"That is true," my friend said.

"I was young then, much younger than I am now. I don't think I knew then... I suppose I'm trying to say that I don't think I knew then what course my life would take, and I most certainly didn't know then how I would feel on a day such as today when my son is about to graduate from high school, and then... Mr. Morris, I feel as if my son is leaving me. For good. Will he come back? Will he want to? Where is he headed in life? Will he be happy? I have so many questions and no answers. And I have so many feelings, and although I have a pride for my son that can't be explained, I also feel like my heart is breaking."

"Ah," Mr. Morris said. "I see. You feel like you are losing him."

I nodded. "I do."

"And yet, he is still here."

"In a way, yes, I suppose he is. But he'll be going to school soon. Did I tell you about school? He was looking into the program that my husband took, but Matthew has decided a different program would suit him better, and I'm proud of him for making that decision for himself. And yet... he'll be so far away."

"Not so far."

"It feels like it, though. Since the very day we took him home, Matthew has been under our roof. He's lived with us, grown with us. I've witnessed firsts and lasts. The first tooth he lost and the last. His first smile, his first step. The first time he said my name. The first time he reached for me. His first fall. His first day of school. His first friend. And each day, Mr. Morris, each day has been a step farther and farther away from me, and I don't like it. Not one bit. Each day has led us here, to today. To my son graduating from high school and starting his life without me and without his father."

"Ah," Mr. Morris said, holding up a finger. "But will he be without you?"

"No," I admitted. "Not entirely. I know he will call. I know I will see him from time to time. But Mr. Morris, it just isn't the same, is it? My house is going to feel so empty when he leaves. And I know this is just a part of life. I know this is my son growing up, beginning his journey as an adult. But I suppose… I just didn't think it would be this hard. It's just so hard." My lower lip quivered. I tried very desperately to keep the welling of my eyes to a minimum, but the tears soon spilled over and onto my cheeks. I swiped them away.

"I'm sorry," I said. "I don't mean to cry."

Mr. Morris stood and walked to my side. He placed an aged palm on my shoulder. "Cry away, my girl. Cry away. No shame in that, is there?" He paused and watched me swipe at another tear before he said, "Elizabeth and I don't have children. You know that. So maybe I can't fully comprehend the feelings you have right now. Haven't been through it, you know. I might be a clown—again, that's something you already know—but doggone it, got some emotion left in me still, haven't I?" He squeezed my shoulder again. "I've felt loss in my life. It's true. Felt a loss when you had Matthew and stopped working for me."

"You… what?" I looked up and into his brown eyes.

"Maybe not the same. No, not the same. But in a

way..." I watched as his hand slipped from my shoulder and began to fidget with his trouser pocket. He cleared his throat and retreated to his chair. He sat down and trained his gaze on his desk. But golly, if I didn't see the blush on his cheeks then.

...

"Matthew, are you ready? We're going to be late if we don't hurry."

It was time.

"Coming," Matthew called from up the stairwell.

I watched as my son descended, all long, lanky legs and his grandfather's broad shoulders. He wore a pair of black trousers—a crease at their front from my ironing—and a white button-down shirt. His father's blue tie was neatly knotted at his neck and hung almost to his belt. His graduation cap was held in one hand, and his gown was slung over a shoulder. "I'm ready," he announced.

I looked at Merle standing beside me and sensed the pride he felt in our son; it permeated from his countenance and in the emerald eyes that he had passed down to Matthew. "To the car, we go," Merle said.

We arrived at the high school soon thereafter. Merle parked the car, and we exited. We walked into the building, and Matthew led the way to the gymnasium where the ceremony would take place. "You go in," he said. "I'm supposed to meet in the cafeteria."

"Oh," I said. "All right."

"See you after?" Matthew was beaming.

"Yes," I agreed. "We'll see you after. Will we meet you somewhere?"

"I'll find you," my son said confidently.

"All right."

"Bye!" Matthew set off, his back to his father and me. I turned to Merle. He smiled down at me and took my hand, and together, we walked into the crowded gymnasium and found two unoccupied seats. After a few minutes passed, I spotted my mother, who I flagged down with a hand. She sat beside me and clutched her purse to her lap. By this time, Merle's parents lived out of state and rarely traveled.

"Oh, my," she said. "How did this day arrive?"

"That's what I was asking myself this morning," I said.

"I imagine you were," she said with a sigh. "But really." She turned to look at me. "Your father would be so proud."

And instead of feeling a fresh set of mournful tears well in my eyes, I smiled. My heart felt light in response to my mother's statement. They say time heals all wounds, but I disagree. Time does not heal. Not from a loss so great. But with the passing of time comes a sense of peace, of acceptance. With the passing of time, the memories cease to be a torment and instead fill your heart with joy amidst the lingering sorrow. And that was how I felt right then, sitting in a chair at my son's high school graduation with my husband on one side of me and my mother on the other.

"I know," I said. "He would have been very proud of Matthew."

My mother took my hand in hers and didn't let go.

The ceremony began, and I spotted my son, looking so handsome in cap and gown. When he stood on the stage in front of me and received his diploma, my heart felt close to bursting. I wanted to leap out of my chair and clap, to call his name. To yell in front of all the other attendees that I was proud of him and loved him. But of course, I remained in my chair.

After the graduation ceremony, we had a small gathering of people over at the house. My mother was there, of course, and so were Barbara, Joseph, and the girls. Mr. and Mrs. Morris shared in our celebration, as did Annabelle and Fred and their two children, and Mary Lou and her husband, Lewis—who she had married in her late twenties—and their son. Matthew had been eager to celebrate with his friends after the ceremony took place, but when I explained to him that the graduation was almost as much for me and his father as it was for him and that we were also eager to share this day with our closest friends and family, he had relented. I saw it in his expression, in his eyes, that he would have rather skipped out on our little get-together, but he made no verbal complaint.

That evening, I felt elated in my home, surrounded by those I loved most in the world. We ate the cake I had made for my son, snacked, drank, and laughed. A lot. Matthew accepted the praise showered down upon him with modesty, but then it was over. Just like that. Why some of the most wonderful moments of life have to end so quickly, I will never know. But there we have it.

Most of our guests left, leaving only my mother and Barbara. Joseph departed with the girls when Barbara said she wanted to stay longer with me, and my mother offered her a ride home.

The door had closed behind the last guest, discounting my mother and Barbara. Only minutes afterward, Matthew said, "I'm off."

"Already?"

Matthew laughed. "What do you mean, 'already?' It's been all day!"

"I suppose you're right," I said. "I was just having so much fun."

"And now I want to go out with the guys."

"Yes, I suppose you do," I remarked. "Be safe, now. And have a good time."

"Always," Matthew said.

I walked him to the door. Before he could leave the house, I cupped his jaw with my palms, the tips of my fingers lingering on his temples, and said, "I am so proud of you, Matthew Arthur Mayhew. And I love you very much."

I knew my son just wanted to leave the house. I knew he wanted nothing more than to celebrate this momentous day with his friends. And I understood. I had been that young once too. But by golly, when I'm feeling the way I was feeling that day, I'm not one to hold it in.

I stood on tiptoe and kissed him on the tip of the nose before removing my hands from his face. He winced. "Really, Ma?" he said.

I laughed. "You will never be too old for me to hug and kiss you," I said playfully.

"Don't know about that."

"Well," I said, "I do. Now go and have yourself a good time. I love you."

"Love you, too, Ma," he replied.

And I held those words, that voice, with me even as he closed the door behind him, and I saw our car disappear in the distance.

. . .

"I'm heading to bed," Merle said to me later that night. "You coming?"

"No," I said. "I think I'll stay up a bit longer."

"Suit yourself," Merle said. He leaned down and kissed me on the head. "Goodnight."

"Goodnight," I said.

I knew that Matthew would be out with his friends for a while still, but I couldn't sleep until he was home safe. It had always been that way for me, ever since he was old enough to be out without me and especially since he had begun to drive. I didn't know how I wouldn't worry when he no longer lived under my roof, but I'd deal with that when the day came, even though I knew it was so very close to arriving.

The phonograph was playing, the music soft and melodious. I listened while I read a book. Even though years had passed since my youthful discovery of my love of reading, I enjoyed it just as much as I did then and devoured the written word when I had time to do so. Eventually, I turned the radio off and headed upstairs and to my son's room. I opened the door and slowly walked inside. It wasn't the cleanest of rooms; my son was not a neat individual by nature. But it was his. I looked around, at the small desk under a window, textbooks stacked on top. I looked at his unmade bed, at some clothes strewn across the floor. And then I caught sight of a small bookcase, one of those Merle and I had purchased when Matthew was just a little boy. There were only a couple of books in there. The bookcase was otherwise used to display figurines and unnecessary paraphernalia that he had collected throughout the years and had no desire to part with just then. But as my eyes roamed, I saw a familiar sight, one that set a smile on my lips and sent a little flutter that tickled my heart.

I walked over to the bookcase and removed that item, an old copy of *Curious George*. This had been the book that I had read to Matthew even before he could read it himself. He had nuzzled against my side on the living room couch, sometimes leaning into me and placing his head on my bosom as he peered down at the illustrations. We had read this book so often that the pages had frayed. I had even read it to Matthew when he lay unconscious in his hospital bed at the age of seven.

I took the book to my son's bed and sat down. I opened it, ran my finger against the worn paper of the first page. And then I began to read out loud. When I had finished, I felt hot tears wet my cheeks, but I let them run. I leaned back against the wall in my son's room, closed the book, and brought it reverently to my chest. I sighed. And I smiled.

We had done all that we could do, Merle and I. We had raised our son to the best of our ability. And now he was going out into the world as a young man. He was beginning his life as such. And I had to trust.

Oh, I was nervous. You'd better bet your buttons I was! And rightly so. This world is a big bundle of uncertainty, is it not? But I trusted my son, and I also had to trust that all would be well.

It was just another gigantic step in this thing we call life.

BARBARA

"*W*hat's wrong?"
I could hear it in her voice when she said my name on the other end of the telephone line. Something was worrying my best friend.

It was the summer of 1965. Matthew had graduated three years prior and was now twenty-one years old. Barbara's girls were growing up, too, and that hit me anew every time I saw them, which was often. Her eldest, Hazel, was now eighteen and had graduated from high school just a few weeks prior.

"Can I see you?"

"Of course you can," I said. "Barbara, are you all right? Is everything all right?"

"Yes." But I heard the sniffle in her voice.

"I'll come. Right now. I'm grabbing my purse. You're home?"

"Yes." It was but a whisper.

"I'm on my way."

I drove to Barbara's house, faster than I should have, I

admit. Barbara was family to me. When it came to her well-being, I was more than invested emotionally. I had known my best friend almost as long as I had known myself, and I cared for her deeply and dearly.

She opened the door even before I had the chance to knock. I hurried inside, and she closed the door behind me. As it was the weekend, I expected to see her husband, Joseph, and at least one or two of their four girls, but as I looked around the room, all that greeted me was silence and Barbara's anguished expression. "You're alone?"

"Yes." Her lower lip quivered.

"Where is… What is going on?" I grabbed her hands and squeezed. "Please tell me what's going on. I see it in your face, and I heard it in your voice when you called."

Barbara bit her lower lip, and a single tear dribbled down her cheek. She led me to her couch, where we sat. I was still clutching her hands with my own. "Would you like some coffee?"

"Oh, pish-posh," I scolded my best friend. "I'm no guest. And since when are you so formal with me?"

Barbara gazed down at her lap. "I'm sorry, Martha," she said. "I'm just so… I don't know…"

I dipped my head and caught her eye, imploring her to look up at me. She obliged. "Please tell me what's going on. I'm worried."

Barbara nodded. She removed one hand from my grasp and swiped the tip of a finger under her eye. Then she wiped the tear she had caught on her dress. "It's Hazel," she said, offering no further information. I saw her inhale a sharp breath.

"What about Hazel?" My voice was soft, though I was screaming inside.

My best friend looked into my eyes, and I marveled, as I often did, at the beauty of her own. Unshed tears only intensified the speckles of green within the brown, and they seemed to beckon to me, to plead with me, to speak of their own volition what Barbara had not yet divulged to me. I searched those eyes, and in them, I found the depths of my best friend's grief.

Eventually, Barbara exhaled and said, "Hazel is pregnant."

My chest constricted, though I held my gasp inside. I nodded, slowly. Once. Twice. "Tell me," I said, softly. I brought my free hand up to my friend's cheek and lovingly wiped a fresh tear away.

"Apparently, she's been seeing a boy."

"I didn't know she was seeing anyone."

"Neither did I," Barbara said. And then her face transformed from a mask of grief to an almost amused pain. Her nose scrunched, and her brows creased. "She didn't tell me, and she didn't tell her father. She's been sneaking around. She had to have been sneaking around with this boy, Martha. Otherwise, how would she have gotten herself into this predicament?"

"And you…" I had to tread lightly. I did not want my best friend to place any blame on herself or Joseph for their daughter's lies and stealth. "You didn't know she was sneaking?"

"No," Barbara said. "I didn't. I don't know if she left the house at night to meet this boy or if she skipped school from time to time. I have no idea, Martha. All I know is that she came to us today and told us that she was pregnant, that she had been seeing this boy for a while now, and that she was in love. In love, can you believe that? In love. And with a boy that she has never introduced to us, a boy that she felt the need to sneak around with. What kind of love is that?"

I shook my head but said nothing. I wanted Barbara to feel that she could expunge all the feelings that she bore within, let them free, let them go, let them out. I was listening.

"I don't know what 'a while' means. I don't know how long it has been. I don't know when this started. I don't even know how far along she is, though I could not tell she was expecting. And I..." My best friend looked me directly in the eye, and I saw the torment she felt. "She's my daughter, Martha. Why did my daughter feel that she had to sneak? Why didn't she come to me? Why did she lie? Why... How did this happen? Am I not a good mother? What is wrong with me that my very own daughter felt she had to keep this relationship a secret?"

I had to speak then. Had to!

"It's not you!" I exclaimed with an abundance of fervor. "Please, Barbara, please don't think this is because of you. This is not your fault. You are an amazing mother. Just amazing. I've seen you with your girls, I've seen you and Joseph raise them. They are lucky to have you. You are an incredible woman and an incredible mother. Please don't think this is because of you."

My words apparently sent my friend over the edge, since a fresh set of tears welled then fell, too fast and furious for her to wipe them all away. Eventually, she surrendered and let them fall freely.

"Then why?" she asked me. "Why did this happen? Why to Hazel? Why to us? Why, Martha? Why, if I'm such a good mother, did my eldest daughter keep this from me?"

I shook my head, tears welling in my own eyes. "I don't

know," I admitted. "But it pains me to hear you speak of yourself this way."

"I'm not sure how else I'm supposed to speak. Or how else I'm supposed to think. I cannot wrap my head around... My daughter, Martha. My eighteen-year-old daughter is going to have a baby with a man that we know nothing about. How is that going to happen? When am I going to meet him? *Will* I meet him? Who is he? Is he older than her, younger? Where did they meet? When did this happen? How did it start? I'm going to be a grandmother to a baby who... Oh my gracious! I'm going to be a grandmother! I'm too young to be a grandmother."

Despite myself and the heaviness of the conversation, I smiled. "Neither of us is too young to be a grandmother." I leaned in and gently swiped at my best friend's cheek once again, though the tears continued to fall.

"This baby—boy or girl—what kind of beginning will they have?" Barbara continued. "Hazel just graduated from high school. She doesn't even have a job yet, for goodness' sake! You and I were just talking about this a few weeks ago when she graduated, how I was concerned for my daughter and her future because she didn't seem motivated at all. Maybe it wasn't a lack of motivation after all? Maybe I just assumed it was? Maybe she already knew? Oh, Martha, did she already know she was pregnant then and kept it from me?" Her face contorted, displaying her pure and unadulterated grief.

"I don't know," I told her. "But whatever it is, whatever happens, we have to trust."

Barbara shook her head. "I don't know if I can. Just a couple of hours ago, everything was okay. Everything was fine. My biggest worry was when Hazel would get a job. I worried about the other girls falling and hurting themselves when they went out to play. I worried about Joseph when he went to work, always hoping he'd come home safely to me. But never—never—did I worry about Hazel falling pregnant from a boy I know nothing about! And then I can't help but think about myself, think about my father and my mother. I feel that *I* had a reason to keep things from them, and yet I never did. So what does it say about me that my daughter kept this from me, kept *him* from me? Why didn't she trust me? What is it about me or about her father that made her think she couldn't come to us?

"I've always dreamed, you know. I've always dreamed that my girls would grow into women and find their place in this world. I dreamed that they would be happy, would meet good men, would start families of their own. But never did I dream this, Martha. Never. In my dreams, these young men came to our home, met Joseph and me. In those dreams, I knew them. My dreams consisted of crying tears of joy on wedding days. Oh, God, Martha!" She dropped her head into her hands. I nudged myself closer to her side and took her in my arms. My best friend rested her cheek against my bosom. I let her weep. For minutes, we sat like that on her couch. Eventually, she righted herself, wiped her red-streaked eyes, and breathed deeply.

"Thank you," she said.

"You have nothing to thank me for."

"I do," she said. "You have always been the best friend anyone could ever ask for. When I found out... all I wanted to do was talk to you. You understand me. You always have. Sometimes I think you understand me more than my husband does, God bless him."

I smiled. "I know how you feel."

And then Barbara chuckled. We embraced, and she

204

laughed into my neck until she calmed and looked at me. "I don't know what to do."

"I'm not sure there's much you *can* do," I told her. "Hazel is an adult now. She can make her own decisions. If she claims that she and this boy are in love, then perhaps all will be well."

"Perhaps," Barbara said. "But I fear for her, Martha. I do. Very much. If she kept this from Joseph and me, what does that say about this boy?"

"I don't know," I admitted. "But let's let this play out. Where is she now?"

"She left."

"Left?"

"Yes," Barbara said. "We shouted at each other. I couldn't help it, Martha. I can't describe how I felt when she told me the news. She just let it out there, and it was such a shock. I was so hurt and angry. I felt deceived. I thought Hazel and I had a good relationship, and now I question it all."

I shook my head. "Don't do that," I told her. "Don't you dare do that."

"What would you do?" my best friend asked. "How would you feel?"

I took this in for a moment and then nodded. "I see your point," I said. "But please, don't think the worst. Try not to, anyway." After pausing, I asked, "And you have no idea where she is right now?"

"No. Probably with this boy somewhere."

"Yes," I said. "I would imagine so."

"I wish I knew where that was," Barbara said. "It pains me to think my daughter is out there somewhere with a boy I don't know, doing God knows what. And in her condition. Where are they going to live, Martha? Here? Somewhere else? Is he a good man? Will he stay by her side? Will he take care of her and the baby? Oh, God, Martha, I just don't know!"

"Where's Joseph?" I asked.

"He took the girls out. After Hazel and I fought, the girls… They were scared. There were lots of tears. And I'm afraid… Martha, I said some words I shouldn't have said."

"Anybody would have in your position."

She shook her head. "I'm unsure about that," she remarked. "But they were said, and I can't unsay them. I just hope she comes home soon. I need to see my daughter. I need to… Please tell me everything will be okay."

"It will be," I assured her. "It will be." I placed my palm on her thigh, felt the coarse material of her dress. "She'll come home," I promised her. "How could she not?"

"I hope you're right," Barbara said. "I'm so… Martha." She looked into my eyes. "I'm just so scared."

I didn't know what to say. I had no further words of reassurance then, so I placed my hands on the back of Barbara's neck and gently led her head to my bosom. We sat—two women, two companions—in silence, each of us with our minds reeling.

And I desperately hoped I had not just lied to my dearest friend.

. . .

The wedding took place at the end of the summer, a rushed affair that sent Barbara into another flurry of tears that wet

206

my blouse. By this time, Hazel was showing, though her dress hid the bump well.

Hazel didn't come home the evening my best friend told me that her daughter was pregnant. I left Barbara's home later that evening when Joseph returned with their three younger girls. By the look on Joseph's face, I knew that Barbara's husband was hurting just as much as his wife, and it pained me anew. By the time of their arrival home, the girls did not seem affected, so Joseph must have pushed his anguish aside to reassure them that all would be well, and my heart went out to him, sending a fresh flurry of emotion, of love, welling within me for my best friend's husband. One thing was for sure: Barbara and I had both been lucky in love when it came to our husbands.

Although Hazel wasn't my daughter, I was her mother's best friend. A kindred soul. We shared a bond that I still wish every woman possessed but am sure not many have been fortunate to have had. I was therefore present in Hazel's room directly before the marriage ceremony was to take place. She would marry Kenneth—yes, we had since learned that her beau's name was Kenneth—in the Groggles' backyard, yet another area of contention between Barbara and her daughter. Barbara had always assumed that her girls would marry in the church, but Hazel had been defiant, claimed she wanted nothing to do with their church, and refused to enter one on her wedding day. Barbara had been hurt but had conceded. It wasn't her wedding, after all, and she had to respect her daughter's wishes on her special day. And that was what Barbara hoped it would be, after all: a special day. She wanted only the best for Hazel, no matter what that would be, no matter where her life and her choices would take her. She simply wanted her daughter to be happy.

There was a knock on the door, then Joseph poked his head inside. "I think it's time," he said. "People are getting restless."

"By people, you mean Kenneth," Hazel said, looking rather annoyed.

Her father smiled in return, though his expression was closed-mouthed and weak. "Yes," he said. "Your husband-to-be has made it known that you're running late."

Hazel flung her hand in the air dismissively. "He'll get used to that," she said with a light laugh.

Joseph opened the door more fully and entered. "You do look beautiful," he said.

"Thanks, Dad."

Joseph opened his arms, and Hazel entered his embrace. He planted a light kiss on his daughter's forehead. "A married woman, eh?"

"I will be," Hazel said.

"Hard to believe."

"You've been saying that all week," Hazel remarked with a slight roll of her eyes.

Joseph nodded. "Still hard to believe."

"Well," she said lightly, "believe it. I'm getting married. Having a baby. You're gonna be a granddad soon."

Joseph tried to hide his reaction behind a smile, but I saw it, fleeting though it was. For just a split moment, my best friend's husband had looked like someone had slapped him across the cheek.

"Well," Barbara said, eyeing Joseph. I knew that she, too, had seen his masked reaction. "You won't be getting married anytime soon unless we head downstairs."

"True," Hazel said with a grin. "Ready, Mom?"

"I am ready," Barbara said, and she plastered a smile on her lips.

Hazel proceeded to the door but suddenly halted and spun around. "Almost forgot my bouquet," she said. Her two bridesmaids tittered. Hazel walked toward her dresser, a hop to her gait. She bent forward and reached for her bouquet. The collar of her dress twisted slightly, revealing an ugly yellow bruise.

Barbara gasped. "What happened?" she asked her daughter, hastening to her side.

"Nothing," Hazel said, quickly fixing her dress.

"That's not nothing," Barbara said.

"It's nothing, Mom!"

"What happened?" Barbara asked again in a more demanding voice.

"Nothing!"

"Don't tell me that nothing happened, Hazel!"

"Oh my God, Mom. It's nothing. I was being stupid and walked into a door."

Barbara eyed her daughter suspiciously. "A door doesn't do that."

Hazel placed her hands on her hips, her bouquet squishing against her dress. "And how would you know that?"

For a moment, Barbara was silent. Then she said, "We will speak later. But Hazel, are you... Are you sure you want to get married?"

"Are you kidding me?" Hazel said incredulously, her eyes wide and her lips curled into a sneer. "You ask me this now?"

"I..."

"No," Hazel said. "I can't believe this. Thanks, Mom." She walked toward the door, her two bridesmaids following hesitantly in her wake. "You've just ruined my wedding day."

"I—" Barbara lunged at her daughter. Her fingers attempted to clutch Hazel's arm, but they grasped only air. Hazel was already out the door.

"I—" Barbara looked from me to her husband. "What have I done?"

Joseph took a step toward his wife. "What are you thinking?" he asked, his voice tentative, almost as if he didn't want to hear her reply and instead wished to believe in his ignorance.

"I grew up in an abusive home, Joseph. You know that. My father, my brother... I don't even speak to my father any longer. Haven't done so in years. And my mother... She's been so beaten down that she... She's stuck, Joseph. My father has stripped her of any happiness in this life. I..." She shook her head. "I've seen it. I've lived it. Joseph..."

"Maybe," Joseph said in a cracked voice. "Maybe she did hit a door?" But I could tell that even he didn't believe his daughter's lie.

Barbara shook her head, slowly. Ever so slowly. She pressed her lips together. Joseph took a final step toward his wife and held her in his arms. I slipped into the hallway to offer them some privacy.

Twenty minutes later, in front of a diminutive crowd of well-wishers, Hazel was a married woman.

. . .

Hazel gave birth to a baby boy in January of 1966, just a couple of weeks after I celebrated my forty-fourth birthday.

Barbara spent as much time in her daughter's small apartment as she could—the apartment that Kenneth had lived in for a couple of years by then—helping Hazel care for her newborn son, while Kenneth worked. Hazel asked her mother to leave before Kenneth arrived home during the week and to also keep her distance on the weekends. Hazel had assured her that all was well, that she just wanted to bond with her husband and son, but Barbara knew otherwise. She attempted to speak with her daughter, tiptoe around the heavy words she knew she had to impart, but Hazel was having none of it. Barbara, God bless her, felt it was prudent to be near her daughter for as long as she was allowed. She knew that if she pushed herself too far, Kenneth would exert his dominance over his wife, and that would seep onto Barbara herself until she was unable to see her daughter and grandson at all. That was what she feared, day in and day out. The anxiety consumed her and began to affect her relationship with her husband and her three younger daughters, who were still living at home. They all saw the way Barbara fretted, the toll it took on her mental well-being. And my dear friend felt that she couldn't do anything. If it was up to her, Hazel would leave her husband, take her newborn son, and move back in with her parents, but Barbara knew that scenario would not come to fruition. She had heard and heeded her daughter's words. She knew that Hazel had been manipulated. She knew that her daughter was in no position to leave her current circumstances.

Barbara prayed the abuse wouldn't intensify.

And she prayed fervently, too, that it would not affect her grandson.

And yet, she knew that he eventually would be if Hazel remained at her husband's side. And that only proved to escalate my best friend's worry.

"I don't like him. Not one bit!" Barbara spat at me one Friday evening in February.

We had made plans to grab some dinner together, just the two of us. I sipped my martini and then placed the glass down on the restaurant's table.

"I know," I said.

"I don't understand," she said. "Any of it. I've seen this happen with my parents. And I've told her about my childhood. How could she... How could she let this go on?"

"I think..." I attempted to sort through the thoughts floating in my head. "Perhaps she does believe that he'll change? Maybe, like your mother, she believes that he loves her. And maybe he does, in his own twisted way? I don't know, Barbara. I don't know what to tell you, my friend. I wish all was well with Hazel and with your grandson. I see how hurt you are. And I wish I could do something for her and for you. I don't like seeing you like this. It pains me. I feel your pain *inside* me."

Barbara reached for my hands across the table. "We have always been like that, haven't we?"

"Yes," I said, with a soft smile. "Always."

"My mother is a broken woman. She isn't well."

"No?"

"No," Barbara repeated. "I spoke with her the other day. Her health is declining. I think it has been for a while now. Physically. And mentally, well... We both know she hasn't been mentally well for a really long time. And I fear... Martha, I fear that the way I see my mother, I'm looking at Hazel's future if she stays with Kenneth. And then I think of my brother—"

"Eugene?"

She shook her head. "No," she said. "Robert."

"Oh." My voice was low, barely above a whisper. My

chest felt heavy.

"I'm sorry to bring him up," Barbara said, leaning over the table. "I know you don't want to think about him. I know that you don't want to think… about what he did to you. I know that after all these years, you're still haunted."

"It's all right," I assured her. "I admit that I still have trouble at times, yes. Especially if someone surprises me, when I don't know they're beside me. But what he did… That was a long time ago now."

"Some things stay with us forever."

"Yes," I agreed. "They do."

"So forgive me," Barbara said, "but I fear that my grandson will be like his father. He's so young, Martha. So impressionable. And right now, he's this tiny, beautiful bundle that has his entire future ahead of him. And I want that future to be filled with happiness and love. I want my grandson to grow up and lead a life that he's happy to lead, and I want him to be a kind man, much like his grandfather. I don't want him to be…" Barbara swallowed. "I don't want him to be like Kenneth. I don't want him to grow up and be like my father. I don't want him to be cruel to his mother, or to any other woman he comes across. But that's what I fear will happen. And I feel helpless to stop it."

I sighed. I felt sick inside, my stomach flopping. I played with the rim of my martini glass. "But we can't be sure what type of person your grandson will grow up to be."

"No," Barbara admitted. "And that is the only thing giving me hope right now. I believe either of two things will happen: he will grow to be a kind man despite his father, or maybe because of his father, because of how Kenneth treats his wife. Or—and this is the one that keeps me up at night— he will be just like Kenneth." She sighed. "That's the thing about being a grandparent. And it wasn't something I had really thought about before now, but you have no control. I have no control over how my grandson is raised. I am not there, in his home, to protect him, to teach him. I have to leave that up to my daughter and her husband, but oh, how that stabs me, just like a knife to the heart. I feel it prickle every day. I feel the fear spread within me. Every day. I want my daughter to knock on my door, the very door that was hers for the first eighteen years of her life. I want her to knock on that door, and when I open it, I want her to be standing there with my grandson tucked under her arm and with a suitcase in her hand. I'll know then that she has left him... that man. But then in my mind's eye, I think my daughter, my Hazel, is knocking on the door, but when I go to open it, it's not my daughter at all, but the police, come to tell me that something terrible has happened, that—" Barbara choked on a sob.

"You haven't lived through what I have lived through, Martha," she said, "so it's hard to explain with words, this feeling I have inside each and every day. This fear. This foreboding. But as a mother, I can't let this go. I can't. And I have three other children to raise, and because of Hazel, I question everything I'm doing with them. Everything."

"Please don't," I pleaded. "We've been here before, Barbara."

"I know," Barbara said. "I know. But it can't be helped."

I looked at my friend intently and said, "I promise you, I am here. Whatever you need from me, whenever, any time of the day or night, I am here for you."

"Thank you."

"I'm not sure how I can help, or if there really is anything for me to do, but I'm here for you, Barbara. Always."

"I know you are," she said. "And I appreciate it. I love you."

"I love you too," I said, meaning every passionate syllable. And that's just the thing, isn't it? By golly, I might not have been raised in a home like hers, and thank goodness for that! I might not have had a sibling like Robert, but when you're as connected to another human being as I was to Barbara, well, then, you just feel it, don't you? I felt her pain and her sorrow. I felt her angst and her fear. I felt it when she was happy, and I celebrated with my dear friend when celebration was called for. So no, Hazel was not my daughter, and no, it wasn't my kin that was in the position Hazel was in at that time, but if something was happening to my friend, then by golly, it was happening to me too! I loved Barbara like she was a very part of my being, my soul. When she was hurting, it ripped at me, as though something was tearing a piece of my body from its rightful place. And I grasped to get it back, to piece my being back together. To place it where it belonged. But my beloved Barbara was in limbo, hovering between an existence of happiness and contentment and a world in which the very worst scenario played out for her daughter and only grandson.

...

Time passed. Barbara saw less and less of her daughter and grandson. In fact, she wasn't even informed of Hazel's second pregnancy straight away. Instead, she had been told during a phone call her daughter had finally answered. The conversation had been short and stilted, but Hazel had relayed that in just a few short months, Barbara would once again be a grandmother. Hazel gave birth to another boy in February of 1968, just over two years since her first son had entered the world. Barbara was not at the hospital at the time. She had not even known that her daughter had gone into labor. She found out after the fact, once Hazel had already returned home, and the news had brought with it such an intense sorrow that Barbara would not leave her bedroom for the following two days. Hazel had then refused her mother the opportunity to come by and meet her newborn son. Instead, Hazel had promised that she'd visit her mother soon so that Barbara could meet the new addition to her family, but Barbara knew when she hung up the phone that Kenneth dominated their relationship and had complete control over his wife's whereabouts. She knew she wouldn't meet her grandson anytime soon. Barbara and Joseph had spoken time and time again about what they could do to remove Hazel from her abusive husband, but with each conversation, they came to the same conclusion, once even after paying a visit to the local police station: nothing could be done. Hazel was an adult. She made her own choices. She could not be forcibly removed from her current situation, no matter how much Barbara wanted her to be. Now, if Hazel had spoken of her desire to extricate herself from her husband, that was another thing entirely, the police had assured her. Then, something could be done to keep Kenneth away from his wife. But no, not now. Not when Hazel had made no move to separate from her husband. Not when Hazel claimed she wanted to stay.

And thus, the cycle continued: Barbara attempting to reach her daughter, Kenneth keeping them apart, Hazel— on those occasions that she spoke with her mother—

assuring her that Kenneth wasn't "all that bad" and never meant to hurt her, and yes, she wanted to stay right where she was. It was better for the boys, after all, was it not? Barbara could expound until exhaustion set in, and she could try her very hardest to convince her daughter otherwise, but to no avail. And so, Barbara wallowed in a deep state of depression, fearing the worst for her eldest child and her grandbabies, while also attempting to be a wife to Joseph and a mother to her three younger girls. Under Barbara's watchful gaze, they had grown. Only the two youngest remained at home, one aged sixteen and the other fourteen. Thank the Lord, it appeared that Barbara's three younger girls, having seen what both their sister and mother had endured and were enduring still, had steered clear of domineering boys and men. That gave poor Barbara's heart a reprieve.

1968 morphed into 1969, one year into another— quickly, as years were wont to do, in my experience. And then, in December of 1969, came the draft.

Our country had been fighting in Vietnam for several years up until then. This I knew. But the war had kept its distance from our small New Hampshire town. Sure, I had seen images on the television screen and heard the news on the radio, so I wasn't entirely naive about what was going on in our world. Oh, no. But up until that point, I had only known a couple of boys who had gone off to fight. They had been the sons of acquaintances of mine or of Merle's.

Our own boy, Mathew, had graduated from medical school by that time. He worked so hard with the internship he had procured for himself in Boston, Massachusetts, and I heard the weariness behind his voice every time we spoke over the telephone, which was often. Our conversations made my heart smile, even though I knew how very tired and worn out my son was. "You be careful," I always warned him. "Take care of yourself."

"I am, Ma," he'd say back. "I promise. Matthew Mayhew disease won't ever happen to me again."

Matthew might have been a twenty-five-year-old man and was surely making light of my concern, but I was still his mother, and a mother's worry never ceases.

I did not get to see my son very often those days, what with his busy schedule and all, but Merle and I periodically made the trip into Boston—oh, how I hated that city traffic! Merle drove into the city when our son had first begun his internship, but I was so frazzled by the sporadic lane changes, heavy brake usage, and swerving of other cars— not to mention the shrill sound of maddened horns!—that I found myself clutching onto the side of my seat with my jaw clenched and my heart racing. Soon, I was the one behind the wheel, offering my mind some semblance of control, though I knew I hadn't much! Goodness golly, was I nervous. And I didn't calm until our car was parked and we had safely arrived. Oh no. Only then could I breathe. But of course, I digress...

So yes, Merle and I visited our son when we were able, and Matthew came to us from time to time as well, bless his heart. And so, on December 1st, 1969, Merle and I found ourselves in our home with Matthew, his best friend from childhood, Edward, and my dear Barbara and her husband, Joseph, who, by that time, had become my husband's closet male confidant. We adults shared the couch—a bit squished with the lack of room for all four bodies—while Matthew and Edward took to the floor. The six of us sat there and watched the television set in the living room as a man in dark-rimmed glasses and a black suit stuck his arm into a large, clear container that held blue vials, one for every day of the year. The papers within were read and the dates announced by an older man sitting behind a small desk. September fourteenth was the first date chosen, and my heart ached for the boys that shared that birthday, the first to be drafted. Those young boys, aged eighteen to twenty-six, whose destinies had been written on a sheet of paper, encapsulated, and chosen at random. Matthew was born in July, and so I breathed a sigh of relief when that September day was announced. But my heart ached still. Those boys had people that loved them dearly, as Merle and I loved Matthew. Those boys had mothers and fathers, aunts and uncles. Some had sisters and brothers. All, I was sure, had friends. And with the announcement of their birthday, they had been stripped of their choice whether to enter this war. Matthew was twenty-five and therefore in danger of being drafted himself. He was no longer in school, had no dependents. He wasn't about to flee to Canada, as I had recently heard some boys had been doing. Yes, he had graduated from medical school, and thank goodness for that, because I held hope that my son fell under the category of essential worker, but I still fretted greatly, since he was not yet a practicing physician. My fears had been allayed a bit by the efforts of his coworkers and friends, who told me time and time again that our son was safe, but as a mother, I still worried.

And then there was Edward. He was neither in school nor what the country deemed an essential worker and was therefore not offered the choice to remain safely on our side of the ocean.

We sat with bated breath, Merle clutching my trembling hand. Number ten passed, then twenty, then thirty. I exhaled a breath I hadn't realized I had been holding, though my hand still trembled, my chest felt tight, and the muscles in my neck strained.

Thirty-one, thirty-two, thirty-three. Thirty-five came, and when they called the birthdate of May seventh, my free hand clenched into a fist. I looked immediately at Matthew, sitting beside his best friend, who was staring at the television screen with a hollow expression. I watched as my son slowly reached his hand out to Edward and touched his shoulder. And I watched as Edward turned and looked at my son. I saw the pain in his eyes, watched his slightly freckled face contort. He ran a hand slowly through the thick locks of his red hair. "Well," he said, his voice cracking, "there we have it."

"Number thirty-five," Matthew said in a mere breath.

"Thirty-five," Edward confirmed. "Not so good, huh?"

"Not so good."

Edward shrugged. "It is what it is," he said. "Not much I can do about it now." But I saw the expression on his face. Oh, how I saw his expression!

"There's gotta be something we can do," Matthew said.

"No," his best friend replied. "There's not. You know it as much as I do."

Matthew sat there, staring at Edward as the commentators announced more birthdates, revealing the fates of the young boys and men that had been born on those days. Eventually, he said, "I suppose not."

A tear trickled down my cheek as I watched the scene play out before me, my son and his dear old friend, both knowing that soon, Edward would be gone. That soon, he would be fighting a war that he didn't believe in. That soon, he would be required to answer his country's beckoning call.

I had lived through war before. My heart broke anew

that we were here once again.

Matthew was given the lottery number one hundred eighty-eight. It was on the higher end, which gave us hope if, for some reason, his essential worker status was revoked, though our hope had fleeted a bit with the realization that Edward would soon be conscripted into the army.

As it turned out, my son was indeed exempt from the draft because of his work at the hospital, so my fretting for him had been unnecessary, though as I said before, a mother never ceases to worry. But now my motherly heart showered its love upon Edward and on my son, who was living with the newfound knowledge of his best friend's conscription and the uncertainties that it would bring for the future.

If memory serves me well, Edward was required to receive a physical examination before basic training, and much to our surprise, this happened rather quickly, a month or two after the draft was called. He passed, of course. Edward was a healthy young man. During one of our frequent phone calls with Matthew soon thereafter, we learned of the letter that Edward had received in the mail. A letter stating that it was time for Edward to be inducted into the army.

And then he was gone. He was at basic training and safe for a time, we knew. But we were also cognizant that the dear boy would soon be on a plane and headed for Vietnam. Technology had advanced by this time. Oh, we had known what had occurred during World War Two, yes, but I seem to recall that I knew so much more about the war in Vietnam than what I had been apprised of during the Second World War. Maybe it's my memory. I am one hundred one years old, as you know. But I recall images on a television screen. I recall hearing voices of the atrocities on the radio. And I recall, with clarity, conversations on the streets and at work. I knew what was going on overseas. Oh, I knew.

And it only made me worry all the more.

I was still working at Mr. Morris's office at the time, but it was not Mr. Morris for whom I was working. A colleague of his had taken over the practice. I was a personal assistant to him and not my dear friend and mentor, Philip Morris.

In the fall of 1971, when Edward was in Vietnam and Matthew's only communication from him was via delayed letter, when Barbara's daughter Hazel seemed to have fallen off the face of the Earth, when my darling Merle's practice was flourishing, when my dear mother announced that she had met a man and that they were dating—oh goodness!—it was then, when the world was revolving around me, that Mrs. Morris gave me a call informing me that her husband was ill and in the hospital.

Mr. Morris was in his eighties. I had known for a while that he was ailing, but he was a hearty little man and had always jumped back, so I assumed he would do so that time as well.

I visited him on a Saturday morning. I remember the day well, even the weather: sunny and unseasonably warm. Why is it that we remember with such clarity days like these? Days that alter the course of our lives? Days that prick a hole in our hearts that never seem to mend?

Mr. Morris was sitting up in the hospital bed when I arrived. To my great amusement, he had a smearing of what looked to be chocolate pudding on the chest of his gown. "Look at you," I said. "I would have expected nothing less." And I motioned to the stain.

"Ah, yes," Mr. Morris said, his voice scratchy and low. He rubbed the stain as if his finger boasted a magical remover, but of course, it remained. "Always was a clown, and don't you know it."

I chuckled. "Yes," I said. "I know it."

"Calling me a clown now?"

I smiled warmly at my dear friend.

"Have a seat." He motioned to a chair by his bedside, and I sat, crossing one ankle over the other and placing my hands upon my lap, feeling the soft material of my flowy patchwork skirt. Oh, but I loved patchwork designs then. Still do. There's just something about them that appeals to my eye.

"How are you feeling?" I asked Mr. Morris.

"Not so good," he said.

"No?"

And then he looked at me. Really looked at me. Through his spectacles, I saw the intensity in his gaze, a change, a sign. Mr. Morris was telling me something important. My friend was speaking to me without the use of words.

And then I knew.

Somehow I knew.

My friend wasn't bouncing back this time.

A lump swelled in my throat, and I found breathing hard. Eventually, I was able to mutter a feeble, "Why?"

"Happens when you get old, my girl. This body of mine's been through a lot. Tellin' me I've worked it hard enough."

"But—" I stammered, feeling tears well in my eyes. "I don't understand."

"'Course you do," he said and offered me a wistful smile.

"Yes," I said, my voice but a whisper.

"Been blessed," Mr. Morris said, and I could tell his

voice was already failing him. He was struggling to get his words out. He laid back on his pillow and closed his eyes for a moment, taking a deep breath. When he opened his eyes, he looked back at me.

"Couldn't have asked for more in this life," he said. "I've been... happy." His breathing became ragged.

"Mr. Morris," I pleaded with him. I leaned over and placed a palm on his mottled arm, feeling the soft, sparse hair under my touch. "Please don't talk. Rest."

"I'll have time enough to rest soon enough," my friend said.

And those words did me in. I covered my eyes with my hands and wept. After a time, I removed my hands, swiped at my cheeks, and looked at Mr. Morris. "I'm so very sorry," I told him.

"Nothing... to be... sorry... about," he said. "You always... did... make me feel good."

Mr. Morris lifted his hand feebly and held it in the air. I took it within my grasp, one hand under and the other over, cocooning it. "Had I known," I said, "I would have had Merle visit with me today."

Mr. Morris smiled. "He's a... good bloke," he said. "But... it's you..."

When Mr. Morris didn't complete his thought, I asked, "It's me what?"

I felt Mr. Morris's hand move, his fingers pressing weakly into my skin. His eyes bore into my own. "You..." he said. Then he exhaled a slight cough. "You... always like..."

Fresh tears pooled and dribbled down my cheeks.

"Clumsy... flawed... I am... but..."

I leaned forward, inching myself closer to my dear friend.

"Always special… you are… like a daughter."

"Mr. Morris…" My tears flowed freely, and I made no effort to wipe them away.

"You're a… good girl." He closed his eyes, inhaled.

He drifted off to sleep soon thereafter. His breathing became steadier, and I felt his hand relax between my own, but I did not release my hold. I stroked his aged, paper-thin skin and ran my finger along the length of a protruding blue vein. I watched my friend sleep, watched the blanket rise and fall with each breath. I stayed by his side until Mrs. Morris entered the room.

"He's sleeping," she said, though it was not a question.

I nodded. "He is."

"He loves you," Mrs. Morris said to me as she stepped to my side.

"I…" I thought my tears had dried up, but I my eyes welled once again. It couldn't be helped. "I know," I said.

"Always has."

I looked up at Mrs. Morris. "Really?"

Mrs. Morris smiled down at me, a close-lipped, gentle, smile. "Yes," she confirmed. "Always. Since that first day you walked into his office. He came home and told me, he said, 'Elizabeth, I met a girl today,' and wouldn't you know, I just laughed at the man."

My lips curved upward, and my cheeks rose. I still held my dear friend's hand in my own.

"He knew you were special," Mrs. Morris said. "Even then."

"But how could he have known that?" I asked. "We only spoke a few sentences to each other. Barbara was there, and so was Poppy. Oh, Poppy was there, sitting in Barbara's lap."

"Yes, my dear," Mrs. Morris said. "But he knew. Philip

has a way about him. He always could read people. Better than me, I can tell you that."

I looked over at Mr. Morris sleeping in his hospital bed. And I understood. He and I shared that, didn't we? My heart, though breaking, swelled.

"Is this... Is it really time?" I asked.

"I'm afraid it is." Mrs. Morris sat on the edge of the bed and gazed at her husband.

"How... how can you be so composed?" I was attempting to stifle the heaving of my chest. My emotions were prolific, and I was unsure how to manage them.

Mrs. Morris glanced at me with a wistful look on her face. I watched as her shoulders rounded, relaxed. "It's the way of life," she said. "Philip has led a good one, and I've had many, many years with him at my side. I'm not saying goodbyes aren't hard to take—they are—but they must be made, and I'm able to make mine here, with Philip still looking at me that way he does. His mind is with us. It's his body that is failing. It's the way of things. We're old, my dear. Philip has led his life, and now, when he departs, he just hopes that he's left an imprint. I know he's left many on me. And I think"—she looked at me—"he's left some on you, too."

I nodded. "He has."

"Then he'll be remembered. He won't ever be forgotten. Guess Philip and I, we've always believed that if you leave your imprint in this world, even if you think it's small, even if some days you don't think you're leaving much of an imprint at all, well, we've come to believe that just isn't true. We all leave our imprints. Lots of them. On many, many people. On the world. Day by day. Step by step, we leave those imprints. We meet people for whatever reason, and we leave one. Maybe something changed in them, maybe not. But there's some sort of impression on their soul, and that impression might be left on another. And so on. Maybe I'm talking hogwash, but I don't think so. No. I don't think so at all. Philip imprinted on my life. I can't imagine what it would have looked like without him. And that's it, isn't it?"

"That's what?"

"That's what life is all about. If you've made even one person's life better with your presence, then you've lived a good one. Person to person. Human to human. Words, actions. Those are what life is all about. So, yes, I'm sad. My Philip won't be with us much longer. But I also celebrate the life we have been blessed with. I know not all get to say such a thing when they look back on theirs. But I do." She looked at her husband. "Oh… I do."

I called Merle to tell him I would be a while and explained to him what had occurred. He was quite concerned for my well-being, bless him, and urged me to stay for as long as I wanted. I remained with Mr. and Mrs. Morris until Mr. Morris slipped into a coma in the middle of the night, at which time I told Mrs. Morris that she should have her privacy and be alone to say goodbye to her husband.

The wonderful woman told me I could stay and said I was welcome, but I thought otherwise. I was honored by her invitation. Truly honored. But she was going to lose her husband, and I wanted to offer her privacy to mourn when the time came.

Leaving Mr. Morris's side was ever so hard. I cannot even put into words what I was feeling, the heartache, the sorrow that seeped all the way into the very center of my being.

Merle held me in bed early that morning and stroked

my hair as I wept. The moon offered its diminutive glow through our bedroom window, a halo of light into which I gazed when my eyes were not shut with sorrow. I found it hard to sleep, but sleep eventually took over, and I was awakened by Merle when the sun began to ascend. He sat on the edge of the bed and gently said my name. When I opened my eyes, he told me that Mrs. Morris was on the telephone.

I extricated myself from the bed with a heavy heart. I knew what this phone call entailed, and I dreaded the words.

Some deaths hit you hard. Some seem insurmountable, even when that person has led a long life filled with joy. Whatever brought Barbara and me to walk that road on the day I saw the sign in Mr. Morris's office, it was truly serendipitous. Perhaps I was meant to be at that very spot at that very moment on that exact day. Perhaps. But I do know now that Mrs. Morris was right: having Philip Morris in my life imprinted on me. And for the better. My life was improved because of his presence in it.

I have seen a lot of death in my one hundred and one years. Oh, have I! And by golly, do some hit you like my father and Mr. Morris, while others seem to spark within you feelings of a different sort, I suppose. Like Robert Brown. And his mother.

Mrs. Brown passed shortly after Mr. Morris. I did not know Mrs. Brown well, only that she was Barbara's mother and that she had led a very sorrowful, wretched life. I suppose my regret at her passing wasn't so much a regret that I had lost her from my life, for she wasn't really much in my life, was she? Rather, I felt a sadness for my dear friend. Oh, the feelings that must have flourished in Barbara the day she received the news: the regret of missed opportunities, missed life, missed experiences. A sorrow for a woman that Barbara was not entirely close to but whom she still loved dearly. There are so many feelings one can possess, are there not? And sometimes, we cannot sort through them well, or understand them entirely. But they are there.

I attended Mrs. Brown's funeral. I was there for my dear friend, offering her comfort in her time of need. Even Hazel attended her grandmother's funeral, which I know filled my friend's heart. I only regret that it took a death for Hazel to see her mother and to allow her mother to spend time with her grandchildren. Even to this day, I wonder if Hazel's husband knew where she was or if Hazel had dared fabricate a lie to get out the door.

When I saw Mr. Brown in the church pew, I thought my heart just about stopped beating. Though much older than the last time we had met, he reminded me so much of Robert that a flurry of emotions crept their way back in. Emotions that I hadn't felt in a while, that I had kept at bay, that I had tried to forget.

I felt it in the pit of my stomach as it roiled. My knees even shook ever so slightly in the pew as I sat beside my dear friend, her husband Joseph on her opposite side, holding her hand in his own. Their girls sat in the pew directly in front of us, the youngest shedding tears that I assumed then were spent out of confusion about death instead of the loss of her grandmother, whom she had not known well.

It was at the reception in the church's community room that it happened.

Since her father hadn't stepped up to take over most of the arrangements for his wife's funeral, my dear Barbara placed it upon herself to take control. She arranged for food to be made and delivered and even provided some of it herself. I helped, too, though I have never been able to pride myself on my cooking or baking skills—my mother's specialty sauce excluded. My friend appreciated my overtures nonetheless, and they were the least I could do. I felt at a loss for how to help her beyond lending a listening ear and a shoulder on which to cry. I was very thankful at this time, as I was through the entirety of their marriage, that Barbara had met and wed such a wonderful man in Joseph. He proved to be an emotional crutch when his wife needed it.

I was standing in the community room speaking to a man I had never met, Merle at my side, when I heard a sudden shuffling and a commotion. I turned my head, and there, in the near distance, I watched as Barbara's brother's face contorted into a look of outright disgust. "Are you seriously drunk right now?" Eugene was nearly yelling, and his cheeks were turning red. He curled his hands into fists at his side.

Barbara rushed to stand beside him, placing a comforting—or perhaps a pleading—palm on Eugene's shoulder. She whispered in his ear, and a look of concern took over her countenance.

Eugene shook his head and clenched his jaw. "No, Barbara," he said. "Not this time." He turned back to their father, who was smiling self-righteously at his son.

"I ain't drunk," Mr. Brown said, but even from across the room, I could hear him slur.

"How could you?" Eugene asked him. "This is Mom's funeral. She's dead, or didn't you notice?" He was seething, and as I walked forward, I noticed a small speck of spittle lining his lips. I had to get to Barbara. I don't think I was in my right mind at the time, but despite the nausea that

230

swelled within me at the altercation taking place, all I could think of was my dear friend and ensuring her comfort. Joseph beat me to Barbara's side, and my steps slowed until I was near enough to grasp her if need be, but I stayed out of the way.

"I know that," Mr. Brown spat. "My wife, ain't she?"

"She was," Eugene said. "No good that it did her."

"Don't you—" Mr. Brown stumbled forward and made to grab Eugene by the shirt, but Eugene was light-footed and retreated out of his father's reach.

"I don't think so, Pops," he said. "Not this time."

"Pfft," Mr. Brown muttered. "Just like your damn mother. You ain't nothin' but a sissy. Should be Robert here right now. Should've been you that was killed."

The next moment seemed to play out in slow motion as I watched Eugene's curled fist swing from his side and meet his father's elderly cheek. I was convinced I heard the very moment knuckle met skin, and I jumped in surprise and fear. Mr. Brown's head snapped back, and he lost his balance, stumbling backward and to the hard floor. A collective gasp sounded throughout the room just before Barbara screamed. She stepped toward her father, but instead of kneeling to ensure he was okay, she placed her hand over her mouth, hovered over him, then turned her head and looked at Eugene. Her eyes welled with tears. She looked at her father once again as he sat on the floor, wiping blood from his cup lip. His cheek was already beginning to redden.

"You're nothing!" Eugene yelled. "You hear me? Nothing! Everything I went through… everything you did. You and Robby… I'm done! The only reason I came here today was because of Mom. But that's it, Pops, you hear? I'm done!" He turned aggressively on a heel and walked out of the room.

"Good riddance," Mr. Brown yelled after his son. "Didn't want ya here, anyway." He wiped his lip once again then looked down at his bloodied finger. He reached a hand up to Barbara. "Help me up, girl."

Barbara stood staring down at her father's hand, and I watched as the tears dribbled from her eyes and down her cheeks.

"You deaf?" Mr. Brown asked. "I said, help me up."

Barbara shook her head ever so slightly then hastened toward the doorway through which her brother had exited. Joseph followed in her wake with two of their four girls. Hazel was cradling her youngest in her arms, her third child, a girl that she had borne just a few months prior. She stared at her grandfather with an expressionless face. Mr. Brown was left stupefied, sitting on the cold floor. I didn't stay to see what happened after that time. Instead, I, too, made my way to the exit to meet my friend, while Merle led an elderly woman to a nearby chair.

I caught up to Barbara, Joseph, and the girls outside. We had all left our coats indoors, and since it was winter at the time of Mrs. Brown's funeral, the chill hit me with a sudden force that left me with widened eyes and arms hugging my chest. Of course, that did nothing to stave off the cold. What a strange instinct it is to wrap one's arms around one's chest, is it not?

Words were truly never needed between Barbara and me. Just a look was all it took. With one look, we knew the other's thoughts. Such was the relationship that we shared. Sisterly souls, that was what we were.

I noticed that Joseph was consoling his girls, while Eugene was nowhere to be found. I would later learn that he had taken off in his vehicle, and goodness gracious, was I relieved that nothing ill had befallen him. What an irresponsible thing to do, speeding off when he was in such a mood. But I suppose there are times we don't think straight, and for Eugene, this was one of those times. He connected with Barbara later that day, apologizing profusely for his role in how the day had soured, but she was understanding of his plight. She had also grown up with Mr. Brown as a father and knew some of what her brother had endured as a child under their father's roof, though I suspect she didn't know all of what had transpired. With what Robert had attempted to do to me… No, no, I don't even want to think about the possibilities.

I walked toward Barbara and hugged her close. She reciprocated, resting her chin against my shoulder. Tears had clumped her lashes together, and her red nose ran, though from emotions or from the cold I did not know.

When it was time for us to leave, Barbara took my hand. From the look in her eye, I just knew she wanted me with her. Joseph, God bless him, had become accustomed to our relationship by that time and made no protest. In fact, I think he thought of me as an extension of his family, and for that, I will always be truly grateful. Merle encouraged me to accompany Barbara to her home.

I held my dear friend close to me that evening. She, Joseph, and I talked well into the night. When he saw Barbara rubbing her red eyes, Joseph encouraged her to head to bed. She obliged, though hesitantly. I don't know why Barbara wanted to stay awake. If I had been in her position, I am sure that I would have desired nothing more than to drift away to forget what had occurred at the funeral that very day. But Barbara was not me, and she tackled life's issues in a different manner. Perhaps she was comforted that both her husband and I were there. I don't know. But she did walk up those stairs, and when Joseph checked on her five minutes later, she was asleep.

Since Merle and I had driven to the funeral together, and Merle had not accompanied me to Barbara's house, Joseph drove me home that evening. The blackened roads vacant of other vehicles lent a silence that I did not find comforting.

By the spring of 1972, I was ready for a reprieve. My best friend was still mourning the life and loss of her mother. Barbara missed her brother, though they had never been close and had rarely seen each other. His presence at their mother's funeral and the altercation between Eugene and Mr. Brown had brought with it a plethora of emotions for my best friend, and along with those emotions inevitably came a sweltering of elicited feelings from memories she would have much rather suppressed.

Merle was working hard in his practice but showing his age. My husband was fifty years old, and his medium-hued brown hair had dulled. He now had a splattering of gray interspersed throughout. And golly, but he was losing it too. I can chuckle to myself now as I close my eyes and remember my beloved husband. I know that I, too, had aged, also being fifty years old at the time. I was no longer a spring chicken, mind you. But, for whatever reason, I always saw the physical transformations of others before I noticed them in myself. Call me foolish, if you will, but I was never one to scrutinize my face or figure in the mirror. I did, however, look intently upon those I loved, and Merle was one of the people in my life that I loved most. Those eyes, though—those gorgeous, striking green eyes. They never dulled. Even when they were lined by sagging skin

234

and wrinkles. And he always had a knack for gazing at me intently, making me feel… well, *seen*.

Matthew had left home. He was almost twenty-eight years old. Oh, goodness, twenty-eight! At one hundred and one, I know how young twenty-eight truly is, but then… oh, then, I thought he needed to stop growing up! My son, my baby boy, was an adult in his own right, practicing medicine like his father. Though, unlike his father, Matthew had chosen pediatrics. It was all about that mysterious Matthew Mayhew disease! When I thought about my son, tall and lean, with his father's incredible green eyes, cradling an infant in his arms, I have to admit that I felt nostalgic for times long past when I held my own darling boy in my arms, when he needed me, wanted me. When I would kiss his knee after a fall and everything was once again miraculously right in the world. And when I thought of Matthew holding an infant, I admit, I dreamed of the day I would become a grandmother.

But that day seemed long away, if it ever was to happen. Matthew hadn't yet taken a girl home to meet Merle and me. I knew he was a busy man. I knew he had a particular set of priorities. And I knew he had time still. But my mother's heart was aching, and my maternal arms were yearning. I never did share my desire with my son. I didn't want to place any pressure on him. He didn't need that from me. And anyway, it was his life to live, not mine. He would live it the way he chose. But I did speak with Merle from time to time, and he shared my desire. Merle had been such a wonderful father to Matthew and was a wonderful father still. And I yearned to witness him as a grandfather. My Merle…

I was happy in my job at the lawyer's office, but it had not been the same since Mr. Morris had stopped working and especially since my dear older friend had passed. Not the same at all. Mrs. Morris was still with us but was aging fast. I saw her about once a month and loved every moment we were together. She was slowing down, and I feared she would join her husband within the next few years, though it was she that had taught me that death was merely a part of life, that in death, we could still view beauty. And I knew that when she passed from this world, it was those thoughts that my mind would hold on to, those thoughts that would console me. And I knew that I would see that beauty, the beauty of remembrance for a life well lived.

So yes, by the spring of 1972, I felt I needed a reprieve of sorts. And that reprieve came with the reunion of Matthew and Edward. Edward had finished his active duty overseas, thank the Lord, and was now stateside.

And it was Edward who would give me one of the largest shocks of my entire one hundred and one years of life.

MATTHEW

*O*h, how I've always adored Christmastime. Everything about it, really. Merle wasn't much for decorating, though he did love that Christmas tree. He humored me, though, and encouraged me to decorate the house, both inside and out. He helped me with the outdoor lights, which I found a bit difficult to string, but he allowed me to instruct him on what to do and where to put them.

I love Christmas music, and because Bing Crosby was such an integral part of my upbringing and reminded me of my parents—my father especially since he was gone from this Earth—I often found myself frequently listening to him throughout the month of December. I also enjoyed Dean Martin, Johnny Mathis, and Kay Starr: popular artists from the '50s and '60s. They were always my favorites. They remain my favorites still.

On the first weekend in December, it happened.

I had already decorated for the Christmas season, and Merle and I were expecting Matthew over for a nice family dinner. I had a turkey in the oven—I was hopeful I wouldn't burn it—and music playing in the background, seeping from the living room and into the kitchen. Spices filled the air from the chutney I was stirring on the stove. Although my culinary accomplishments have always been few and far between, I do pride myself on my chutney! And the chutney is my very own recipe, not one handed down to me by my mother, like the aromatic and tasty pasta sauce that Merle loved so much. Merle was vacuuming the living room. My husband never was one for conventional roles, and I loved him for it. In that way, he reminded me of my father. "You vacuumed yesterday," he had protested to me when I removed our vacuum cleaner—a clunker of a contraption—out of the living room closet.

"I know," I replied. "But Matthew's coming over."

Merle rolled his eyes at me, a smirk lining his lips. "Matthew couldn't care less," he said. "You really think Matthew is going to notice the state of the house?"

"Well, probably not," I admitted. "But *I* will. And you know me…"

"I know you," Merle said. "You're my turkey."

"I'm no turkey. You're the turkey!" I threw his child-hood word back at him. Even after all this time, I still thought it the funniest saying. Turkey? What did that even mean? But his father had used the word with Merle, and so, in his youth, Merle had adopted it. The word reminded me of when we first met, and that brought me joy. A simple little word brought me joy. Merle kissed me on the cheek and took the vacuum cleaner from my possession. I smiled to myself mere moments later when I heard it *whoosh* from the living room as I stirred my delicious chutney on the stove.

About half an hour later, someone knocked on the door. I jumped up in anticipation, wiped my sudsy hands on my apron—which I still wore at the time due to my clumsy nature in the kitchen—and clapped my palms together. "Oh," I exclaimed. "He's here!" I didn't see my son nearly as often as I would have liked, and I looked forward to every moment we were able to spend together.

I ran to the door—well, I couldn't run. My home wasn't nearly large enough for that pace. But I hastened to the door, feeling a sense of immense glee. I whipped it open, and there, on the threshold, stood my handsome son, a brown suede trench coat snug around his lithe frame. It was the style of the times, I must say. And through all the decades I've been blessed to live, the '70s had the fashion I hope never returns. Or maybe the '80s. By golly, those were some interesting trends. The hair, all that product. The neon clothing, the jelly shoes…

But once again, I digress. It's common for me to do so these days, and isn't that the truth?

"Why did you knock?" I asked Matthew. "You know you're welcome here anytime. This is still your home!"

"I know." He smiled at me. "But the door was locked."

"Oh, my," I said. "Silly me."

"Sill you." He walked inside, and I shut the door behind him.

"Oh," I said. "I'm so happy to have you here!" I threw myself at him, my arms wrapping around his ribs, my cheek resting against his chest. Like his father, he was tall. Nearly six feet. That was almost an entire foot taller than me! And golly, now that I think about it, I've shrunk since that time, haven't I? I wonder how tall I am now…

"I'm happy to be here, Ma," Matthew said. "Hi, Dad."

Matthew turned his head, and I noticed Merle had sidled up next to me. He placed a palm on our son's shoulder and then pulled him in for a quick hug. Before parting, they patted each other on the back.

"Good to see you," Merle said.

"You too," Matthew replied.

"Come in, come in," I said. I ushered Matthew farther inside.

"Ah," he said. "Still playing the same songs, I hear."

"Of course," I said. "They're the best."

"Bringing back some memories for me, Ma."

"I'm bringing back memories for _you_? Matthew, do you know that I listened to Bing Crosby as a little girl?"

"I do," he replied. "You've told me tons of times."

"Yes," I agreed. "I know. And I do suppose that a lot of the songs I play now were played during your childhood. I'm sure they do bring back memories for you."

"Good ones, though."

"Well," I said with a little laugh, "I'm glad to hear that!"

We chatted for a while longer until the turkey was done cooking. When I pulled it out of the oven, Matthew said, "A whole turkey? There's only three of us. How the heck are we gonna eat that entire thing?"

"Turkey is one of your dad's favorites," I said. "You know that. Leftovers, that's how we'll eat it all. I'll send you home with some, of course. You might not live at home any longer, but you still have to eat well. And your dad will happily eat turkey until he turns into one!"

Matthew chuckled. "I'd like to see that day." He looked at his father with a grin.

We sat down to dinner, the three of us under one roof again. My heart was happy. So very happy.

I was about halfway finished with the food on my plate when I noticed Matthew shuffling his stuffing around with the tines of his fork. His smile had faded, and he seemed to be shaking. Just a bit, but I noticed it nonetheless. "Matthew?" I asked, attempting to catch his eye from across the table. "What's going on?"

He looked up, and I saw that he was trying to hide his discomfort behind a facade. But I knew my son. "Matthew?"

He inhaled sharply and released a very expressive sigh. The fingers holding his fork were trembling. He placed his utensil down on his plate. "I need to tell you something."

"Matthew," I said, "you're scaring me."

Matthew shook his head. "It's nothing like that."

"What is it?" Merle asked. He, too, had paused his eating to offer our son his full attention. My stomach quaked, and I wished Matthew would just get on with it already. I needed to know what was going on with my son! Was he sick? Had something happened at work? Had he lost his job? Had he been in some kind of accident? My mind, in just those few moments, traveled far and wide, every terrible scenario playing out in my head. I couldn't take it!

"I…" Matthew paused, the silence hovering in the air between us, foreboding. He rubbed his cheeks and eyes with his hands and then ran his fingers aggressively through his hair. "I don't know how to tell you this…"

"Tell us what?" I demanded. "Matthew, I feel sick. Please, please just tell us."

"I…" He looked from me to his father then back at me again. "I want to invite someone to come here with me on Christmas Day. To… I want to… because they are impor-tant to me."

My fear began to subside, and I felt a weight lift from the pit of my stomach. But I still didn't understand. "What do you mean? Why was that hard to say?"

"It's..." He took a deep breath in then let it out slowly. "It's... I..." I wanted to scream at my son to get it out, but I sat there, clenching my fists against my lap, hidden beneath the table. I would give him time. I wouldn't help him at all if I berated him, no matter how anxious I was feeling.

Merle reached across the table and placed his palm on Matthew's hand. I saw him squeeze it before retracting his hand and steepling his fingers. I could sense my husband's body language and knew that he, too, was apprehensive.

"The person I want to bring with me is... It's Edward."

I relaxed. Edward. Matthew's best friend. "Well," I said. "Of course you can bring Edward along."

"But," Matthew continued slowly. Ever so slowly. "I want to bring him because... because... I love him."

I smiled. "Of course you love him," I said, my shoulders rounding. "We love him too. He's been such a wonderful friend to you all these years. He is more than welcome here on Christmas Day."

"You don't get it," Matthew said. "I love him like... He's... I love him, love him."

I just stared at my son. "Yes," I said. "We know."

Matthew shook his head. "Edward and I... We're in a relationship. Have been for years. Like... like the kind of relationship you want me to be in with a girl." I could see the quake in his body, hear the vibration in his voice. "I... I..." he stammered. "He's my boyfriend."

I continued to stare at my son, realization dawning. His boyfriend. Relationship. Love.

"We're together," Matthew said.

Together.

"I…" Merle said. "I don't understand."

Matthew looked directly at his father, though I saw his lower lip tremble. "I think you do."

Merle paused for a few moments then stood from the table and retreated to the living room. Matthew placed his head in his palms, dejected.

"Matthew?" I reached over and touched my son's arm. He looked up at me, his eyes red-rimmed. I saw the angst clearly displayed on his face. "I… Give us time," I said. "This is… You've surprised us. Just give us time. But Matthew?" My son looked into my eyes, the emerald hue of his own intensified with the tears that pooled in them. "I see you."

A single tear dribbled down his cheek.

"I see you," I repeated.

Matthew nodded. I squeezed his arm with the tips of my fingers.

And then Matthew's shoulders heaved, and he openly wept. I walked to his side and knelt beside him. I held my adult son in my small arms and offered soothing shushing sounds that I had used often when he was just a small child. He needed them then.

When Matthew had calmed, we talked, he and I. For a long time. Our meals had been forgotten. All that mattered was us, what was between us. "Why didn't you say anything?"

"I was scared."

I nodded. "I understand," I said. "But I'm your mother."

"I was still scared."

"I love you, Matthew," I assured him.

"I know," he said. "But—" He motioned toward the living room, where we both presumed Merle still lingered.

I nodded. "I know," I said. "Give him time. Give us both time. This is…" I searched for an appropriate word. "Different."

Merle entered the room then and looked at our son. He sat across the table. "I was born in the early '20s," my husband said without preamble. Matthew nodded. "Times were different. What I saw, what I was taught…" I could tell Merle was still sorting through his feelings, his thoughts about what our son had just confided to us. It was 1972. And it was shocking.

"I know," Matthew whispered, his eyes trained on the table.

Merle nodded. "I'm sorry I left."

"I get it," Matthew said.

"Still wasn't good of me to do," Merle replied.

"I get it, though."

"Then that speaks to your character," Merle said. "What I did… I'm afraid it speaks to mine." And my husband, just then, looked ashamed. I felt a burst of renewed love and appreciation for the man I had chosen to spend my life with. "I am sorry."

Matthew attempted to hold back a fresh set of tears. "Thanks, Dad."

"You're my son," Merle said. "My son. And that… I'm sorry."

"Thanks. I bet it was… not expected."

And Merle laughed. Outright. A big, hearty burst. "You can say that again."

Matthew swiped under his eyes before his tears had a chance to fall, and he smiled. My son smiled. And my heart swelled.

"I'm going to need to… talk with you," Merle said. "To understand. I… I've never known…"

"I bet you have," Matthew said. "I bet you have known others. Actually, I guarantee it. We tend to… hide. The way society treats us…"

Merle nodded. "And I was just one of those people."

Matthew shook his head. "You weren't. You're sitting here with me now. And *that* is who you are. *That's* your character."

After a lull in the conversation, Merle said, "So. Edward is joining us for Christmas?"

And oh, but I thought my heart would burst out of my chest when I saw the look on my son's face after his father spoke those words.

"Yes," Matthew said, so much spoken in just that one little word.

Merle nodded. "Guess he's always been part of the family, yeah?"

Matthew laughed. "Yeah," he agreed.

"Now I guess… it's just… different."

"Better," I added.

Merle looked at me then back at our son. "Better," he agreed.

. . .

"Welcome, welcome!" I exclaimed as my son walked into our home on Christmas morning with Edward at his side. His boyfriend was clearly uncomfortable, and I knew immediately that Matthew had informed him of our conversation a few weeks prior.

I hugged my son fiercely, my way of reminding him that I loved him, that I accepted him for who he was. Then I turned to Edward. "I'm glad you're here," I said.

"Thanks for having me, Mrs. Mayhew."

My eyes opened wide. "What is that nonsense?" I asked. "'Mrs. Mayhew'?" I pulled him in for a hug and felt his body go stiff. When I released him and looked up and into his eyes, noticed the freckles that still sprinkled his cheeks, my smile was warm and genuine, and Edward noticeably relaxed. I took him by the hand and pulled him farther into the room.

Matthew and Edward spent hours with Merle and me that Christmas day. I will not lie and tell you they weren't awkward at times. Remember, this was 1972! But those hours were filled with love and acceptance. Since the night that Matthew had confided in us, we'd had other opportunities to speak with him about his feelings and his relationship with Edward. And we were fortunate to have known Edward for countless years by that time.

Yes. We were blessed.

I was nervous to tell Barbara about my son's relationship. Not because I thought that she would judge Matthew; I knew that she would not. She was not typically the type to harbor bias. I was uneasy to tell her because I knew that my son was in a loving, healthy relationship, and her eldest daughter, Hazel, was not. In fact, by that time, Hazel had attempted to get out of her marriage but to no avail. She was too terrified of her husband and what he would do to her and their three children. It was a daily struggle, a daily stressor for both Barbara and Joseph. I did not want to throw my son's happiness in her face.

But I told her. She was my best friend, after all, and we kept nothing from each other. Nothing.

"Wow" was the first word she spoke aloud after I relayed the news.

"Yes," I said. "Wow."

"That is… interesting."

I laughed. "To say the least."

"Well," she said, sitting straighter on her couch, "I am happy for him."

"You are?"

"Of course I am," Barbara insisted.

"I thought… I was nervous to tell you."

"But why?" She looked affronted. "You didn't think I'd take well to your son being a homosexual?"

I smiled. I loved my dear friend's bluntness. "No," I said. "That's not it."

"Then what is it?"

"I was afraid…." I took her hand in my own and scooted closer to her side. "Oh, Barbara! I know that you're struggling with Hazel. I see how it's affecting you day after day, and I didn't want to… I don't want to spite you with my son's happiness."

"Oh, nonsense!" Barbara removed her hand from my grasp and flung it in the air. "Don't you know that news such as this is only going to make me feel better?"

"It does?"

"Yes, it does, you goose," she said. "This will give me something to be happy about. Matthew is happy, which makes you happy, and you're my best and dearest friend, Martha. You always have been. Don't you know your happiness brings me happiness?"

"I hadn't thought of it that way," I admitted. If the

roles had been reversed, though, I would have felt the very same.

"Well, you should have."

"I'm sorry."

"You don't need to be sorry," Barbara said. And then she smiled. "But you do need to bring me details! I want to hear about Matthew."

Oh, how I loved my best friend!

"I have to admit," I said, "I was blind as a bat!"

"I am sure you were," she said with a giggle. "But why would you have known if he didn't say anything?"

"Matthew dated a couple of girls in high school, you know," I said. "I'm sure that threw me off, though those relationships, if you can call them that, didn't last long, and he hadn't mentioned any other girls in all these years. Edward has been over at our house countless times. We have known him since he and Matthew were just boys. But there were never any indications."

"When did this begin?" And I knew what she meant. When did the relationship take a turn?

"He told me it was years ago when they were in their late teens. After high school."

"Ooh," Barbara crooned. "I wonder who made the first move and how they realized they were both feeling the same way."

"I don't know," I said. "We've talked about their relationship a bit, but we haven't gone that far. I want to give Matthew some privacy, let him decide what and when to tell us."

"I want to know."

I laughed. "Honestly, so do I!"

We collapsed into each other, our shoulders touching,

our heads resting together at our temples. We laughed that day. A lot.

I left Barbara's house feeling light and carefree.

And hopeful. Hopeful for my son's future. Scared, too, I'll admit. This world can be cruel. But I *had* to hope. Hope is what takes us forward. Hope motivates us to get out of bed in the morning. And my hope was that my son's life would progress with love and promise and happiness.

But of course, that is not always the case, is it?

...

The 1970s flowed smoothly into the 1980s. Quickly too. So quickly that the new decade arrived before I even had the chance to ponder how swiftly the previous one had passed. By the mid-'80s, I was in my late sixties, and Matthew was—and this boggled me: how could my son be so *old?*—early forties. He and Edward had made a comfortable home together in the next town over, and I will always be grateful for that happenstance. How many mothers are fortunate enough to live so close to their adult children? Oh, many, I suppose. But not all, and I counted myself as fortunate. Especially because times were changing. Families no longer lived in such tight-knit communities. Homes no longer consisted of generations under one roof but of nuclear families instead. And children grew up and moved out of homes, towns, and even states and countries.

By this time, Barbara's younger girls were married and had children of their own, a constant comfort to my dear friend. Hazel had been in and out of her relationship with her husband but could never seem to escape fully, which was a persistent stressor for Barbara and Joseph. As I've said before, it does not matter how old your children are. Once you are a mother, you are always a mother, and a mother's worry never ceases.

Matthew and Edward expressed interest in raising children of their own. Unfortunately, that dream hadn't seemed attainable at the time. There was such prejudice, such turmoil relating to the gay and lesbian community in the '70s, mind you, and that only seemed to intensify for my darling boy and his partner during the '80s. It was when the AIDS pandemic first came to light, and that terrible disease had first been blamed on the gay community. Oh, I remember it well. Matthew and Edward had only confided their relationship status to a handful of people by that time. Both boys feared any repercussions that would be made by angry, ignorant people. They listened to the news, and they had other gay friends, one of whom had been beaten bloody in the early '80s as he emerged from a gay bar in Boston. So yes, my boys were scared. And that was what Edward had become to Merle and me: our boy. And what a wonderful man he was, I tell you. He deserved our love, right and good! I had known even when he was a little boy that Edward had a good heart, a good soul. And he never did anything to make me think otherwise.

Matthew was our only biological child, yes. I felt blessed beyond measure to have him in my life. After my son had fallen ill, after that terrible time in which I wasn't sure of his fate and wondered if he would depart this world and join my father, I felt a sense of contentment blossom. An experience like that will change someone, I tell you! But now we had Edward too. And by golly, we were happy.

The progression of time didn't change that my son

wanted a child of his own. Countless times we would talk, he and I, and together with Edward and Merle as well. I knew their desires, their struggles. They wanted to adopt but had been unable to find an agency that would accept them as prospective parents; many stereotypes remained even after the movement for gay and lesbian rights in the '70s and '80s. They sadly still remain, don't they, though we've made incredible progress since then.

Matthew and Edward were getting along in age, and Merle and I had resigned ourselves to the fact that we would probably never be grandparents. That saddened me greatly, but I held on to the very many blessings I had in life, and they saw me through. Oh, but to cradle a grandchild in my aging arms...

Matthew and Edward joined us for dinner at our home one weekend evening in late December of 1985. Although Christmas had come and gone, we still had our tree up. Decorating was a bit of a struggle for both Merle and me then; we were in our sixties, after all. Merle was showing signs of arthritis in his hands, and my body had slowed down considerably. I often found myself nostalgic for my younger days, those days when Merle and I strolled through town, or went dancing with Barbara, Annabelle, and Mary Lou. Those days when we were young, lithe teenagers. When we had our entire futures ahead of us. The nostalgia came from the sense that we were aging and didn't know how long we had left in this world, I'm sure. It came from those body aches, from watching our son grow into a man. It came from the wrinkles that lined my face and the veins that protruded from the pale skin of my small hands.

And, for me, it came as the memories of my father faded over time—not all my memories, and thank goodness for that, but many memories still—and as my elderly mother ailed in the bedroom upstairs that had once been my son's.

But never, not once, I am happy to say, did my nostalgia stem from unhappiness and discontent.

And for that, I know I am a lucky woman.

"I'm so happy to see you!" I exclaimed as I flung my arms around Matthew's back and pulled him toward me. He stumbled and laughed.

"You said that just a couple of weeks ago when we saw you."

"I know," I replied. I pulled back and looked up at my son. Into a face that was a bit worn, into eyes marked with fine wrinkles and a mouth surrounded by laugh lines.

"Good to see you, Edward," Merle said as he held out his hand. Edward shook it. It had been their thing, this shaking of the hands, since we had first learned that Edward was our son's partner.

I released my son and embraced Edward. I then placed my palms on either side of his face, pulled him down, and kissed his cheek. A soft redness swept across his freckle-lined skin, only exemplified by the hue of his hair. He always blushed, and I gleaned a sense of pleasure from eliciting that. Oh, I'm terrible, I know! But that boy—how giddy he made me.

We chatted amiably for a while and then sat down to dinner in the kitchen, Merle and I on one side of the table, and Matthew and Edward situated on the other. My mother hadn't had a good day and was resting in her room.

Matthew swallowed his first bite of stew. "Good, Ma," he said.

"Sorry it's not anything big tonight," I apologized.

"Doesn't always have to be big," Matthew said. "It's just

Edward and me. I'm sure you cook enough, even for just you and Dad."

"I suppose," I said.

"'Cause I know Dad doesn't cook much."

Merle grimaced, which made our son laugh. Though Merle did various household chores, he never liked the kitchen.

A few more bites were taken, and then Matthew looked knowingly, almost conspiratorially at Edward, and his partner nodded.

Matthew rested his spoon in the bowl of stew, laced his fingers together with his elbows on the table, and said, "We've got some news."

"Oh?" I asked. I ladled a large spoonful of stew into my mouth, relishing the strong flavors on my tongue.

"Yeah," Matthew said. He looked at Edward again, pleasure evident on his face. His body was held more erect in his chair, and he was… Well, he was beaming.

"Goodness," I said. "What is it, Matthew?" I gazed at Merle beside me, and he raised his brows.

"Remember I was telling you about a friend we've got? Amanda?"

My eyes rolled upward as I pondered the name. "Oh, yes. I believe you've mentioned her before."

"Well," Matthew said, elongating the word and letting it hover in the air.

It was my turn to lift my brows.

"Amanda is expecting," Matthew said. "The baby's father… He's…" Matthew tilted his head. "Not the best. He doesn't want anything to do with the baby."

"Oh, no!" I said. My heart immediately went out to this Amanda and her unborn child.

"She's in no position to care for a child," Matthew

continued. "She's estranged from her family, unfortunately. So she thought over her options, and she came to us. She knows about Edward and me. And she knows that we've been wanting a child of our own, that we haven't been so lucky. And... Amanda has asked us if we'd like to adopt her baby!"

My fingers raced to my surprised lips, and my eyes widened immensely. "No! Matthew, are you being serious?"

Matthew and Edward both laughed. "Yeah, Ma," Matthew said. "I'm being serious."

"But how... You've been trying to... what? How will this happen?"

"She's already looked into an agency that will work with us. They're good to go, so everything will be legal. The father will turn over his rights, and once the baby is born... I'm telling you that you're going to be grandparents."

I leaped so swiftly out of my chair that it tumbled to the floor behind me. I bounced—up and down, up and down —and placed my palms on my warm cheeks. "Oh, Matthew!" I exclaimed. "Edward!"

Matthew stood, walked around the table, and hugged me. In that embrace, I sensed his happiness, every ounce of anticipation he felt for what was to come, and every bit of struggle that he and Edward had endured until that point. I wished with my entire being that they would have no hardships from there on in, that nothing would hinder them from this adoption.

"When will this happen? When is she due?"

"She's due to have the baby in May."

"So soon!" I exclaimed.

"Yes, it's soon."

"Oh my," I said, my fingers finding my lips again. And then I began to shake, and tears streamed down my cheeks.

Matthew reached a finger out and swiped them away. Gently, lovingly. "Oh, Matthew," I said.

"I know, Ma."

Matthew walked behind me and embraced his father. Merle was standing, though I hadn't noticed that he had left his chair. Merle hugged him right back and then looked across the table at Edward. They shared a look, a look I will never forget. Merle nodded slightly. He sat back down, eyes still trained on Edward, and I watched as a single tear lined his cheek. I knew then. Between that look and that tear— my husband was overcome with emotion. And it sent me into a new fit of tears and expressed joy.

And of course, my son just stood there laughing. Oh, not at me, mind you. At the situation, I am sure. He laughed from happiness and contentment. He laughed at the culmination of his hopes and dreams. He laughed at his lot in life.

My dear son.

...

It started with a feeling of weakness and fatigue. Merle didn't have his usual, hearty appetite. Then he began to feel nauseated to the point that he'd often find himself rushing to the bathroom to get sick. "Just fighting a virus," he said. It was February, after all, so I didn't question his reasoning. Yet, something nagged in the back of my mind. Merle had been sick like this before.

When his symptoms didn't seem to clear up but only appeared to intensify, and his skin held a sickly yellow pallor, even he knew this was not a simple virus. Merle was a physician, after all. Close to retiring, yes, but he was still in practice, and this sickness had forced him to miss one too many days of work. He knew something was terribly wrong.

With Merle's resources and connections, he acquired an appointment at a renowned hospital in early March. Tests were administered. And about a week later, we were given a diagnosis.

Pancreatic cancer.

Stage 4.

The worst possible. The cancer had unknowingly spread. Throughout his belly and into his liver. My darling Merle was given only a few short months to live.

To tell you I was heartbroken would be an understatement. There are no words. Not for this. I met Merle in 1937. 1937! I was a mere fifteen years old, just a little thing. But my heart was big even then, and despite my initial misgivings about this new boy in school on whom my friend had a crush, that heart of mine soon learned to love. Merle and I had been connected, a pair, for nearly forty-nine years. That is a long time to love someone, to share your life with them. That is a long time to feel them seep into your very soul. And it is a long time for you to envision your life ending with them still in it.

But I had just been told that would not be the case. I had just been told that my beloved, darling Merle was dying.

Merle, God bless him, accepted his fate.

I did not. Even knowing what Mrs. Morris had taught me when her husband was close to passing, I did not accept Merle's fate.

I ranted. I raged. I screamed. I cried until exhaustion overwhelmed me, and I crumbled to the floor in a heap.

I could *not* lose my Merle. My darling Merle! And Matthew could not lose his father.

And oh, good Lord! Merle had to see his grandbaby born. He just had to! What kind of fate was this if an incredible man like Merle, a man who did only good in this world, who left an imprint on so many souls, passed on before he could lay eyes on his only grandbaby?

My heart shattered, the pieces pounded against my constricted chest.

"Let it go," Merle said to me gently one night as we lay in bed. "Let it go." He held me close and kissed the top of my head.

"I can't," I said, tears pooling on my pillow. "I can't lose you, Merle."

"You won't," he promised. "You will never lose me."

"How can you say that?"

My husband whispered into my ear, "There's nothing we can do. Let's not waste the time we have left on tears."

I clung to him, and eventually sleep found me. And in the morning, I vowed to do better by Merle. He had seen my pain, my utter torment. Now it was time to be strong, to lend Merle my unwavering support. To care for him, to love him, until he took his last breath.

How he could hold it together so well eluded me. And yet, I thought that perhaps he wasn't holding it together so well after all. Perhaps, Merle being who he was, was attempting to put on a strong face for *me*, since I had no problem expressing my grief. I felt guilty at the thought. If anyone needed support, it was Merle. And here I had gone and taken that from him. Oh, but goodness… Things are complicated sometimes, are they not?

From then on, it was usually in private that I wept, that I grieved.

And with Barbara.

My darling, wonderful Barbara.

She was there for me in those darkest of days. She and Matthew took turns caring for my home—grocery shopping, cleaning, running errands—so that I could turn my full attention onto both Merle and my continuously ailing mother. There was so much grief, so much anticipatory loss hovering in the air of my house, that I was surprised I could go about my daily tasks at all. But I felt it: Merle's love for me. And I felt my mother's too. And I felt the love of both Barbara and my son. It still amazes me that in a time of such sorrow, love has the tendency to break through.

Although my mother preferred the solitude of her bedroom, Merle could not stand to be alone, confined. We acquired a hospital bed and made my husband comfortable in the living room, right where we had spent most of our time together as a couple in that house. Even when Merle's practice had taken off and we were doing well financially, we never desired to move into something bigger and better, for that little home was all we needed.

While Merle lay in bed, we watched television and listened to music, both current tunes as well as the music of our courtship. The memories that old music elicited washed over me and sent me spiraling all over again. But those memories also filled my soul with a contentment I hadn't known I could possess at such a time.

On an unseasonably chilly morning in early May, Matthew called. "Ma?"

"Yes," I said. "I'm here."

"It's time." I could hear the smile in my son's voice.

I gasped. "It's time? You mean... Matthew, is the baby coming?"

"Yeah," Matthew said. "Edward and I are headed to the hospital now."

"Oh, Matthew!"

"I know. I can't believe this is happening!"

"Go on now," I said. "You're about to become a father, you know. Get on going."

"Thanks, Ma," Matthew said. "I'll call you, okay? I'll call when the baby is born?"

"Yes, of course," I said. "I'll be waiting. And Matthew?"

"Yeah?"

"I love you so much."

"I love you, too, Ma."

I hung up the receiver and rushed to Merle's side. He was propped up in bed. "Merle!"

My husband nodded, a feeble gesture in his state of weakness. "I know," he croaked. "I know..." And then he smiled, lips dry and cracking. His emerald eyes welled with tears.

That evening, I sat beside my husband. "Merle?"

"Hmm?"

"Look outside," I instructed.

"What?"

"Outside," I repeated. "Look out the window and up and into the stars. Do you see them?"

"I see." My husband's eyes softened, and a smile lined his lips.

"That's Cassiopeia," I said. "Do you see her?"

"I see her." His deep voice was hoarse.

"And the North Star, and the dippers."

Merle glanced into our past at that moment. I was sure of it.

"You're up there, you know." I looked at Merle.

"Hmm?"

I grinned. "I named a star after you, you turkey. I paid a fee and sent it in the mail and voila, there's a star named Merle Mayhew. Can you believe it?"

"What's this?" Though his expression was weak, I could see him attempt to crease his eyes and pinch his lips, a tell-tale sign of my silliness.

"I speak the truth," I promised him. "We'll even get a certificate in the mail, and I know right where to put it."

"And where's that?"

"Right here," I said, indicating an end table with my hand. "Right next to your bed, so every time you turn your head, you'll see it. And every time we look into that sky, Merle—every time…" My voice caught.

Merle slowly lifted his arm and placed his palm over the top of my hand. "I love you," he said slowly and with a sigh.

"I love you too. So very much."

Matthew and Edward visited with baby Nicole just a couple of days later when Amanda had been discharged from the hospital. They hadn't even gone home first; instead, they chose to visit us on their way. Matthew knew that his father was running out of time.

I sat on the couch and eagerly stretched out my arms. Matthew handed the tiny bundled infant to me, and I immediately cradled her to my chest.

Nicole was perfect. In every way. Those little eyes roaming under paper-thin lashes. That gorgeous olive skin. I gently peeled the blanket off her teeny body, ran my fingers down the soft, bare skin of her cheek, touched the miniature sock lining her foot. I pulled it off and stroked her toes. I marveled at every portion of that little girl, at the miracle of humanity, of birth. When so much can go wrong in utero, and everything goes right, is that not a miracle in itself? This world we live in, the people we love: they are all miraculous.

After a time, I could barely see my granddaughter through the tears that blurred my vision. I wiped my eyes with my hand, stood, and walked to Merle. He was sitting with his back against several pillows pushed against the headboard, a blanket resting on his thighs. His hands shaking, he asked to hold his granddaughter.

I sat on the edge of the bed and slowly lowered the infant into my husband's arms. My hand remained on her tiny bottom until I was convinced Merle had the strength to hold her on his own.

I watched as Merle gazed down at Nicole. One minute, two. Time ticked by as we watched the scene play out before us, watched the love in my husband's expression.

And then Merle slowly lowered his head and kissed his granddaughter on her temple. He righted himself, though the maneuver looked painful. And then I watched as my husband began to shake. I placed my hands on our granddaughter as a means of extra stability, and then Merle lost himself to his emotions.

My husband wept. Loud and unapologetically. His face contorted, and he pressed his eyes closed.

But through it all, he had a large smile of thanksgiving on his lips.

...

Merle died on a Tuesday in early July, as I cradled his emaciated body in my arms. For once, I did not regret that my stature was so slight. Rather, that was why I was able to curl up beside my husband in his hospital bed, in our very own living room, and nestle my cheek against the top of his head. I stroked the thin hair from his forehead and kissed his skin. I spoke words of love and comfort. Merle's breathing became labored, and I called Matthew, who came straight away to his father's bedside. We were both there as Merle slipped out of consciousness, and we were both there when a large gust of breath was expelled from his lungs and his chest went still.

Burying my husband, the man I had met when I was fifteen years old, the man I had made a life with, took the very last ounce of strength I had. And perhaps that's not right, is it? I lacked any strength whatsoever to bury Merle. I merely did what had to be done, as we all do, mustering up the ability from goodness knew where to do it.

Matthew and Barbara were my rocks during this time. My mother was too weak to leave the bedroom, so she missed the funeral. I knew she had little time left in this world, and grief often hit me anew at the thought.

"I'm… sorry," she croaked when I sat in the chair by her bedside to spend time with her after the funeral. Matthew had gone home to Edward and Nicole, and Barbara, dear girl, was cleaning up in the kitchen after attempting to get me to eat. She had not succeeded, but I appreciated her kind gesture nonetheless.

"I know," I said.

"No… I'm sorry… not going…" She struggled to speak.

"Hush, Mom," I said. "No more talking." I rested my

hand on her bare arm. "There is nothing to be sorry about."

She pinched her thin, chapped lips together, the prolific wrinkles around her mouth appearing more concave. With her aged hand, she gently patted mine. She made no further vocalization, but she looked at me, her gaze deep, and she nodded ever so slightly.

It was all I needed then. And it proved an immense amount of comfort from a woman who had already given me so much in life.

I had loved Merle. With every fiber of my being, I had loved my husband. I love him still. Yes, I had loved my father, and his loss had been immense. And yes, I had loved so many others. But the love that encompassed my soul, the love that set my heart pounding when we had first started dating, and, when we were married, the love that settled into a sense of familiarity and comfort—that love, the love I had for Merle, was so very different from the love I felt for others. And the emotions I felt after losing him tried to break me. Oh, yes they did.

But I held on to the memories of my dear Merle. Of us together. Of his smile. Of his words and the voice that spoke them. Of the way he looked at me, both decades ago and just prior to his passing. I held onto the way he made me feel, the little things he did for me to express his appreciation: The way he'd slip his hand into mine, the way he'd palm my lower back, and the way he'd remove the vacuum cleaner from my hands and take up the task. And I held onto the memories of Merle as a father to Matthew. Of the early days when Merle would swoop our son onto his shoulders. Of the way he'd hug our son, unlike so many other fathers I had known growing up, save for my own. I held onto the memories of how he treated those around him, the difference he made. Those imprints he left.

I held tightly to it all. And, with the help of Matthew, Edward, Barbara, and my mother—with the help of people I am blessed to have had in my life, I persevered. Oh, I sit here now at one hundred and one years of age—old as the ocean, it seems, day after day retreating into the distance just to wake and splash my presence onto the shore—and the loss of Merle still aches in my heart. It is a distant ache now, but a memory. But it is there. It always will be.

But oh, how I was lucky in love. So very lucky…

EPILOGUE

I sit here at my beloved best friend's funeral now, wearing an oversized black dress, the only kind that I can slip over my head with my aching skin and joints, and I reflect upon my life.

What do I say about the years since losing Merle, since 1986? By golly, have they flown by.

I remained in the home that Merle had purchased and taken me to directly after our wedding, the home in which we raised our son. The home in which we met our granddaughter, this amazing minuscule bundle of new life. And the home in which two lives, two beautiful, well-lived lives, had ended, since my mother passed on shortly after I lost my husband.

I stayed in my home until the upkeep became just too daunting of a task. But, goodness, this body of mine has done me some good, you know! I didn't move into my current living situation at the center until my early nineties. Holy moly, just thinking about that makes me grin. Matthew and Edward wanted me to move in with them many years ago, and I sincerely thanked them for the offer, but I'm just too independent of a woman, aren't I? I rather like the little arrangement I have at my current facility.

My darling Matthew still lives, and I thank the heavens for that every day. He isn't the sprightly little boy he once was. He is seventy-eight years of age, after all. But he's doing well, and so is Edward. I look at my darling son now as he holds my hand in the church pew. I scrutinize the wrinkles that line his face, and I wonder: Do I look that old? Oh, but I am giggling to myself now.

"What is it, Ma?" Matthew asks, his voice having morphed somewhere down the line into a hoarse, croaking sort of thing. If I didn't know better, if my son was a stranger to me, then I would assume that voice implied its owner was an elderly curmudgeon. Oh, but that makes me giggle again.

"Ma?"

"Nothing," I tell him. I pat his shoulder. "You're a good boy."

Matthew furrows his brow, bushier now in old age, which reminds me of dear old Mr. Morris. I merely brush Matthew off and attempt to hide my smile. I still remember, though. I still remember holding the man beside me—this old man who walks with a slight hunch now—in my small arms.

I remember…

Edward is beside his husband—oh! Did I tell you that my son is a married man? Oh, yes. They gave them that right, they did. What a happy day that proved to be. Makes my heart smile to remember that day.

And beside Edward is their daughter, my wonderful granddaughter, Nicole. She is thirty-six years old now—or is that right? Oh my… Sometimes I misremember details.

You can't blame me, though, can you? If Merle was here right now, he'd thwack my shoulder gently and call me a turkey. I can almost hear him now...

Nicole is a mother herself. And of three children! Can you believe that? I have been blessed three times over to be a great-grandmother! I see them fairly often. How lucky is that? And when I hear their voices, see their faces, and look into their eyes, I am awash anew with the sense that life is but a miraculous mystery. That days pass us by before we know we've lived them. Those days morph into years and years into decades, and before you know it, you're sitting at your best friend's funeral wondering where the time has gone.

Sitting behind me is Deidre, my nurse. She didn't have to be here today. But she chose to be. Deidre is not only my nurse but has become a darling friend. Even at her young age. Sometimes age doesn't matter, not when you can see into someone's soul...

I am surrounded by love. Friends and family alike. Most of these people did not know Barbara the way I knew her. I look around now and realize that's an under-statement, isn't it? *None* of these people knew my best friend the way I did, not since Joseph's passing and Hazel's too. We are all gathered here today to say goodbye to a woman that I met when I was three years old. Three years! Can you believe that? Sometimes I cannot believe this to be true, and I'm the one that's lived this life!

They are here for me. I know this. My family—they are here for me. To lend me support. To say goodbye to the woman I held so dear. They are here because... Well, it's because of love.

I was given this time for a reason, I know. I am lucky.

But sometimes, when death surrounds you so prolifically, it's hard to understand why you're the one to survive.

I have lost so many people. I cannot help thinking this thought. Not today. Not when death is staring me in the face as I look upon my best friend's casket. We are all mortal, and yes, I have struggled with the notion of my own mortality. Especially after I lost Merle and when I became an old woman. And especially as I look upon my son's aged face.

But I think my old friend Mrs. Morris was right: we all leave our imprints.

And when I depart from this world, I can only hope that I have left mine.

I close my eyes and can see them now: Merle, Barbara, Mr. and Mrs. Morris. I see Annabelle and Mary Lou, my school-aged friends. I see Joseph. I see Mrs. Brown and Eugene. I see my mother and father. I see countless cousins, aunts, and uncles. Friends.

I will join them soon. This I know.

And I am not afraid.

I slowly open my eyes and look at Matthew beside me. Then Edward. I smile at Nicole, so beautiful, so dear to me. I look at my great-grandchildren. I glance from face to face in the pews around the church. I watch movements and hear the shuffling of bodies. I see tears. The signs of life are all around me.

I look down at a small, weathered black-and-white photo clutched in my hand, a photo given to me by my dearest Barbara when we were but girls. A photo taken on our first day of school, when our futures were bright, and we held the world at our fingertips, ready for the taking. A photo snapped in front of my home, the home with the bright red panels that now make me smile as I remember the mother that insisted upon them.

I don't need to look at the casket before me. I simply have to close my eyes. It is there that Barbara lives, behind my lids, in my mind. I can almost reach out and grasp them now, images of the two of us as children then as young women. I remember her smile and the small dimples on her cheeks when that smile was wide. I remember those eyes: light brown with a splattering of green; gorgeous, welcoming.

I think of them all now, those I have loved. When I take my last breath, whenever that might be, I know, I just know, that I will join them.

Not only that—I will also be leaving behind a legacy. One does not have to be famous in life, or known to many in order to leave a legacy. When I look at the people surrounding me, I know I have been blessed beyond measure.

My legacy is this: the love I have given. Freely and with my entire heart. It will be passed from generation to generation. It will have its effect.

Yes, I have made my imprint with this life of mine.

Barbara. My dear, beloved Barbara. I will join you soon. I will close my eyes. I will embrace sleep as it encompasses me, just so I might dream. Dream of those that left me behind. Dream of those I will be reunited with soon.

I am tired now.

So very tired.

And I am ready.

But while I am here, I will seize every moment given to me.

I feel my son's hand in my own. I blink.

And I let the tears come, though a smile lines my lips.

THANK YOU

Thank you so much for reading *I Will Close My Eyes*. With so many choices out there, I am humbled that you chose one of mine.

If this novel has brought you pleasure, would you please rate or review it on the social media platform of your choice? Ratings and reviews help get my books in the hands of new readers. I appreciate them more than I can express. Thank you!

ABOUT THE AUTHOR

Never miss a book release or important news! Sign up here to stay informed: http://eepurl.com/gPCU1X

Visit Amy at https://www.amyfillion.com.

An author of both adult and children's fiction, Amy Fillion graduated from the University of New Hampshire with a degree in psychology. She worked in the field of early intervention before making the decision to leave and stay home with her growing children. Amy has an insatiable appetite for reading, and you can easily find her juggling between three books at any given time (paperback, ebook, audiobook.) When she's not reading or writing, she loves to walk and cycle outdoors. She lives in New Hampshire with her husband, three boys, one rescue dog (best office companion ever!), and two crazy rescue cats.

ALSO BY AMY FILLION

Adult Novels

The Marks You Made

Grace and Ally

Surprise Me (Grace and Ally Book 2)

One Day (Grace and Ally Book 3)

Secrets of Spaulding Lane: Nancy

Secrets of Spaulding Lane: Marni

Secrets of Spaulding Lane: Rose

Little Things

Broken and Breaking Free

Children's Books

Fairville (Room of Reveries Book 1)

FenneGig (Room of Reveries Book 2)

Esmerelda and the Courageous Knight (Room of Reveries
Book 3)

Wonderwell (Room of Reveries Book 4)

SkyTopia (Room of Reveries Book 5)

The Ancient Curse (Room of Reveries Book 6)

A Magical Farewell (Ro0m of Reveries Book 7)

Made in United States
Orlando, FL
08 February 2024

43389448R00171